MW01254460

Return to Circa '96

Bob Sawatzki

Winner of the 2014 Kenneth Patchen
Award for Innovative Fiction

Journal of Experimental Fiction #58

JEF Books
Depth Charge Publishing
Geneva, Illinois

Copyright 2014 by Bob Sawatzki

All Rights Reserved

Special Color Edition
ISBN 1-884097-06-5
ISBN-13 978-1-884097-06-5

ISSN 1084-547X

The Journal of Experimental Fiction
"The foremost in fiction"

Return to Circa '96 is a work of fiction. Jeremiah D. Angelo is not me. Any resemblence between the characters and events depicted in this story and people and events in the real world is coincidental. River Bend exists only in the the imagination of the author. The dilemnas, delusions, and illusions of its citizens have nothing to do with what really goes on everywhere every day, do they?

Copyright © 2014 Bob Sawatzki, all rights reserved. No part of this manuscript may be reprinted without author's permission except for excerpts used for review purposes.

Return to Circa '96

Jeremiah D. Angelo

Associate Specialist, River Bend Public Library

River Bend, Iowa

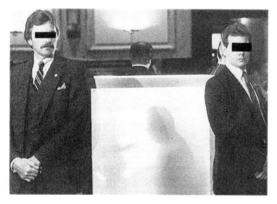

Jeremiah D. Angelo testifying during
FCC hearings in Washington, D.C.

The Witness Security Program was authorized by the Organized Crime Control Act of 1970 and amended by the Comprehensive Crime Control Act of 1984. The U.S. Marshals have protected, relocated and given new identities to more than 8,500 witnesses and 9,900 of their family members, since the program began in 1971.

Part One

000: Generalities

Brunch at the Acropolis 1

100: Philosophy and Psychology

In the Archives 4
The Spirit of Library Science 5
Elevator Interlude...7
Down the Up Escalator 8
Stamp, Strip, and Display 9

200: Religion

Redevelopment Day..12
Ethical Group Decision Making 16
What Would Dewey Do? 18

300: Social Sciences

Down By The River...22
A Shielded, Twisted Pair..23
Doctor Wu's Workshop...27

400: Language

By Statements 31
The Journal of JeremiaD 33
riverrunning 35
Afterbirth...44
Elevator Interlude...45
New Users Group 46
        Virtually There 49

500: Science

riverrun

Summer   1996

ALA @ NYC

600: Technology

Down on the Killing Floor...67
The Brooklyn Girl's Guide to Manhattan 70
To The Lighthouse 72
Classified Information...74

ALA:
Summer Camp
for Librarians

24 wide-eyed visitors from River Bend Public Library were among the 22,000 Librarians attending the 120th conference of the American Library Association recently in New York City.

It was summer camp for librarians as they attended panel discussions and poetry readings, hobnobbing with authors, workshopping concepts, exploring new paradigms, celebrating all things library-related.

Most librarians still found time for shopping, sight-seeing, and watching shows, both on and off Broadway—a road with 350 years of history.

The street that Walt Whitman compared to life itself is alive as ever, but changed in every way, no more so than at the intersection of Broadway, 42nd Street, and Seventh Avenue; known since 1904 as Times Square. After decades of decline, Times Square is being re-born in a controversial process known as "Disneyfication."

The evidence was all around us, and we came to know the neighborhood well during our week in the city. Thanks to a generous donation from our new partners at KeyCo, rooms were reserved for library staff at the fabulous Hotel Millennium.

Times Square, New York, New York. Photographs in the Carol M. Highsmith Archive, Library of Congress, Prints and Photographs Division.

VOL. 130
NO. 2
SUMMER
1996

500s:
Science

riverrun

Part Two

700: Arts

Meetings, Dreams, and Hidden Agendas.................................77
Social Capitalists @ Work 82
Hostile Work Environment?...87

800: Literature

Storyville...90
The Mississippi River Writers Confluence 93
Inappropriate Behavior?..94
The Late Great Age of Café Mauve 97

900: History & Geography

The Gambler, The Sheriff, and The Library Director 104
Where's Wally? 105
Re: Your 1996 Performance Review......................................108

riverrun

Fall/Winter   1996

Commemorative

Disaster Issue

Where's Wally? Conclusion...127

Scholarly Apparatus

92: Biography...........129

Acknowledgements...131

DreamReport.doc......133

Ropes Course
Training Memo........134

References.................136

Shout-Outs.................174

Voter Information

General Election:

November 8, 1996:

Initiative #1
21st Century
Library
p. 167

Initiative #2
Raise the
Magnolia!
p. 169

Initiative #3
Build the
Panopticon
p. 171

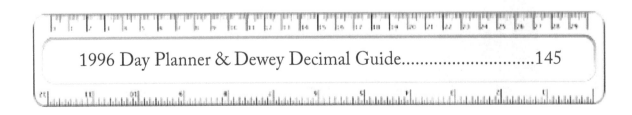

1996 Day Planner & Dewey Decimal Guide...........................145

Part One

Part One

OOO: Generalities

Brunch at the Acropolis

—In the beginning, there were Generalities, said the director, squinching her eyes.

—You're a hell raiser, is what you are, I said. I can't believe they let you run the library. How much longer till you're out of here?

—Maybe five years, according to Plan A, said Helena, holding up her right hand, five fingers stretched out and wriggling. Two years, at least, for these personnel changes to take effect. Then the campaign for the new library begins, that's where you come in, Jeremy.

I nodded astutely. Clueless. With that listening face upon which so much depends, wanting to believe in her dream, just a sparkle then in Helena's eye.

—Then the design phase; lots of public input on that. It takes longer, but you get more buy-in. The architectural competition and public hearings will take a full year. Another year, at least, for construction...

Helena got that Vision Statement look in her eyes, gazing off into the middle distance.

—And then instead of this bombed-out inner city, we'll have a new community center and a public library, like two hands clasped together. If all goes according to plan, we'll open for business on January 1, 2001. And then I'm out of here.

—Then your turn at the helm is over.

—Exactly.

Helena brought her hands down again to her paper placemat, picked up the fragment of wooden swizzle stick, and began methodically breaking it up into smaller and smaller bits. Her nervous habit while drinking peppermint schnapps and coffee with Zelda, Nancy, and me, meeting for brunch at the Acropolis Bar & Grill. We sat at a banquette surrounded by artificial pinewood walls decorated with etchings of Greek temple ruins. No natural light intruded into this cave-like setting, as the big-screen Sunday afternoon football game gently flickered on the wall; an electronic window onto a brightly lit and more perfect world.

It was January, 1996, and the digital tide was rising. We had no idea then of how the internet was about to rock the world of library science. Odd globs of flotsam, such as myself, were being lifted, beginning to drift and merge with other bits and bytes in a world unmoored.

I had no previous experience working in a library, but I had plenty of experience in freelance writing and odd-jobbing since dropping out of Great Northwest State College. After a decade of drifting I was back in River Bend, my home town, baking bread at Wally's Whole Wheat World. When the editor of the library newsletter abruptly quit and left town—for reasons that remain unknown—my life was forever changed.

After an extensive interview with these three ladies, I had been hired as editor of *riverrun* and was assigned to the Serials Department as an Associate Librarian. This informal meeting was a chance for me to learn more about Library

Science and about the great changes ahead for River Bend Public Library. Among many other things, we discussed the signage system for the new library:

—I'm thinking neon signs, I said. One for each decade of the Dewey Decimal system, in a spectrum of colors. We'll have art and famous quotations.

—*It Was A Dark And Stormy Night*, said Helena.

—Okay, great, I said, writing it down on my placemat. That would be for what? The Eight-hundreds?

—Sure, said Zelda, Or the Five-hundreds, and we could put it with books about Weather. No. The Five-hundreds should be Einstein: *Energy equals M-C squared*. And the Four-hundreds could be *Parlez Vous*. Or, *Qu'est Que C'est?*

—What I don't get is what we do with the Ninety-twos, I said. Biographies? Do they go with the Nine-hundreds? Or do they go before the One-hundreds? With the zero-zero-whatever-you-call-thems.

—Generalities is what those are called, said Nancy, a big, quiet, middle-aged girl. Dictionaries, reference works, all encyclopedic knowledge.

That's when Helena said, with that gleam in her eye:

—I know what we want there: *In The Beginning, There Were Generalities.*

001: Knowledge

Zelda turned to me brightly, like a wizened old bird with one glass eye.

—Ask me about the Dewey Decimal Sys-

tem, she said, her beak poised, ready to pounce.

I could never remember which was her good eye, so I kept close watch on both her eyes and said:

—What about the Dewey Decimal System?

—Take anything. Take architecture, for instance. Look in the Seven-hundreds if you want to learn about its history and development. If you want to learn how to build your own house, just go to the Six-hundreds. It's all so integrated, you see.

She smiled, her head tipped happily sideways like a bird dreaming of an ideal birdhouse.

002: The Book

—Have you seen this book…I said, pulling a volume out from my shoulder bag and showing it around the table: *The Androgynous Manager*?

The three women looked like I had brought out a bomb. They were afraid I was going to talk about sex.

—It must be fifteen years old, I said, hoping to defuse the situation. Jordy and I are reading it, to help, you know, get adjusted to life in a library.

—If it's that old, I probably ordered it, said Zelda, taking the book in hand and flipping it open toward the library bar code on the back page. Holding it up to her good eye—it was the left—she scrutinized the page closely in the dim light, looking for her mark.

003: Systems

The talk veered toward By Statements,

re-organization, and the interviews to be held the next day for the new Associate Director positions.

—I still don't get why you want to…to let go of direct control, I asked Helena. What do the new jobs do that you don't already do?

—Can you say "Bad Guy?" said Helena.

—Can you say "Fall Guy?" Zelda chuckled gaily.

—You're going to interview for all three positions in one day? I asked.

—Only seven staff members applied, said Helena. I'm looking forward to it.

Gleaming eyes and white teeth shining out at me across the table; her moment of apotheosis as all the pieces of the grand design began to coalesce.

021: Library Relationships

I told them about Marian's stalker. How I had responded like a stereotypical male, charging over to the Art Department to rescue the ladies from a creepy guy who needs mostly just to work on his social skills. Standing fast by the females in their paddock, walled-in with fat reference volumes, I had been stern-visaged, arms-crossed, feeling like a fool. One more example of what androgyny in the workplace would more usefully resolve.

—You know, Melvil Dewey was the first library stalker, Nancy said, her eyes downcast, hint of a smile on her lips.

—I heard about that, I said. It was on the cover of *Library Journal*!

Nancy only smiled and nodded her head, cheeks flaming red in embarrassment.

—There was like a cult of women around

Dewey, I mused aloud. He hired women because they're submissive. I mean, in those days they were, I quickly corrected myself.

—And they'd work cheap, Zelda peeped.

093: Incunabula

When the waitress brought the bill, Nancy said it was her turn to pay.

—Won't be another time for me, I said. Not until there's another staff re-org, anyway.

—Could be next week, said Helena, laughing. Who knows? If the board has that necktie party for me.

She twisted her head sideways and made an upward yanking motion with her right hand, like pulling tight a noose around her neck: Then we go to Plan B.

—What's Plan B? I asked.

—It's just like Plan A, but instead of five years, we only have one year to get it all done!

Everybody had a good laugh at that, and we adjourned. Soon we were outside in the parking lot, Sunday afternoon stillness along the waterfront. As others walked away toward their cars, Helena held out her closed fist toward me.

—Something for you, she said. To remember me by.

I held my palm out and Helena let loose, like a shower of confetti, the fragments of pulverized wooden swizzle stick she had been grinding up. Sun-stunned and hung-over, I stared dumbfounded at the stuff sprinkled across the palm of my hand. Not knowing what else to do with these infinitesimal bits of information, I pass them on to you, Gentle Reader.

100: Philosophy and Psychology

In the Archives

101 Theory of philosophy

—I had no idea that Library Science involved so much moving stuff around, I said.

—It's like working in a warehouse, said Barney, but without lift trucks or a union.

—Libraries are warehouses, said Jordy, wiping sweat from his prematurely balding head. Except what we stock is books and our inventory is always growing. That's the problem; how to stuff ten pounds of shit into a five-pound bag.

We were deep in the underground archives, Jordy, Barney, and me; shuffling serials, churning through newspapers, journals, and magazines. After discarding duplicate copies and throwing out boxes of moldering ruins, what remained was a cross section of two hundred years of popular culture.

110 Metaphysics

Jordy was one of those little wise guys who seem to burn inside with a lifetime of resentment against people who are taller and not as smart or hard-working. Jordy wore black Levis, pearl-button cowboy shirts, and rolled his own cigarettes. He had a neatly-trimmed beard, high-heel cowboy boots, and a Masters degree in Philosophy from the University of Texas at Austin; apposite education for a cross-county truck-driver,

Jordy had been wondering whether finishing his doctoral dissertation was worth the bother, when he parked his rig at River Bend Library. He was only looking to borrow books on tape, but became intrigued by the collection of deep river blues, including out-takes from River Bend's legendary Bluesville Society & Marching Band. By closing time, Marian, the fine arts librarian, had agreed to meet Jordy at the Acropolis. When she showed up at the bar that night—with Helena, Nancy, and Zelda in tow—Jordy found himself being converted to a new career.

114 Space

Charged with new meaning in life, Jordy turned his rig around and headed back to Austin, finishing a two-year Master of Library Science program in twelve months. Returning to River Bend as a professional librarian, he had been hired as head of Serials. But Jordy's first assignment, to clean up the archive, was taking longer than planned. We had been shifting stacks for weeks, attempting to impose order on motley lots of history. Jordy decided what to toss and what to keep. We were moving everything before 1900 to one side of the archive, everything after 1900 to the opposite side, and discarding as much as possible.

115 Time

—You know, a robot could do this, said Barney. They don't need light or fresh air and they can work twenty-four seven.

Barney was built like Barney Rubble, and

had a similar cheerfully cynical attitude toward life. He was married, with two pre-school-age kids and a third on the way. He was taking night-school classes toward certification as a computer network manager.

Barney stretched his arms out robot-like toward a shelf of bound copies of *The Tatler*, 1726-1760: pasteboard boxes with incomplete volumes standing out among their calf-skin bound companions like false teeth.

116 Change

I was loading up a book truck loaded with bound boards holding *Leslie's Weekly*, circa 1856-1895.

—What should we do with this old fish wrap? I asked Jordy.

—Just take it to Franny. She'll know what to do with it. And try not to get lost on the way back this time.

The Spirit of Library Science

118: Force and energy

I put my shoulder into it and began driving the book truck through the dimly-lighted, dusty aisles, trundling down a long hall and around a corner into the gloom of Special Collections. That was when I first started hearing the whispering voices.

—...signal-to-noise...

—...information half-life...

—...see what I'm saying?…

130: Paranormal Phenomena

River Bend Public Library had been built in the flush years of River Bend's youth, a glamorous era of riverboats, runaway slaves, and Civil War. Legends had been accruing to it ever since. With each addition to the rambling structure came more stories; such as the time Harry Houdini stayed over night. After his performance in the ballroom adjacent to the library, Houdini had staged an impromptu seance in the archive. "Houdini Enchanted by Library Spirits" was the headline of the *River Bend Forward-Progress* the next day. Now, with the library on the cusp of the digital era, the spirits seemed restless once again.

I was tracking the voices back to a dark corner of the original edifice, and could almost make out what they were saying when the ancient, coal-fired furnace started up with a groan and a hiss of steam; snapping me back to earth. There I was wandering off again, just as Jordy had warned me not to do. So I turned the book cart around and got back on track.

141: Idealism and related schools

Somewhere out there Franny was cataloging the rarest of rare volumes, her last assignment before certification as Master of Library Science. Seeing a light in the distance, I steered toward it, and found her in a little room within a room that might once have been the janitor's hideaway. There was a World War II vintage desk and a bunk bed and calendars from long ago with faded pictures of leggy dames.

Franny was bending over a rare and curious volume of forgotten lore, entering the data on a luminescent laptop. Glancing up as if in a daze, agate-eyed gaze fixed on the contents of my approaching cart, she said:

—Come to me, my little darlings.

Franny was an elfin figure, golden hair tied up in a practical ponytail, tips of her ears sticking out, elvishly. She was fresh-faced and without adornments. Some days she wore jeans and t-shirts, other days Franny came to work in a student librarian outfit of leotard, black skirt, black leggings, and black nun's shoes, with big, clunky heels. Franny was the product of a Virginia prep school and an east coast ladies college. Our mid-western, inner-city, public library, falling apart from decades of over-use and ever-diminishing funding, was her first job as a professional librarian. For Franny, every day here was an education in itself.

150: Psychology

—Jordy is really stressing, I said. He's losing it.

—You have to excuse Jordy if he seems ornery today, Franny said. He just got rejected as an associate director.

—Serves him right for extending my probation another six months. He said I'm not "dedicated to accurately entering data."

—You know, Jordan's not completely anal-retentive. Last night he played his banjo for me.

—I didn't know Jordy played the banjo.

—He's got a mandolin, too. And an electric bass. There's more to Jordy than you might think.

Franny gave a shove to an empty book-truck, rolling it toward me, saying:

—You can take this one back to the boys.

I wandered back through the labyrinth. Once again, I heard voices. Screwing up my courage, I tracked the sounds to their source: Jordy and Barney, stuck with a truck full of serials and no more available shelving.

—Fuck, crap, shit, piss, Jordy was thoughtfully muttering, as he measured shelves and scribbled quick calculations with pencil and paper.

—Bit of a sticky wicket here, said Barney.

—This whole range is whacked, said Jordy.

—Unless we toss about sixty years of *Reader's Digest*, said Barney, waving an arm toward shelf upon shelf of the chunky, red volumes. I mean, who really needs this, unless you're waiting in a doctor's office for like, eternity?

—What about those boxes after *Reader's Digest*? said Jordy. Five feet of shelf space right there.

Stepping up on the stool, I pulled down one of the crumbling cardboard boxes. Blowing off the dust and carefully folding back the flaps, I pulled out a yellowed sheet of newsprint.

—Holy shit, I said. It's *Riverrun*, Volume One, Number One, 1866.

—Clear that lot out and our problem's solved, said Barney.

—Don't chuck it! I pleaded, cradling one of the boxes like a babe in arms.

Jordy was casually flipping through the musty-smelling issues.

—Completely useless unless catalogued, he said. Anything in *Reader's Guide to Periodical Literature* we have to keep; that's the Categorical Imperative. *Catelog ergo sum*. Librarians exist because of cataloging, and vice-versa. You might say this box of old news has the potential of being indexed, and therefore useful, information. But without an organizing principle, it's useless for a library.

Setting the box down on the cart, I started pulling out issues at random, stirring up dust. There was something strangely alluring about these remnants from another age. Barney glanced at his watch and said:

—School's out ten minutes ago. Barbarians at the gate in five.

—Sorry Jeremiah, said Jordy, but separating wheat from chaff is our mission here.

—Okay, I said, in desperation. What if I made an index of the issues?

Barney sneezed and laughed at the same time, emitting such a strange sound it made Jordy laugh, too.

—Sure! Why not?, said Jordy. If you can organize this sorry mess, well, hell...I could take you off probation.

—Even cooler would be if you scanned the pages, said Barney. Save them as digital documents and mark 'em up in html so they're searchable on-line. That might be really useful.

—Just get them out of here, said Jordy. At least we'll have more shelf space. But you guys better head back upstairs to help with the after-school rush. Franny and I can sort out the rest by ourselves.

Elevator Interlude

152 Perception, movement, emotions, drives

The freight elevator was a steel cage with hand-operated gate and splintered wooden floor dating back to the first World War. Barney closed the gate, punched the button for the second floor, looked at his wristwatch and blew air out of compressed cheeks like a jogging man stuck at a red light. With a jolt, and then a steady *rrrrrrrrrrrrrrrrrrring* sound, the elevator lifted us up for a long, slow, ride.

—I'll be driving Bonnie to a doctor's appointment at four o'clock, said Barney. From five 'til nine there's my class on Windows NT. Guess we'll get dinner at the drive-through and eat in the car on the way back and forth. The kids always make such a mess in the back seat, he sighed.

160 Logic

—I don't get why your wife can't drive herself to the doctor? I said. You stay home and feed the kids?

—Bonnie can't drive 'cuz of her MAO-inhibitors.

—Oh, right, I said. What do you suppose that does to the embryo, anyway?

—You don't even want to think about stuff like that.

161 Induction

—Don't forget, tomorrow is Revelopment Day, I said. Starts at eight a.m.

—Could be an announcement about the library and a certain computer software company whose name I can't say, said Barney.

—Like I would even know the names of any software companies, I said. Except Micro-

RETURN TO CIRCA '96

soft. It's not Microsoft, is it?

—I can't say.

162 Deduction

—It is! We're being acquired by Microsoft!

—You didn't hear me say that. And don't think "acquisition," it's more like...a convergence of interests. And it's not Microsoft. It's an offshore dummy company they set up so there's no liability.

174 Economic & professional ethics

—Is that legal? I mean the part about a public library hooking up with a corporation?

—It is if the state creates "enabling legislation." But it all depends on the outcome of the bond election this fall.

—How would you know about all this shit?

—I can't say.

The elevator lurched to a stop, there was series of clicks and the sound of latches unlatching. We rolled back the gate and the outer doors rolled open onto the mezzanine *mes-en'-scene*.

Down the Up Escalator

138 Physiognomy

Three Latino kids running by, laughing hysterically, speaking rapidly *en espanol* and heading straight for the escalator, which was blockaded by orange pylons, a bright yellow plastic chain, and a big red and white OUT OF ORDER sign.

—Stop those kids!

It was Cody, wheeling out of the men's room, holding his pants up with one hand, brandishing cans of spray paint in his other hand.

The leader of the pack, Esteven, (easily recognizable as they swept past us from the reek of cologne, the pomaded and hair-netted head, and wearing his customary white silk tank top even in the dead of winter) leaped the chain like a hurdler in a track meet, came down running, and hip-hopped down the steps.

Esteven was followed by a skinny kid (Leonardo in his big green hooded parka) who leaned over the railing and pommel-vaulted sideways onto the escalator track.

The fat kid in last place was Carlos #1, wearing his gangsta football jersey in red and black with his name across the back: CARLOS #1. Dropping to his knees, Carlos #1 slid on the polished marble underneath the chain. Jumping up again, he raised his arms in victory. Chuffing like a tiny locomotive, he followed his friends down to the lobby and outside through the front doors.

Cody was gaining speed, heading toward the top of the grand staircase, where I met him.

—Look at this! Cody said, waving red and black spray paint cans at me, one in each fist. The little bastards were tagging the men's room!

A mestizo of Native American and Latino descent, Cody had tawny skin, hooked nose, virile mustache and long, flowing, jet-black hair. He wore a turquoise stone on a leather thong around his neck and a silver earring in his left ear. Love-struck ladies frequently exclaimed that he looked just like Yanni, the New-Age musician. Cody had a previous career in the construction industry, but after years of sheet-rocking, he needed a sit-down job. Taking night classes, Cody had earned his MLS while working at the library, and now was manager of Main.

177 Ethics of social relations

Cody was ranting all the way as we ran down and around two flights of creaking oak staircase:

—I was on the can! I could hear 'em laughing and spraying, but they took off before I could get out. Recognize any of 'em?

—Not really. They all look alike, know what I mean?

—Jeez Jerry! Cody said, snorting with laughter. You can't say that!

117 Structure

We arrived at the lobby, its design an amalgam of cathedral, train station, and department store. There were arches, stained glass windows, marble floors, and carved wooden benches. The chrome-plated escalator was an addition from the 1950s, out-of-order more often than working. As we passed by the circulation desk, Cody barked commands to the staff:

—Call the cops. Fill out Incident Reports. Describe what happened and what they were wearing.

It was rush hour at Main. Phones were ringing, families with children were milling, coming, going, meeting and moving on. Patrons lined up for the circulation desk like housewives at a supermarket with egregiously slow and tedious service.

—Well, you know, Cody equivocated.

When you guys get a chance. Okay?

Patrons waiting in line were looking at each other like: Does that mean us, too?

Other staff joined the posse as Cody and I advanced to the front doors and stepped outside onto the majestic front portico. There we paused among marble columns and broken statuary overlooking the traffic-jammed parkway. The sky was leaden with smog except for an orange smear of sun sinking into the steaming river. Outside; all of us complicit in a momentary secret joy just to be outside again.

Stamp, Strip, and Display

169 Analogy

Reluctantly, we returned to our battle stations inside the library. My department was the north end of the second floor, home of newspapers, periodicals, microfilm, vinyl records, audio and video tapes, framed art reproductions, and black and white WPA photographs mounted on cardboard; a wacky mix, but that was how the department had evolved over time as new media piled on top of old.

Evelyn Wood was at the front desk with the phone cradled on her shoulder. With her left hand, she was carefully turning the front pages of a magazine, searching for its volume and issue number, reliably printed in the tiniest font and well-hidden. Her other hand was poised with a pencil on a shelf of the Kardex, ready to record the number on its title card. The Kardex was a big blue box with a swivel base upon which it rotated like a battleship turret. Jordy once described the Kardex to me as the "brain" of our department:

the essence of 19th Century Library Science.

It was our common nemesis, representative of mind-numbing library traditions soon to become obsolete: twelve gray, metal trays, each with a creaky little hinge. On the trays were rows of yellow cards, one for each of the hundreds of titles in the Reader's Guide to Periodical Literature. Each card fitted onto its own little hinge, so that cards could be flipped up, revealing the next title in alphabetical order, from *Ad Astra: the Journal of the Space Age* to *Zyzzyza, Journal of West Coast Writers & Artists*. The Kardex was the center of our universe; keeping it up to date was our Sisyphean chore.

156 Comparative Psychology

Evelyn Wood was six feet tall and built like somebody who would have been a good college offensive lineman, if girls played football. Compensating for her bulk, Evelyn wore pink chiffon sweaters, pearl necklaces and pearl earrings. By always moving within a cloud of Channel No. 5, Evelyn disarmed from afar.

Evelyn had worked at the library since high school, when she had been hired as a library page. After twenty years, she was a seasoned support staffer, never advancing beyond assistant librarian, and still living at home with her parents. Keeping her head down, avoiding eye contact, Evelyn spent the days maintaining obsolete machinery and crumbling collections.

After finishing a task, Evelyn liked to buff her nails while briskly reviewing movies and news of the day; developing story lines, character arcs, and recurring themes in the lives of the rich and famous. It was all material for

Evelyn's other life as a romance writer, attending writer's conferences across the country and on cruise ship excursions where she learned tricks of the trade from the pros.

158 Applied Psychology

The final steps of our daily routine were known as "Stamp, Strip, and Display," which meant stamping the covers, sticking a magnetic security strip into the binding, and setting out each title for display. Evelyn and I enjoyed working on this together because we shared an inherent love for magazines, that aspirant marketplace where we had each known small success. Side by side we processed periodicals, inhaling a rich mix of ink and pulp and the heady scent of sample perfume inserts in the ladies magazines, ripped out by Evelyn and collected in her top desk drawer to be distributed as necessary when the vagrants got too ripe. We had just about finished with stamping and stripping, when Evelyn said:

—Don't look now, but Tippi is back!

In the dim light of the alcove was the silhouette of a woman in red leaning into the drinking fountain. Her head turned away, tangled blonde tresses tumbling over a strapless top, with broad shoulders and buff biceps; taking a deep, slow drink, her short skirt showing off long legs and tall, tippy, heels.

Tippi looked best standing still. Because when at last her drink was over and she swirled around and began to walk, anybody could tell that this was a man. Keeping her head down, hair obscuring her face, mincing in wobbly steps, Tippi made her way past the transients and across our department; heading straight for a shadowy corner back in the stacks of bound periodicals.

145: Sensationalism

When we were done with processing periodicals, I left Evelyn to work on her latest romance, while I took the cart around the great circle surrounding the reading area, setting out titles for display. Each magazine had its own red plastic jacket secured with a lock opened by a steel key: a simple fin of folded metal and a circle-shaped grip. Each of the new jackets came equipped with a copy of this key. There were hundreds of these stashed in the same drawer where perfume inserts were kept.

Springing locks and scanning pages, I caught a flash of movement from the corner of my eye. Tippi was lounging at a study carrel, chair turned sideways, stretching out long legs, and slipping off high heels with nylon-stockinged toes; first one, then the other. Then she was massaging her feet, crossing her legs, leaning back and squeezing her thighs together. Tippi smiled, sighed, gazed at her magazine, idly turning pages while teasing a strand of hair.

Suddenly, I realized other eyes than mine were watching Tippi's show. There was a guy in the stacks peeking over the bound volumes. There was a man in a chair by the big windows, his hands under the table. We were all part of Tippi's show.

135 Dreams & mysteries

After work, I walked home to the apartment I lived in nearby. I set the box of old newsletters from the archive on a chair next to the kitchen table, pulled out a single torn and stained printed broadside sheet with an all-caps masthead identifying itself as *RIVER-RUN*, VOL. 1, #1, 1866, and started reading.

That night, I dreamed of the Golden Key: the key that unlocks all knowledge. There were pages turning, dresses swirling, perfume strips unfuling, and the golden key within my grasp.

200: Religion

Redevelopment Day

The hallway outside the ballroom was jammed. It was eight a.m. and the combined staffs from the Main library and all four branches—more than a hundred people—were arriving for this annual event. Staff Association ladies were doing a brisk business selling cakes and cookies, brownies and fudge, along with raffle tickets for handmade quilts displayed along the corridor.

An early addition to library, Keystone Hall served also as a basketball court and community events hall. Long tables were set up for the meeting, with a buffet of fruit, breakfast rolls, hotpots of coffee, and pitchers of juice. Seeking out other guys in the room full of ladies, I headed toward the back to sit with the maintenance crew. They had been cleaning library buildings since three a.m.

Knute was an immigrant from Amsterdam, and had served in engine rooms of merchant marine ships during World War II. Because Knute knew how to keep obsolete machinery working, he was held in high esteem at the library. He was as handsome as he was modest, and in much better shape than most employees, despite being well past retirement age.

Tom was a chunky cowboy in a feed-store cap who worked at the library to support his farm and three horses. Crapped-out next to Tom, like some rough beast in a safe place, Vern softly snored.

Everyone else seemed to be talking and not listening, waving to one another and calling across the room. One thing I noticed from the back of the room was lots of hair, all kinds and styles; curled, straightened, colored, and *au natural*. A woman with prematurely gray hair pulled up in a tortoise-shell clip and falling to her shoulders. A rather severe looking lady dressed like she was going to church with plain brown hair flowing like a waterfall all the way down her back. A girl with an auburn rooster-do, and next to her, a henna-red poof.

Handouts being passed down through the ranks included our Library Mission Statement, patronage statistics, Venn diagrams of income and expenditures, and Dewey Decimal updates and revisions. Up on the stage, Barney and his cohort in Information Service, Stanley, were setting up an overhead projector, focusing on the title card:

Revelopment Day, 1996:
A 21st Century Library for River Bend!

Stepping down from the stage, Barney and Stanley worked their way to the back of the room toward our table. Barney was the junior partner, a chubby, chuckling, assistant network systems manager. Towering behind Barney, Stanley was outdoorsy and over-sized, sporting a goatee and blow-dried hair because he liked to think young. Stanley started out as a librarian and was now a certified UNIX guru. Under

Stanley's direction the old card catalogue had been replaced by a barcoded, cross-indexed, machine-readable database. Anything was theoretically possible in the clear blue skies behind Stanley's eyes.

As Barney and Stanley were sitting down next to me, a covey of late-arriving lady librarians burst through the doors and took the remaining seats. Marian sat at the end of the table, blue eyes beaming from within an aureole of flaming red tresses. A Renoiresque figure in a silk business suit with big shoulders and a lace bustier. At Marian's right hand was her assistant, Betty, a peppy, blonde, former cheerleader in a V-neck sweater, tights and sneakers. Veronica, another red-headed extrovert, but approaching retirement age, sat at Marian's other hand, sporting some kind of square-dance outfit with a hoop skirt. Veronica put on puppet shows and school programs, taking kids on library tours because she was about kid-sized, and had worked in every department.

251: Preaching

Helena Montana strolled out from behind the curtains dressed in a black leather vest and pearl-button shirt, black Levis, and hand-tooled red leather boots. Still an Iowa farm girl at heart, she, too, had started out as a library page.

Gazing around the room at the chattering crowd, Helena took something out of her pocket and set it on top of the overhead projector. A gleaming blue blob of plastic appeared on the screen. Casually giving it a counter-clockwise spin, Helena instantly got our attention. We stared in mystified silence at the projected image of the spinning bright blue thing. It lost momentum, paused an instant, then reversed direction for a few more turns, then rattled to a stop.

Helena picked up the blue blob, and holding it between finger and thumb, showed it around the room, a mysterious smile playing on lips. Then she put it down and set it spinning counter-clockwise again. We could all see it and faintly hear it spinning, pausing, reversing directions, and rattling to a stop.

—Any idea what this is? asked Helena, picking it up and showing it around again.

No one dared speak.

—This is a paraboloid, one of those little deals they give away at leadership school to demonstrate principles. And the principle this paraboloid demonstrates is that it can only turn in one direction: clockwise. See, like this...

Giving it a clockwise spin, Helena looked triumphantly around the room as the blue blob kept merrily spinning clockwise, round and round and round.

—When it's going in the right direction, it keeps spinning as long as you like. That's the way our library should function. That's how we know we're going the right direction. That's why we have these principles.

Helena brandished the sheaf of printed sheets at us, challenging:

—How many of you actually read this stuff?

Muffled laughter. All the managers obediently raised their hands, while the rest of us looked around sheepishly, equivocating, saying things like:

—Well, I read parts...

—Some pages were missing...

—My copy is up in the office...

—Who needs to read the fine print? Right? said Helena. That's what lawyers and managers are for. Right?

Helena laughed, and we laughed with her.

—Paraboloid shares the same Greek root as parable, which is a fable or story told to illustrate a doctrine, or to make some duty clear. You could call this the Parable of the Paraboloid. The principles of this piece of plastic are inherent in its design, just as our library has principles. We use them daily. We embody them in the thousand little decisions we make each day. There isn't any big, long list of how you're supposed to react to every situation. You wish it was that easy!

Helena paused to look all around the room, seeming as if to peer into our souls.

—No, that's not ethical decision-making. That's having decisions made for you. So, a review of ethical decision-making skills is the first order of business today. We're going to test our understanding of fundamental principles against hypothetical situations. All the tools you need to solve these problems are in the handouts. Raise your hand if you didn't get a copy of *The Complete Idiot's Guide to Ethical Decision Making.* That's Dewey Decimal two-thirty-two, point-one, R, for Rawls, John.

210: Natural Theology

—We want you to brainstorm among yourselves, said Helena. Assign one person at each of your tables to be a scribe. There's sheets of newsprint for the scribe to write down key concepts. You have fifteen minutes to solve these problems. When you're done, have a spokesperson from each table stand up and share your decisions.

Helena set up a slide on the projector:

Top 10 Ethical Decision-Making Situations

#10: Little black girl and white adult male college professor both want to use the microfilm reader.

#9: Important donor complains about a book in library collection.

#8: Transients bringing food and drink into the library.

#7: Street gangs spraying graffiti in the bathrooms.

#6: Transvestites cruising the stacks.

#5: Patrons fighting over last available copy of a best-selling novel.

—I got tired after five, said Helena. Let's just skip the rest. I know you'll have enough scenarios in the course of any day at work to get my drift, which is that responsibility for ethical-decision-making begins with you. But there's one more ethical dilemna facing our library. How we respond to this opportunity could change everything.

Giving us all that long, searching, look again, Helena set the next slide onto the projector:

#1 Ethical-Decision Making Situation:

Multi-national corporation tenders offer to acquire public library.

There was a collective gasp of air from the staff, a muffled cheer, a clash of shocked outrage against whoops and calls.

262: Ecclesiology

—Our three new associate directors will facilitate your discussions, said Helena. Meet your new leaders! Please show your support as I introduce them, because they've already proven they can handle their new jobs.

Gesturing toward the table where Nancy sat among the sage hens of Technical Services, all dressed unobtrusively as possible in dowdy browns and grays, Helena said:

—First among equals is Nancy, Associate Director of Collection Management. She will make final decisions about everything that does and does not belong in our library.

Heart-felt applause and cheers as Nancy modestly rose to her feet, shyly smiling, cheeks flaming red in embarrassment.

As the applause diminished, Helena continued:

—Our Associate Director of Facilities is Cody Cordova. That includes maintenance of existing buildings and construction of new buildings.

Whistles, cheers, and sustained applause erupted from the staff. One by one, and then en masse, we found ourselves standing and cheering as we dimly sensed what Helena was leading up to.

—That's right, said Helena. The great day is at hand. A new main library is in the works. Cody will be our "go-to" guy out there on the ground, dealing with contractors, architects, and engineers.

—Get 'em Cody! called out a voice from the crowd.

Laughter and more applause as Cody stood and grinned, giving the "thumbs-up" sign. Helena waited for us to calm down before continuing, in a more somber tone:

—Finding the right person for Human Resources was the toughest decision I've ever had to make. We interviewed candidates from all over the country, but the person who finally stood out head and shoulders above the rest was someone from our own ranks. Yes, and it's Trixie, manager of Woodland Hills Branch Library.

There was stunned silence, then a sibilance of whispered voices.

—Just a few years ago Trixie was starting out as a page at Main, Helena fondly recalled. Since then, she has been working her way up and around the system, learning practices and procedures from the inside out. Trixie also managed to earn her MLS along the way.

Trixie stood to acknowledge the polite applause. She was thirty-something, twice divorced, one child by each sperm donor, bleached blonde hair, enveloped in a blue business suit with big shoulders and an American flag pinned on its lapel.

—Thank you. Thank you, she said.

There were tears in her eyes, an edge to her voice, a trembling hand grasping the back of her chair for support.

238: Creeds and Catechisms

—The associate directors will be visiting your tables to answer questions about ethical decision-making, said Helena. They are there to help you in any way that you need. Now, here are three key principles to keep in mind.

Displaying two more graphics, Helena read their messages aloud:

Principle #1:
Ethical decision-making tends to be inclusive and consensus building.
Principle #2:
Ethical decisions must be made from behind "the veil of unknowing."

—The "veil of unknowing" is the "original state," according to Rawls, Helena explained. What we are before we are born into the social conditions of our lives. What we are beneath this temporal and mortal experience, the only place where true equality prevails.

Giving us that inclusive, consensus-building-look, implying we were all of us together behind that veil of unknowing; Helena set the final slide onto the projector:
Principle #3:
The Difference Principle

—When in doubt, invoke the Difference Principle, said Helena. Kant called it the Categorical Imperative. Most people know it as The Golden Rule. Ethical decisions should result in a positive difference for the least fortunate. How best to make a difference? That's for you to decide. Let me suggest that you frame your discussion within the concept of an "ideal library," but balance decisions within limitations of the real world. Remember, there are no "right" answers. What's important is that we all experience the process of ethical decision making.

Ethical Group Decision-Making

233: Humankind (or is it 218?)

There was no question who would lead the discussion at our table. We all looked expectantly toward Marian to start things off.

—I'd tell that white, male, college professor he'll just have to wait his turn! said Marian. He's a teacher and helping that little girl would be a great 'teaching moment.'

—Likely looking for an obituary, said Betty. Or could be she's tracking down a runaway dad!

—Could be she's the runaway, Veronica said quietly. And just killing time till she has to go outside and sleep in the park. I think I saw her there last night.

A momentary silence loomed over our table.

216: Good and Evil

—Well. Ethical decision making is pretty light work, said Stanley. What's the next question?

—We'll be outta here early, said Barney.

—The important donor and the objectionable book, I prompted.

—What about the gangs spray-painting the restrooms! Exclaimed Knute. I'll teach them some ethics!

—Were those little gangstas tagging us again? said Marian.

—Did you see what they wrote? said Tom.

—No, what did they write? said Betty,

ripple of anticipation in her voice.

—You don't wanna know what they wrote, said Barney. Not with the ladies present.

248 Christian experience, practice, life
—Well, they're tagging their turf, Marian suggested. There's competition among other gangs for public space in our very crowded urban environment.

—What they need is love and understanding, Betty chimed in.

—No. What they need is a functioning public social system, said Veronica. Which libraries used to be a big part of a long time ago.

—I sense we're getting off track here, said Barney, glancing toward his watch.

—That rich donor, said Stanley. I think I know who she is. Was the book in question a history of a prominent local family?

—It's not a particular book, I said. It's a principle that she's trying to get us to think about.

—Should we ask Helena for more info? Said Marian.

—If it is who Stanley thinks it is, said Veronica, and I'm thinking he is right-on about this particular lady and her family-damn history, then Helena sure as hell isn't going to talk about it now. In front of all these witnesses?

—Whoah..., Betty surmised.

—Good point, Veronica, Stanley concluded. And well taken.

—Let's assume it was a best selling novel, I conjectured. With a sexy scene to which the rich donor objected.

—That's a nice scenario, Marian said amicably in melodious, rounded tones.

—Then too bad for the rich bitch! Barney pounced. Because if the book is a best seller, then the library must have it in it's collection. Case closed!

—Slam dunk, said Stanley admiringly. What's next?

—The gangs! Insisted Knute. That's what. Ripping-off rapper CDs and packing heat!

—Security cameras in every department and metal detectors at the gate are what's coming next with that, said Tom. Cody told me it's already in the pipeline.

Vern had been sleeping through all this, arms crossed, head down, labored breathing. Now he opened an eye and said to nobody in particular:

—And they breed like rats!

—It's them damn transients and the throw-up that gets me, said Tom. I mean what are we running here, a flophouse?

—I don't think that's in our Mission Statement, Barney started to reply.

—'Cuz I grew up in a flophouse and I recognize the symptoms, Tom concluded.

—How about them transvestites? Knute said in a voice of wonder. Sure, we used to see that kind of behavior on shore leave during the war, but not in River Bend!

—Her name is Tippi, Betty equitably interjected. She's not that bad.

—So long as she keeps her skirt on, I guess, said Marian.

—I think it's kinda funny, Veronica said, dismissively.

—What she needs is some fashion tips, Marian said, decisively.

—Don't we all, Betty agreed.

—Maybe Marian could lead a workshop on that, I suggested.

—What a charming idea, Marian laughed. I could bring in some fashion designers.

—I know I could use some tips, I admitted.

—You need more than that, Barney said.

—We all need help in some ways, I guess, Stanley agreed.

—You know, this ethical decision making is fun, said Betty, but I don't think we're any closer to getting out of here. Let's skip to number five.

—Right, Veronica agreed. The best selling novel. Two ladies fighting over it and I don't know which of 'em is dumber.

—The best-selling novel that the rich bitch in number two is complaining about, I added helpfully.

—I'd say solve the problem the way we used to settle these things, said Betty: Scissors, Paper, Rock.

—That's fair, Marian pointed out.

—And equitable, Stanley agreed.

—Sounds good to me, said Barney. This ethical decision making is cake!

—I guess we're just good at it, Marian agreed.

—Because we're all such superior people! Betty concluded.

One eye opening again, and speaking to nobody in particular, Vern rumbled:

—Is anybody writing this down? 'Cuz I thought somebody was supposed to be doing that.

—Oh crap, said Marian. Jeremy, you're a writer. Just summarize the points we covered.

—Put in lots of bullet points, said Barney. They love that shit.

273: Heresies in Church History

—That leaves only the Number One ethical question, said Stanley: Multi-national corporation wants to buy the library.

—I'd have some serious questions about that! said Veronica.

—Well, of course, you twit, said Stanley.

—That's the point of this exercise, Barney pointed out. She's leading up to the announcement.

—Announcement of what? Marian asked.

—Go ahead, said Barney. Raise your hand and find out.

—Ask, and you shall be answered, said Stanley. Seek, and it shall be given unto you.

What Would Dewey Do?

264: Deus ex machina

Marian raised her hand.

—Marian? Said Helena. You have a question?

—Yes, said Marian. We have a question about the multi-national corporation? Can you give us some background?

—I'm so glad you asked, said Helena. Because we have a demo ready to go.

Stanley and Barney were already moving into position, rolling a cart equipped with a computer and a projector toward the stage. Barney plugged a blue cable into the back of the pc, then backed away, un-spooling the coil across the stage and down the aisle, toward the storage closet at the back of the ballroom.

—Check it out! Barney whispered to me as he passed by our table, then opened the door of the closet.

Taking up most of the space on the floor of the little room was an industrial-size spool of fiber-optic cable, one end ascending through a hole in the ceiling. Barney got down on his knees, plugged his line into a socket at the center of the big spool, saying:

—Houston! We have contact!

228 Revelation (Apocalypse)

Scrambling to his feet, Barney gave the okay sign to Stanley up on the stage. Stanley turned on the projector and fussed with the focus. What we saw projected was a computer desktop screen and the icon of a golden key, seeming to shimmer.

Helena stood by the cart, idly rolling the cursor around the golden icon.

—Can you say, "Paradigm Shift?" said Helena.

We all laughed.

—No, really. Repeat after me: *Paradigm Shift.*

There was muttering and mubling, but nothing like what Helena had asked for.

—*PAR-A-DIGM-SHIFT!* Helena commanded.

A look like I'd never seen before was on Helena's face, the tendons of her neck taut, jaw-clenched with grim determination to get

across this point.

—Paradigm shift! Cody shouted back at her, and everyone laughed with relief.

Whatever Paradigm Shift meant, it was something to shout about. On screen, the moving arrow circled, paused, then double-clicked on the golden key. The icon started spinning, then launched the first internet connection in the history of River Bend Public Library. There was a series of high-pitched telephone *beep-beep-boops,* followed by a crackling, hissing sound before the image finally resolved to this message:

KeyCo® presents.....
A 21st Century Library
SYSTEM

269 Spiritual Renewal

Onscreen, a montage of archtectural drawings and photographs of new buildings pummelled the senses in rapid fire sequence, zipping and darting while the soundtrack played the theme from *2001: A Space Odyssey.*

—We live in an age of wonders, said Helena, but it's important to know when to turn down the volume. So let's just stop here.

Pausing the presentation with the click of a button, and scrolling backwards to the first image, Helena continued:

—The old saying that knowledge is power has taken on deeper meaning today. Knowledge management is now profitable as an end in itself. New businesses such as KeyCo are springing up over night in service of it. There's a whole new Information Economy developing.

Helena had been pacing the stage as she spoke, but paused in mid-thought and turned to face us as if presenting her dilemna.

—And the danger is that if libraries don't make this technological leap, we'll be left behind. Instead of an ethic based on public service, you'll have bottom-line oriented businessmen making decisions about our processes. But not, by God, our mission! Not on my watch. Not if we take the whip hand now by negotiating our own deal with a company like KeyCo.

Helena went back to pacing again, making eye contact with all corners of the room. Even Vern was wide awake now and paying attention as Helena gradually built to her startling conclusion.

—Managing knowledge is what libraries have been doing since Alexandria. If you learn nothing else today, take home this thought to ponder: after all the new information technologies have gobbled each other up in an orgy of money-changing, what will remain—for those who sieze the day—will be a residue of great public libraries!

Abruptly turning her attention back to the screen, Helena began scrolling through the photos and drawings, while commenting:

—San Antonio's thirty-eight million dollar library opened last year. Denver has a seventy-two million dollar building designed by Michael Graves, built in 1992. The Phoenix library was built in '94 and cost forty million. Vancouver, B.C.'s library was designed by Moshe Safde and cost seventy-four million. Note the resemblance to Brueghal's *Building of the Tower of Babylon*. Look at this one: the Science, Industry, and Business Library, or SIBL, in New York City. Originally built in 1919

as the B. Alton Department Store, back when department stores where called "Cathedrals of Commerce." For eighty-five million dollars it's being redesigned as a Cathedral of Knowledge. Those of you attending ALA this year will get a chance to see it for yourselves. And our newest great public library, in San Francisco, costing a hundred-thirty-four million dollars.

Pausing to critically survey the room, Helena brought us back to an acute perception of our antiquated building.

—How can River Bend get in on this boom? Two words: corporate sponsorship. It's "The New Direction in Fundraising," according to a recent article in *American Libraries*. Ameritech, for example, made a six-figure donation just to have their name attached to the opening general session at ALA last year. Another example is *Libraries Online!*, Microsoft's program to help small libraries, such as River Bend, join the world wide web. Here's the key quote: "Companies are going to be knocking at your door, and you're either going to be driven by the program or you're going to drive the program."

268 Religious education

—What it comes down to is the library is at war, said Helena. Poverty and ignorance are chief among the armies arrayed against us. But an alliance with KeyCo may yet save our bacon. What the heck is KeyCo? Good question. We'll soon be learning more about them. But before we decide anything, we need to think about this ethically. And what I always ask myself is: What would Melvil Dewey do? Dewey would think about it with that hard-headed empiricism for which he is justly famous. What's the most practical solution? What new technologies are at hand? How can we adapt to the new information environment and better serve our customers?

266 Missions

Helena was pacing the stage again, as if thinking out loud in public.

—We look back at the accomplishments of Melvil Dewey as across a great and unfathomable chasm. We have come so far since then, and so much has been lost. What we used to take for granted as first principles of society have long gone by. Visit any shopping mall in the land and you can see the kind of behavior that commercial culture reaps, against which stands the public library as a bulwark of civilization. But Nineteenth Century routines just won't cut it in the Twenty-first Century. Here's the bottom line.

Stopping at mid-stage, Helena turned to face us, her right hand out with an open palm:

—The library has received an offer to have all our technology systems sponsored by KeyCo, including financial backing for a new Main Library and community center.

With her other hand out, and opening its palm, Helena said:

—Here's the catch: construction must begin within twelve months.

Scanning our faces again with that practiced look of earnest complicity, Helena said:

—They want rights to our database, our practices, and our historic collections. In exchange, KeyCo will outfit our library with all the best hardware, software, and updates in perpetuity. River Bend will be a testing ground for new technologies and a pilot program for community renewal around the world.

Pausing for effect, Helena said:

—Sounds too good to be true? That's why we want you to think about it first, before signing your non-disclosure forms, and picking up your new keys at the door. They're gold, they're inscribed on the back with your name and Social Security System number, and they'll get you into the KeyMail system. KeyMail will become the library's new central nervous system, documenting all inter-personnel communication. Best of all, KeyMail never forgets. This meeting is adjourned. Class dismissed. That's enough Redevelopment for one day, don't you think?

229 Apocrypha

A mighty cheer erupted from the staff. Tongues of fire descended from heaven and danced over our heads. It was *massteria*, people rolling in the aisles, speaking in tongues, racing for the exits.

234 Salvation

Rapidly clicking through the rest of the show, Helena advanced the images to a black and white landscape photograph of River Bend. With a sound-effect whooosh!, the photograph transformed into the image of a model village built around a gleaming glass library and business conference center. The only thing not changed was the river.

300: Social Sciences

Down By The River

301 Sociology & anthropology

I signed the non-disclosure form and received my KEYCO pass—a plastic card with a magnetic strip allowing entry to the library and access to the KeyMail system. Along with it, I received an orientation folder with this title:

RiverBendPL.com
A 21ˢᵗ Century Library Operating System.

Swept along in the exodus from Keystone Hall, I followed paths of least resistance, down back-alleys, out along the wharf, looking for a place to sit down and think. Passing by the Acropolis Bar & Grill, Helena's voice came echoing back to me from our meeting there in January:

—Then the campaign for the new library begins, that's where you come in, Jeremy.

I finally found a quiet place on the loading dock of an abandoned warehouse next to the rotting hulk of the *Magnolia*, a riverboat from the previous century. There by the river, the auto salvage lot, and the old gas refinery were bits of nature and trees, even, starting to spring up through cracks in the asphalt.

According to the prospectus in the folder, this ruined landscape would be redeveloped, transforming the waterfront into a model community with a library at its heart. The empty warehouse where I sat would become an artists' cooperative. The old ferry landing would be rebuilt as a hotel and conference center adjacent to the new library. A pathway along the riverfront would lead to a village of condos, cottages, and small businesses.

There were reassuring letters of support from the city council, from Mayor Matt, and from the Chamber of Commerce. Funding depended on three sources: twenty million dollars from the River Bend Redevelopment Agency; a matching twenty million dollar HUD grant; and approval of a twenty million dollar bond in a public referendum to be held November 8, the same day as the national presidential election.

There was also this memo from Trixie B.:

KeyMail©.

March 01, 1996
To: All staff
From: Trixie B.
Re: By Statements

Fill out the attached Personality PRO-Filer© and return to Administration by Monday. Your Personality PRO-Files will be individually tabulated and collectively analyzed by a professional consultant, Reverend Doctor Frank Wu of the Riverside Buddhist Temple.

Library staff will assemble at 8:00 a.m. on March 15 in Keystone Hall, where Doctor Wu will workshop our collective PRO-Files, demonstrating how they are used as a diagnostic tool in understanding human personalities and interpersonal relationships at work and at home.

The rest of the session will be spent

in writing your own, unique, By Statements. By Statements are a series of statements describing your job responsibilities and obligations.

As you will see from the results of your Personality PRO-File, everyone of us is special in our own way, just like Mr. Rogers says.

C U soon!

:) Trixie

Personality PRO-Filer©

1. You feel at ease in crowds.

YES   NO

2. What you like best about your job is the social life.

YES   NO

3. Socializing is the thing you look forward to most each day.

YES   NO

4. Group discussions energize you and stimulate your imagination.

YES   NO

8. The center of attention is where you want to be.

YES   NO

331 Labor economics

Jeremy stopped circling NOs to watch the river traffic. Fiberglass party boats motoring up river passing by tugboats towing winding dotted lines of barges. A tiny figure on the poop deck of an oil tanker, pissing over the side. From that guy's perspective, Jeremy would seem a peripheral figure.

9. After an intense social event you want to get away and be alone.

YES   NO

10. You enjoy solitary walks.

YES   NO

11. You'd rather read a good book than go to a party.

YES   NO

12. The problems and concerns of most people don't really affect you.

YES   NO

13. You prefer listening to speaking.

YES   NO

14. You usually sit at the side or the back of room rather than at its center.

YES   NO

338 Production

Jeremy stopped circling YESes, started skipping around and writing in the margins.

23. You never do anything halfway.

YES   NO

37. Talking about your feelings is your least favorite activity.

YES   NO

40. You value truth higher than justice.

YES   NO

62. You know what you want and how to get it.

YES   No

A Shielded, Twisted Pair

304 Factors affecting social behavior

I was downstairs in Administration

sorting out newspapers and magazines from the plastic bins full of daily mail. Hurrying past me toward her office, Helena paused, came back, and said:

—We're interviewing for the staff artist today, Jeremy. Maybe you'd like to sit on the panel? Trixie and Stanley are already on board, but we need a third person and there's a meeting I'm late for.

—But who's going to check-in the newspapers and magazines?

—I'll get someone to cover for you. We need your input. You'll be working with the staff artist more than anyone, especially on *riverrun*. It's our whole budget for public relations, and we want to look our best!

390 Customs, etiquette, folklore

Trixie sat at the head of the conference room table, tapping her pencil, looking at her watch, and snapping her gum:

—Well I hope this doesn't take long, 'cuz I rilly have to get back to the branch.

Trixie was thinking of what she would be cooking for lunch at Woodland Hills Branch Library, her home away from home. Her staff had been clamoring for chili rellenos and Trixie would need to stop at the supermarket to pick up fresh cilantro and *pico de guyo*.

—I'm in favor of that, said Stanley. I mean, jeez. Why is it so hard to keep an artist at the library? Are we that bad?

—Here's your score sheets and interview questions, said Trixie, passing out papers and pencils. We have three candidates. We ask them each the same questions in the same order.

Make notes in the margins, so you remember key points. Then we discuss their qualifications. And then we vote. That's why you need at least three staff members, so there's a tie-breaker. We'll be outa here in no time.

She twinkled her eyes at Stanley and at me. There were little sparkles on her eyelashes.

391 Costume & personal appearance

The first candidate was Irene, a middle-aged lady from Trixie's church. She did the church newsletter. A single mom with two pre-schoolers, Irene would have to work at home a lot. She passed out copies of the church news to us, and asked Trixie about her kids.

The second candidate was a guy named Jake who gave us copies of mountain-bike catalogs he had designed. Jake had his own website and was disappointed, but not discouraged, when he found out that the room wasn't yet wired for the internet. Boy Scout-like, Jake was prepared and had a copy of his website saved on a ZIP disk. Stanley rolled a computer on a cart into the room and helped set up the demo.

The third candidate was Jamie. Jamie was wearing jeans, t-shirt, and sneakers, with a matching necklace and bracelet made of candy on a string. She had inexpertly applied lipstick for the interview—you could tell it wasn't something she had much practice at. When Trixie asked where she was born, Jamie said:

—New Rochelle, New York. You know—the Dick Van Dyke Show? That's where I'm from..

Jamie was small and fine-boned. Her eyes and lips were too large for her head and her head was too large for her body. But her hands were just right; expressive, un-adorned, and always moving. She had attended Bryn Mawr and the Rhode Island School of Design, graduating with a combined degree in Theology and Art.

—I thought you guys might like this, said Jamie with a small smile, setting a box on the table.

Untying white silk ribbons, she carefully lifted out an object for our perusal.

—Oh my heck, said Trixie. A hand-made book!

324 The political process

—Well, it's obvious, said Trixie. We hire Irene. I already checked with her, and she can start on Monday.

—Whoah, said Stanley. What about Jake? We could use a slick-looking catalog like this, he said, opening a gate-fold flyer with a guy on a bike flying over Mount Rainer. Don't you think so, Jeremy?

—For sure, I said. But I just have a feeling about Jamie. She's an artist. And she has a thing for books. Aren't books what libraries are supposed to be all about?

—What Irene's got going for her is you know she needs the job, said Trixie. Jamie seems kinda flakey. Is she for real? Jake is great, but he won't last long in River Bend. He's only passing through.

—If KeyCo delivers on everything they promise, said Stanley, then Jake is just who we need. How about that website? He's already up and online!

After three deadlocked ballots, we ad-

journed to Helena's office.

321 Systems of governments and states

Helena was listening to someone on the phone, but waved us in. She rolled her eyes, tapped her wristwatch, and smiled, gesturing to Trixie, Stanley and me to sit down. But where?

The armchair next to Helena's desk was overflowing with mail and inter-department envelopes. The sofa was covered with framed drawings of the 21st Century Library, propped up by three-ring binders and rolls of architectural plans. The corners of the room were stacked with samples of carpeting, tiles, bricks, steel, glass, and brushed aluminum siding.

While Helena finished her phone conversation, Trixie cleared off a space to sit down in the chair next to the desk. Then she sorted Helena's mail, stacking it neatly on the side table. Stanley and I made a place to sit on the sofa, carefully leaning watercolor visions of the future against the walls.

328 The legislative process

Then there was twenty minutes of discussion, with interruptions for phone calls and business issues that could be decided only by Helena. I had less and less to say, just a feeling that Jamie was what the library needed. When Helena prompted me again, all I could say was:

—Did you see Jamie's book? Her Master's project was her own book with hand-made paper and hand-sewn binding that she wrote aboout Saint Tekakwitha, the first North American Indian saint?

—How about that, said Helena, with

appreciation.

What we had in common was a reverence for books in themselves. Trixie and Stanley had other priorities. Whom to hire as staff artist was an amiable arm-wrestling competition between them to see who had more clout.

—Whoever we end up hiring won't be working with you, anyway...right, Trixie? said Helena. And sure, Stanley, it would be great for you and Barney to have somebody with Jake's experiendce helping you build our website. And that's critical. But Jeremy is the one who will be working with the artist on a regular basis on all our public relations.

Reaching for the phone, Helena paused and asked me one more time:

—You're sure, Jeremy? Jamie is the one you feel will be best for the library?

I took a deep breath, nodded, and said:

—I do.

It sounded like a marriage vow. And Jamie came to work at the library like springtime. She set up her posters and paints and her teapot. She brought in her own Macintosh Performa 368, set it up by herself, and plugged in the dial-up modem. Jamie led me by the hand to the online world. And, as gradually became apparent to all, Jamie grew great with child. Inside and outside, it was springtime in River Bend.

384 Communications & Telecommunications

—Doesn't really matter who the father is. Now does it, Jeremy? said Jamie, smiling serenely.

—I know that, I said. I'm sorry I had to ask, but everybody upstairs wants to know.

They've got a pool going on it.

I was editing a story on a Tangent 368 adjacent to Jamie's baby blue and white Mac Performa. Working late with Jamie in her newly remodeled art department. With a few strategically placed Japanese screens, Jamie had made her own space in the basement, an island of creativity down there among the chattering ladies of the cataloging department, the boisterous loading dock, and Stanley's fortress-like, climate-controlled computer room.

—It was a surprise to me, too, you know, Jamie said. You can tell them that.

—Why don't we just put an announcement in *riverrun*? I suggested.

—Oh sure, I can see the headline, Jamie said: *Library Welcomes New Staff Artist And Her Little Problem.*

—Hey! That's what we call our kid, came Barney's voice from the other side of the Japanese screen. We got dibs on that.

From behind the screen came Barney and Stanley, crawling on hands and knees, carefully laying out thick gray cable on the carpet and covering it with duct tape.

—Oh good! Jamie said. The twisted pair is here.

—Who are you calling twisted, sister? said Stanley.

—Who are you calling a pair? said Barney.

—Twisted pair? I said.

—Twisted pair reduces crosstalk, said Jamie.

—Two independently insulated wires, Barney said, standing up to show us the cable.

—Twisted around each other, see, like this, said Stanley. Peeling back the tough gray vinyl cover, he revealed two wires, red and blue, plaited together.

—Crosstalk? I said.

—When a signal disrupts a signal in an adjacent circuit, said Barney.

—Causes signals to become confused and cross over each other, said Jamie.

—Bottom line is it messes with your signal-to-noise ratio, Stanley said.

—This is shielded twisted pair, Barney pointed out. See, the lines are encased in a shield that functions as a ground.

—Finest kind, said Jamie.

Doctor Wu's Workshop

302 Social interaction

As we entered Keystone Hall, everyone received a Personality PRO-File package with our test results and a nametag with our personality type on it. Mine said *Conceptualist*.

The parquet floor was evenly divided into quadrants by bands of bright red tape. A sign on the left wall said EXTROVERTS and a matching sign on the right said INTROVERTS. At the front of the room was a sign that said THINKIES. At the back of the room another sign said FEELIES.

Some of the staff started bringing out folding chairs and tables from the closets, complaining about the maintenance crew not having the room ready. Others milled about aimlessly, exclaiming about one another's nametags, saying things like:

—What's your sign?

—This is so bogus…

—Can we sit down now?

—When does the workshop start?

Standing quietly on the stage, Reverend Doctor Wu smiled down upon us. Doctor Wu was a little Japanese guy with really great teeth. He was a Buddhist monk, a Jungian scholar, and a blow-dried professional business consultant. He seemed to be waiting for just the right moment, when Pandemonium had reached perfection.

—Greetings, fellow travelers, said Doctor Wu. Welcome to the Personality PRO-File Workshop. Please do NOT sit down.

305 Social groups

—I'm no guru, said Doctor Wu. You all filled out your own profiles. The results have been tabulated and are in your hands. I'm just here to help you interpret what it means in your personal lives and at work.

Doctor Wu was pacing the stage, cordless microphone in hand, dressed in a black mock turtleneck, black blazer, black slacks, white sneakers.

—The PRO-Filer determines, first of all, where everybody fits along this axis, said Dr. Wu.

Doctor Wu put a slide on an overhead projector:

INTROVERT ——————— EXTROVERT

—But that's a little two-dimensional, doncha think? he said, superimposing a second slide over the first:

RETURN TO CIRCA '96

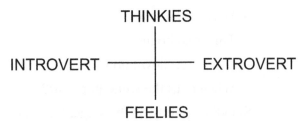

—This is the other axis of possible selves, he explained. When you combine these four characteristics, you see that the realm of possible human personalities is more like a globe.

Flourishing a fat marking pen, Dr. Wu swooshed a bold red circle around the four axis points, building to his grand conclusion:

—There's an infinity of points within. As Hamlet says: *What a piece of work is man! How noble in reason! How infinite in faculty!*

Globe-like, Doctor Wu held out lightly cupped hands, saying:

—Billions and billions of stars. That's who we are!

310 General statistics

At this point, Dr. Wu had everyone shift around the room until we were all organized according to our respective personality types as laid out by the tape on the floor.

—Thanks to the Personality PRO-File, these billions of possible selves can be divided into four subgroups and sixteen personality types, said Doctor Wu. But the types are not evenly distributed. In America, extroverts rule. Comprising seventy-two percent of the population, what a boisterous bunch they are!

The left side of the room burst out into rambunctious good cheer. There was Marian, Betty, Virginia, Barney, Cody, Knute, Trixie, and Zelda, among other colorful figures.

—The extrovert is more influenced by their surroundings, their environment, than by interior motives, said Doctor Wu. According to Jung, the world in general, particularly America, is extroverted as hell. But the results of the survey indicate that your library staff is far from average…because only thirty five percent of your library staff are extroverts. That's right, at River Bend Library, introverts rule!

All of us on the right side of the room smiled modestly.

—Well, of course, said Doctor Wu. The most likely place for an introvert to work would be in a library. *Shhhh!* he shussed us, holding a finger to his lips.

307 Communities

—Introverted Feelies make up about a fourth of the general population, but at your library they are thirty percent, said Dr. Wu. These are the serious, quiet, dependable types you can count on to show up for work on time, stick to their lasts, and go home at the end of the day to their families, because the I-F type is all about Responsibility.

All the ladies in the Introverted Feelie quadrant looked nobly about, smiled graciously, waved shyly.

—But what's most remarkable about your library is the high percentage of staff who scored as Introverted Thinkies, said Doctor Wu:. Twenty percent of your staff. Compare that to the percentage of Introverted Thinkies in the general population, which is just four percent!

Setting up the next Venn diagram on the

projector, Doctor Wu showed that an alarmingly high percentage of the library staff was made up of dark brown Introverted Thinkies.

—There's a reason ITs are such a minority, said Dr. Wu. They carry their own internal worlds around with them. They don't seem to care that the rest of the world isn't always on the same page, if you know what I mean. From among their type come the world's great mystics, charismatic leaders for good and for evil, artists, inventors, cranks and misunderstood geniuses of the world. You know who you are. It's the rest of us who don't.

I looked around at the faces in our quadrant of Introverted Thinkies: Helena, Nancy, Stanley, Jordy, and a dozen others from branch libraries I'd never even noticed before.

379 Government regulation, control, support

Then with a crashing of unfolding chairs and tables and a great grousing sound of setting them up, we were at last allowed to sit down and start writing By Statements. Trixie, Helena, and Zelda joined Doctor Wu on stage to demonstrate how to do it, using Helena's By Statements as an example and showing their notes on the overhead projector.

—All we need today is a rough draft, said Helena. You'll have plenty of time to fill in details later.

—They'll change as the situation changes, said Trixie.

—Depending on the needs of the moment, said Zelda.

—It's a flexible document, Trixie emphasized.

—Everything moves quickly and depends upon a keen ability to manage change, Helena concluded.

—Okay, there's five categories…, Trixie prompted.

—Right, said Helena. And I've delegated three of them to my associate directors.

—That's me, Nancy, and Cody, said Trixie, counting on her fingers: Human Resources, Collection Development, and Facilities Maintenance.

Trixie neatly filled in the names in their respective boxes on the form, then looked up at Helena, saying: That leaves Fiscal Management and Information Technology.

—And that's where KeyCo comes in, said Helena.

—Right!, said Trixie, neatly writing KeyCo in both boxes.

—From now on, I'll be working full time on this partnership with KeyCo, said Helena. Meeting with planners, developers, and fund-raising sources.

—Along with me, at offshore locations, said Zelda, stepping forward and putting her arm around Helena's shoulders.

—I wouldn't dare step into that lion's den without you, Helena warmly responded.

—Raised her from a pup, said Zelda. I can't quit now, just when it starts to get interesting!

—While we're gone, the associate directors will be in charge, Helena emphasized. We'll stay in touch by e-mail and virtual tele-conferencing. You'll soon learn all about it.

—We rendezvous at ALA in New York

City on the Fourth of July, said Zelda. Hope to see many of you there.

390 General customs

And then it was just like high school study hall. We had a two-page form to fill out covering five areas of job responsibilities. Helena and the associate directors were passing out pencils, pocket calculators, day planners, and Mission Statements.

Within the hubbub were pools of earnest quiet, as confused co-workers tried to put what they do every day into words. There were more questions than answers. Reverend Doctor Wu was working the tables, dispensing bits of wisdom, massaging shoulders and aligning chakras.

I noticed that he avoided the table where I sat with Jamie, Evelyn Wood, and the maintenance crew. As an IFSP (Introverted, Feeling, Sensitive, and Perceptive) Jamie was being very helpful at our table and we didn't seem to need his help.

Evelyn was complaining about her aching back. Tom said:

—What's wrong with your back is your chakra's out of whack. Maybe Doctor Wu can help you.

—It's not your chakras that need aligning, said Jamie, it's your sentence structure.

—I think his chakra's kinda cute, said Evelyn.

—I'm acquainted with Doctor Wu's chakras, said Jamie, and he can keep them to himself.

367 General clubs

The extroverts all seemed to have more fun. They were laughing, flirting, and copying each other's work, so they all got out early. It took longer for the introverts, but once we had a pattern figured out, we were good to go. I stayed the longest. I felt like I was really getting a handle on something big.

400: Languages

By Statements

401: Philosophy & theory

When I went back to work the next day, there was blue cable spooling out from a reel on the loading dock. Following the cable down the hall to the staff elevator, I saw Vern and Tom feeding it up into the plumbing raceway. From overhead came the sound of muffled voices. Boarding the elevator, I noticed one of the ceiling tiles had been removed, and as I ascended I could hear voices raising in volume and then fading away as I passed by.

—*See what I'm saying?*

—*What's your signal to noise ratio?*

——*sighing...*

——*singing...*

The elevator abruptly stopped at the second floor, the door rolled opened, and there was Franny, at the video checkout counter.

—Got your By Statements done yet? said Franny.

With a fist full of color pencils, Franny was filling-in the department schedule on a twelve-month calendar spread out over most of the counter top.

—I'm working on my By Statements now, came the muffled voice of Barney. But you wouldn't want to hear 'em out loud.

Barney was laying on his back underneath a desk, his chubby arms and hands yanking on a blue cable snaking down from the ceiling.

Overhead, there was the sound of steps, and then the ceiling tile slid away. Knute stuck his head down from above, and gasped for breath.

——Damn, it's hot up here! Said Knute. Hey, Barney. Is that enough cable for now?

Knute was looking knocked-out. He was too old to be doing this kind of work, but no one else was capable of it.

—Sure, came Barney's voice from underneath the desk. Backing out from under the desk, Barney rolled over, leaned back against the wall, wheezed, and said:

—Time for a cigarette break, anyway. Hey, Jeremy. Got your By Statements done yet?

—Not exactly, I said, but I've been keeping a log of my daily activities and trying to discern a pattern.

—Hold the door! Evelyn Wood called out, wheeling in from around the corner with a book-truck full of *Life* magazines from World War II making their return trip to the basement.

Too late, as the elevator was called downstairs again. Buzzing its feeble alarm, the doors clanged together, and the elevator began its stately descent.

—By Statements done yet? Franny hopefully asked Evelyn.

—No, I didn't get my By Statements done yet, Evelyn said cooly, with a toss of her hair and hand on hip. Maybe tonight, after I finish the Feature Films Index. I've got five hundred titles and it's almost ready for proof-reading. Right, Jeremy?

—So then it goes onto *my* By Statements? I wondered aloud.

—Cody says I can write my By Statements with a pencil and paper, said Knute, thoughtfully.

Head pillowed on the crook of his arm, Knute was stretched out on the tiles above, still sucking in fresh air.

—I don't know how to use a computer, said Knute. I can't even type!

—Also, I also need to know if you're going to ALA, said Franny. KeyCo is sponsoring our group, and I'm penciling-in the schedule for July.

—Count me out of ALA, Evelyn said. I'd rather die by drowning in piles of steaming monkey shit.

—That's a "By" statement, said Barney.

—Wish I could go, said Franny. All the other managers are going. Just me and Jordy left to run the library while they're out of town.

—Marian and Betty are going to ALA, said Evelyn. Betty said, 'I'm gonna shave my legs and hope I get lucky!' Poor kid, she doesn't realize ALA is nothing but heartbreak.

—What's going on back here?, said Jordy, leaning around the corner.

—By Statements, said Barney.

—Waiting for the elevator, said Evelyn.

—Staff meeting, said Franny. The schedule for the first week of July is impossible. We're way understaffed while everybody else will be in New York.

—Jamie's on-call, if we need back up, said Jordy.

—Won't she be on maternity leave? I

said. She gets like six weeks. And her baby is due any day now.

—Does anybody work here?

The harsh voice calling from the public service area was Cody, with Nancy, Tom, and Vern in tow.

—This has all got to go, Cody announced, with a grand wave of his arm. We're clearing out space for cubicles and KeyCo computers.

—Everything? Jordy asked, looking toward Nancy, standing well behind Cody.

—All the LPs are going, said Nancy. The Listening Center is history. All the feature films for sure. So we won't need that index Evelyn was working on. Also we're de-acquisitioning photo files, art, and newspaper clippings.

—What about the microfilm? Jordy asked, hopeful lilt in his voice.

—We're keeping the microfilm and microfiche is what Helena says, said Nancy, crossed arms, shaking her head, lips pursed.

—Oh, great.

—Crap.

—Swell.

—Terrific.

—Helena says the microfilm cabinets are moving downstairs again, said Cody.

—Does she have any idea how much those things weigh? Vern wondered aloud.

—Or how flammable that suff is? said Jordy. This place would go up like a torch if the microfilm ever caught fire.

415 Structural Systems

The elevator doors opened again. Stanley came out backwards, towing a dolly stacked high with boxes of computer gear. He and Barney un-loaded it carefully in a quiet corner, cutting open boxtops with a Swiss Army knife. Sitting on the floor among the components like kids at Christmas, they set about happily assembling pieces, and the pc was soon up and running on a desk in the backroom. The final step was plugging in the blue ethernet cable. When Barney launched the Netscape browser, our Serials Department started moving into the future. Bill, Franny, and Evelyn crowded around the screen while Barney and Stanley demonstrated features and functions.

It seemed the perfect moment to slip away and work on my By Statements, which must inevitably begin:

By taking the long, slow, elevator ride downstairs, listening to sibilant sounds of steam and sighing as if in an interminable Ingmar Bergman film, an elevator ride that takes two hours, imagine that. Until finally it hits bottom, with a clunk, mechanical latches unlatch, and the doors roll open.

Dead silence and darkness in the basement. The adminstration department closed, the cataloging department deserted, and the computer room empty, lighted only by constellations of winking red and green LEDs.

By switching on Jamie's Tiffany lamp. By brewing a pot of Jamie's herbal tea. By firing-up my KeyCo© 386. By opening a new document in Microsoft WORD© and saving it as JeremiaD/ByStatements/1996.doc.

412 Etymology

The Journal of Jeremiah D. Angelo

Monday

Came to work today and discovered a KeyCo 386 tower, monitor, and laser printer in the middle of Jordy's desk.

—Barney set it up yesterday, said Jordy. But we can't log on because we don't have user IDs yet. And he's off today.

Jordy, Evelyn, and I stared wordlessly for a moment at the shiny new machine, Windows 95© logos racheting across the screen in an endless blur.

—Thing'll drive you batty just looking at it, said Evelyn.

Tuesday

Had our first Internet / Intranet meeting today. Barney set up enough chairs for twenty people, but only six of us showed up, equally divided between women and men. Jamie, Trixie, and Stacey Cartwright, the office business manager were active participants, along with me, Jordy and Stanley.

Using a chalkboard, Barney diagrammed our Local Area Networks, our Servers, our library Domain, and then a line up to a fluffy white cloud in the sky labeled INTERNET. We scooted our chairs out to make a circle and brainstormed about what we want our website to look like.

—The key is not letting the internet world get into your UNIX world, said Stanley. I'm a eunich. Don't let it happen to you!

He was leaning back, arms crossed, shaking his shaggy head and beard like a big, brown, laughing bear.

Wednesday

Franny has been summoned to a workshop with the managers and assistant directors to learn about By Statements. They will work as facilitators with the rest of the staff, helping us write our By Statements. Franny came out of the four-hour meeting with a headache and an upset stomach and took the rest of the day off.

Thursday

Evelyn reported that one of the transients was eating in the library. She showed me the sofa with an old army coat resting on it, hiding a can of pork'n'beans sprinkled with Fritos and a plastic spork. Under the sofa was a sack containing other groceries and a six-pack of beer, reduced by one. We decided the ethical thing to do was take it downstairs to Lost & Found. Stacey says that when the guy came downstairs to claim his dinner he was was damn mad about it, too.

Friday

A new KeyCo icon is on the desktop, representing the e-mail program. Barney dropped by to walk us through the log-on procedures. The first time Jordy logged-in to his account, there was a letter waiting for him in his

mailbox from somebody he knew in library school.

Saturday

Now there's a KeyCo computer set up for patron use. Adults and kids are inexorably drawn to it. Some of them have actual writing and research to do. Some prefer the old DOS word processor next to it.

In the afternoon, Franny did an internet search for a man looking for employment in Bosnia. Found tons of stuff on the war there. Nothing about jobs.

Monday

Entered periodicals into the Kardex. Helped patrons use microfilm and bound periodicals from the archives. No public computer use at all except by kids sloughing school.

Wednesday

—Checked your e-mail yet? said Barney.

I haven't, and I asked him, again, what is my e-mail address. He gave me this exasperated look like you would to a child.

—You're JeremiaD! How hard is that to remember?

Friday

Searched on-line for an obituary in the *River Bend Forward-Progress* from twenty years ago. Patron didn't know exact date, so we narrowed it down to a two-week period and got 330 obituaries in chronological and alphabetical order. Scrolled through the list and found the one he wanted.

Monday

Trixie called from the Foothills Branch, requesting recent articles on goal setting and personnel evaluation.

—I do care about how the staff are feeling, Trixie said. But nobody seems to believe me. Can you get material on employee morale? What it is and how to measure it?

It took about fifteen minutes online at First Search® / Business. Some of the articles I printed out for Trixie included: *Employee Contentment, Core Principles of Participative Management, Does Joy Have A Place On Your Balance Sheet?,* and *Hide This Report Card! (Workplace Trust)*.

Tuesday

One of the patrons' KeyCo computers froze up and would not re-boot. Abort? Fail? Retry? is all it would display, over and over.

riverrunning

401.41 Semiotics

—This is so sad, Zelda said, wiping away a tear and looking up at us with a watery smile and one glass eye. She was leaning back in her rocking chair, tea cup at her side, red correction pen in hand, ten pages of manuscript poetry spilled across her lap.

—Seriously sad? Or is it just another stinker? Said Jamie, sitting at her Mac, zooming-in on a the *riverrun* logo, adjusting its color,

pixel by pixel, tip of her tongue touching her lips, poised to laugh.

—This one's pretty sad, too, I said, reading aloud:

> *"Now," said she, "put thine arms around me for the first and last time. Nay, thus; courage, and cling firm."*
>
> *As she spoke her form dilated, the vast wings expanded. Clinging to her, I was borne aloft through the terrible chasm…*

—Aloft through the terrible chasm! Jamie snorted. Could be our new motto. How would that sound in Latin?

—*Sublimimus per terribilis hiatus,* said Zelda, as if reading a line of text in the air not visible to others.

Our motto changed with each issue. Printing the suggestions we received from readers was one of our several contests, winners receiving gift certificates from advertisers in our publication, *quid pro quo*. It was a gift exchange and barter economy floating our boat in those heady days of '96.

—That's beats *Veximus estum in Riviera Urbi,* I said, referring to a recent suggestion.

Zelda closed her eyes, put a hand to her forehead as if massaging her brain to come up with a translation: *Trouble there is…in River City?*

—Sounds like an ominous warning from Yoda, said Jamie, darting her eyes off-screen for an instant.

We were all a little giddy from exhaustion, working under deadline to get the Spring issue finished before Jamie's baby arrived.

—It's not only the cliché emotions and mis-spelled words, sighed Zelda. It's just sad to think of whoever this guy is in Des Moines, wasting his time writing rotten poetry. I mean, really. Why do these people persist against all reason and experience? When they could be outside, you know? Playing golf, puttering in the garden, whatever their fancy.

—But *noooooo*, said Jamie, drawing out the sound like a chill wind. They want to share their loneliness with others.

—Imposing on a poor old half-blind, retired librarian, sniffed Zelda, blowing her nose forcefully into a tissue.

Thoughtfully wiping both nostrils, Zelda bunched up the tissue into a ball, aimed carefully, and tossed it into Jamie's big metal wastebasket.

—She shoots…, Zelda, said to no one in particular, …and scores!

Tissues were always in plentiful supply around Jamie's art department, so useful in so many ways, and around the tissue boxes were usually gathered library staff, cups of tea or coffee, tiny plates with crumbs of food, and people passing by our common work space, pausing to share news of the day, leaning against the hip-high, ten-foot long, stainless-steel countertop enclosing Jamie's art department in its safe haven by the backdoor and the loading dock. Deep down in the bossom of the library, hard by the cataloging department, telephones ringing, calls being transferred, and the backdoor bell binging.

Shelves holding myriad colors of paper lined the walls. Scraps of paper funnelled out of the wastebasket. A giant roll of contact paper was positioned at the far end of the counter, next to the great wooden cutting board with it's twenty-four inch scimitar-like blade, going *whack-whack-whack* as ladies from the cataloging department methodically whacked-off lengths of material for new book jackets, their work going on simultaneously with ours.

The heart of the art department was an L-shaped desk against the wall with a pc for me on the left, a Macintosh for Jamie on the right, and a 14" X 36" scanner in-between. Presiding from a high shelf, among other art department props, was a dust-covered paper-mache Statue of Liberty with golden plates reading:

Freedom to Read Week, 1963
Information is the lifeblood of Democracy.
—John F. Kennedy

We were working our way through submissions received since the last issue of *riverrun*, published by Friends of River Bend Library, Zelda F., President. *Riverrun* had been in and out of publication since the founding of the library, stopping and starting at intervals like an intermittent spring. Now *riverrun* was bursting forth in full flood, overflowing its banks, threatening to wash us away.

While Zelda selected poetry contest winners, my job was to wade through the slush pile, pre-screening piles of fiction and non-fiction. Final decisions would be made by Steve and Jeff in the English department at Keystone College, if I could corner them during office hours and get them to sit, read, and pick the winners.

I was sitting on a high chair in the corner, reading manuscripts at Jamie's tilt-top drawing board. Plenty of room to spread out pages and a series of drawers below, containing every imaginable hue and variety of pens, pencils, paint brushes, eliptoid-stencils, X-acto knives, and other tools of her trade.

—Somewhere in the Republic of Letters, I said, there exists a publication for even so sad a writer as the dude from Des Moines. That's the wonder of desktop publishing: anybody can publish anything. It's just a matter of finding your market.

—Well, we won't have it in *riverrun*! Zelda said adamantly. Bad poetry drives out good. This much we know. But send him your nicest rejection letter. He lives in the vicinity and could be a potential donar.

Rocking forward, Zelda neatly tossed the envelope and its contents toward the growing pile of rejctions. Rocking backward, she picked up the next submission. Slicing it open with the blade of her pearl-handled stilleto, Zelda blew open the envelope and pulled out the pages.

The mail was sorted into three piles: poetry, fiction, and everything else. There were manila envelopes, legal-size envelopes, scented envelopes, and postcards from foreign countries. The contents included poetry by the yard, essays of all kinds, fiction both fabulous and flatulent, letters to the editor, unsolicited miscellania, announcements, advertising, art, and photography.

The addresses were from all over the country, notably New York, California, Florida, and retirement communities across the sunbelt. Most came from the heartland where I distributed, throughout Iowa and Illinois, up and down the Mississippi River; our reader base.

This deluge of material was all in response to a single classified ad in *Poets & Writers* magazine:

> *riverrun* seeks previously unpublished writing, including: short story, non-fiction article, essay, vignette, feuilleton, poetry, or excerpt from your book. Type and double-space. Neatness counts. $100 Publication Prize. Send submissions with SASE to: Friends of River Bend Library, River Bend, Iowa, 51234.

I was gratified, but not surprised by the tremendous response to our call for submissions. What surprised me was the way it continued to exponentially grow long after the ad appeared. It was like planting a single seed of possiblity and reaping a universe of response.

When reviewing submissions, I proceeded by a series of triages. The top third was all basically publishable; if not in *riverrrun*, then some other place or some other time or with another draft:

> *Thanks for sending your story to riverrun. Looking forward to reading it again with the suggested revisions.*
>
> *Sincerely,*
> *Jeremiah D. Angelo, editor.*

The bottom third were instantly rejectable with a form letter and a free sample copy of *riverrun*. It was the middling manuscripts that required the most work, the ones where you had to sit down and diagram how the author started out, where he or she was trying to get to, and what went wrong along the way.

Because I had received so many blank rejection slips in my own experience, I always tried to respond personally, but professionally, as a fellow member of the profession, or belief system, that makes writers write. You can usually tell by the first page, but there's a professional obligation to read the whole thing, speed-reading as necessary in proportion to the amount of time the writer had spent writing. I never learned so much as when I was reading bad writing and had to tell the author how to make it better.

—What should I tell this guy with the "terrible chasm?" I wondered aloud. It's neatly typed. And at least he enclosed a self-addressed, stamped envelope.

—Hey, is there a "starry diadem" in that story? Jamie said, swivelling around on her roller chair, a startled look on her face.

—Why yes, I said, on the final page:

Her voice ceased. I heard the swan-like sough of her wings, and saw the rays of her starry diadem receding far and farther through the gloom.

—That's a blatant rip-off from *The Coming Race*, by Edward Bulwar-Lytton! Jamie exclaimed. I thought I recognized that purple prose. It was on the list of required reading for Early Feminist Literature.

—That's not just bad writing, I said. That's classically bad writing!

—What people won't do to get published, Zelda tsk-tsked. So very, very sad.

Holding the retangular magnifying glass up to her good eye, Zelda was already avidly scanning the lines of the next submission.

•   •   •

The telephone was ringing and somebody over in cataloging finally answered, then called out from the far corner of the basement:

—Hey, Jamie! Merriam shouted,. Dr. Wu is calling from California! What should I tell him?

—I can't possibly talk to Dr. Wu now, Jamie said. Tell him to send me an e-mail.

—Hello, Dr. Wu?, said Merriam, Jamie is not in the building. Can you send her an e-mail? Oh, ….you have been sending her e-mails? Really? Well...when she gets back from lunch I'll tell her you called.

•   •   •

Whack-whack-whack went the blade on the cutting board, as the community service workers cut book jackets for a never-ending supply of new books for the library. New books full of new ideas, new words, new stories, fresh art, and fine photography were always passing through, stacked up in piles, hot off the press, marching across the stainless steel countertop. By mining that material and mixing it liberally with original writing and art, *riverrun* grew from eight pages of library news to twenty-four, forty-eight, and sixty-page special commemorative issues fat with advertising.

So long as we maintained our grant funding and continued to find new advertisers, sponsors, and in-kind donors, *riverrun* was allowed to expand as far as we cared to push the envelope. Jamie's latest innovation was a list of all our sponsors with hot-links to those that had websites. And when Jamie pdf-ed the pages, and posted them on-line, it looked like we were golden.

•   •   •

Jamie was zooming in and out, cutting and pasting, popping down menus, selecting text, changing fonts, snapping gridlines, hovering over pages like a hummingbird on a bed of flowers. I soon learned not to try to follow too closely when Jamie was working, except when she directly asked my opinion, saying:

—Which works better…this way or that? Top of the page, or bottom? Left side or right? Is there a pull-quote with this story? Because the size of the pull-quote could make all the difference.

Screen after screen would flash before my eyes, each with incremental differences of good, better, best, like some mad optometrist insisting on the best possible lens for my eyes long past the point of my own capabilities of discernment.

—Whatever! I'd finally say, it all looks good to me, Jamie!

—Excellent! She'd reply in triumph. Now we're finally getting somewhere.

•   •   •

The telephone was ringing in administration, was transferred to cataloging, and then started ringing next to me. *Ring-ring-ringing*, and I wasn't even technically there. We were far past our deadline and I was working on my own time.

—Hello? I said. What do you want?

—Where's Jamie?, said Dr. Wu.

—She's not here, I said.

—Bullshit, said Dr. Wu. I've heard that before.

—No, really, I said. Jamie is at her birth-

ing class.

—Can you take a message? Said Dr. Wu.

—Sure, why not? I said, grabbing a pen and notepad.

—Tell her I love her, said Dr. Wu.

Then the line went dead and the lights went out.

•   •   •

It was a power outage. All the text that I had entered up until Dr. Wu's phone call was lost because I hadn't saved the document. Ladies in cataloging were cheerfully finding flashlights and making shadow plays. Guys from the maintenance department were cursing spectacularly, running in and out, trying to start the emergency generator, which first needed gas and then a new sparkplug. Two people were stuck in the elevator and a rescue operation was underway. And when I finally found my way out of the darkened building, there was a storm raging, wind blowing, tree branches falling, lines down and power out all over the city. Working in the basement, you lose contact with what's going on outside.

•   •   •

The telephone kept ringing until I finally had to pick-up just to make it stop.

—Will you tell her I'm sorry? said Dr. Wu.

—Sure, you're sorry, I said. She's the one who's having a baby.

—I can't believe she's going through with this, said Dr. Wu. I thought it was a hysterical pregnancy. She'd get over it. Or an abortion, if it came to that.

—You know Jamie could never do that.

—I've been trying to get through to her.

Why did you hang up on me?

　—We had a power outage, I said. Jamie's not back yet, but the power is.

　—I don't believe you people, said Dr. Wu. I know she's getting my e-mails because it shows they've been opened.

　—It shows somebody's reading them, I said.

　—Your e-mail's not secure?

　—We have KeyMail here, I said. They own the rights to everything.

　—Fine. Just tell Jamie I'll be back next week for the birthing class.

　—Where are you calling from? I asked.

　—Somewhere in Silicon Valley, said Dr. Wu. To be frank, I'm not sure. I see orange trees and golden factories.

•　　　•　　　•

　Galley proofs of our Spring issue, laid out on thirty sheets of 11" X 17" paper and arranged in three rows, covered the long counter top. When printed on both sides and folded in half, they would make a sixty-page issue. Most of the pages were full, except for some alarmingly large gaps toward the front and back of the magazine.

　—Don't worry about the empty spaces, Jamie said. Art needs room to breathe. White space is your friend.

　—Maybe some more ads will come in by then, I said. Or letters to the editor.

　—My favorite letters to the editor, Zelda said, were those darling alphabet cupcakes we made at Mrs. Frisbie's Free School.

　It was nearing nap-time for Zelda and she was nodding off in her rocker.

　—Here's another bunch of pages good to go, said Merriam, handing me a sheaf of proof sheets bedizened with her corrections in purple overlaid on top of the red corrections made by Zelda and the blue corrections noted by Jamie.

　Our chief proof-reader, Merriam worked in isolation in the boardroom with *Chambers 20th Century Dictionary, The Chicago Manual of Style, Turabian's Manual for Writers,* and the *King James Bible* close at hand. Normally employed in cataloging, Merry paced herself when proof-reading, working no more than an hour or two at a time, or she would end up going home early for the day with a headache.

　—As for this other fellow, Merry indignantly said, I believe he's making stuff up.

　—What we need is a fact checker, said Jamie, like they have in the slicks.

　—That's not in my By Statements, Merry curtly replied.

　—This is fiction, I explained. You're allowed a little lattitude.

　—That's no excuse for not getting your facts straight, Merry insisted. This guy has Custer winning the Battle of Little Big Horn, Napoleon winning at Waterloo, and America winning the Vietnam War. He's got Kissinger winning the Nobel Peace Prize, for goodness sake!

　—That much is sad, but true, said Zelda, eyes closed, speaking to no one but herself.

　—If we do decide to publish it, and I'm not sure it's right for this issue, I equivocated, we'll have Jamie make sure it's clearly labeled with a tag that says Fantasy.

　Tracking down details was my main occupation when working under deadline. And when I learned to stop freaking-out over people not delivering text or graphics as promised, I discovered a bottomless reservoir of alternative material from across the community. By opening-up the pages of *riverrun* to other community groups and non-profit organizations, our newsletter developed a wide-spread and loyal readership.

Then we scored the NEA grant, lined-up matching funding with in-kind donations, doubled our circulation to five thousand copies, and started selling full-page ads. I was allowed time out of the library for distribution, driving the Staff Utility Vehicle up and down Highway 61, dropping off advertising rate sheets along with bundles of *riverrun* at bookstores, art galleries, coffee shops, and libraries along both sides of the Mississippi.

•   •   •

—Now comes my favorite time of day, said Zelda, refreshed from her nap, as she carefully shuffled from the break room, balancing a tray laden with a fresh pot of tea, hot buttered scones, and jam.

—Since when is reading submissions your favorite time of day? I asked.

—No, dearie, Zelda said. Opening the donation envelopes.

Stanley was wheeling a cart with one balky wheel out of the computer room, squeaking past the long counter, heading toward the back door. An Apple II presided on the top shelf of the cart with a tangle of cables descending to the printer on the middle shelf. A perforated roll of address labels scrolled up from the printer, unfolding in accordion pleats over the side of the cart and into a cardboard box on the bottom shelf.

—Time to see if they can make Frankenstein come back to life again, said Stanley, with a heavy sigh. What we really need is a new pc and somebody to re-key the mailing list in Microsoft WORD.

—Do you think the guys at the PC Palace would make an in-kind donation? I said. They could get a full page ad for a year in exchnge for an IBM Thinkpad. Then I could work at home.

—What they'd really want is a link to our website, Jamie said. Have you seen it lately? I haven't posted the latest update yet, but here's what I've got so far…

Jamie's cursor zipped over to the Netscape© icon on the side of her desktop. With a double-click, the icon opened a window with River Bend Library in a rainbow logo. Around its periphery, a score of icons designated links, some already assigned, others merely place-holders.

—When you're using a mouse and desktop, your hand's natural motion is to move in circles, said Jamie. That's how we arrived at the rainbow logo. But I noticed that it also frames a face. See?

Zip. Zap. Zoom. The rainbow dissolved to show a baby's wide-eyed smiling face. Of non-specific gender and race, vaguely oriental-looking, or maybe just plain alien.

—It looks…

—Fresh…

—Different…

—Radical…

Rainbow / baby / rainbow / baby. Back and forth, Jamie rocked the images, demonstrating the dissolve.

—It looks naïve, Zelda said.

—Is that a bad thing? said Jamie.

—What kind of icon are we using for the donor links? I asked.

—How about a dollar sign? Stanley said. That's pretty graphic.

•   •   •

The backdoor bell was binging.

—Probably my date, said Jamie. Would you get it, I need to use the ladies room again.

Crossing the loading dock and swinging open the heavy metal door, I encountered a Japanese gentleman wearing neatly pressed jeans, white sneakers, golf shirt, sport coat, bouquet of flowers in hand, and that blinding smile.

—I'm here for Jamie, said Dr. Wu. You must be Jeremy. I've heard so much about you.

—We've met before, remember? I said. During the Personality ProFile training?

—Oh, of course, Dr. Wu smiled. You're the introverted intuitive. No wonder you and Jamie make such a great team.

—She's changed my life, I said. I don't know what we'd do without her.

With a mighty sound of the ladies' toilet flushing echoing off a marble floor followed by the creaking-open of an antique oaken door, Jamie approached. She was eight months pregnant, a stick-figure girl with a basketball belly, wearing some kind of flowered tent dress with big pockets.

—Life is change, dude, said Dr. Wu. Deal with it.

—I don't get why you have to take birthing classes, I said. I mean, if you're really a doctor.

—Oh, he's not that kind of doctor, Jamie said, with a laugh.

•   •   •

It startled the maintenance crew at first when they showed up at three a.m. and I would still be there, *riverruning* all night, ransacking the library to make a single issue. I know enquiries were made to the director, but she made it plain that I was not to be disturbed. All that knowledge at my disposal. Sometimes I would literally fall asleep over a pile of books, dreaming strange dreams, you know, like that Goya painting, *The Sleep of Reason*? Just like that.

—*Keep your eye on the ball,* a voice was saying. *Observe that at no time does the hand ever leave the sleeve...*

I could hear bells tolling in the distance and then the back door bell chiming-in, like something was being delivered just for me, if I dared let it in. And then I woke up, because the back door bell really was binging and I had fallen asleep again at Jamie's drawing table.

When I went to open the door, Jamie came bowling in. Rushing ahead of me, powering-up her Mac before taking off her coat. Opening a grocery bag, Jamie pulled out a box of crackers, a grapefruit, and a yogurt cup.

—*Bing, bong, bung*, went the Macintosh, its start-up program sounding like church bells ringing; an audio clip Jamie had found on-line.

—Looks like you've been busy, Jamie said, sorting through her in-box, making soft clucking sounds at each new change and correction.

—How'd your ultra-sound go? I said, wondering once again how big Jamie's belly could expand without exploding.

—*Whump-whump-whump* like a little washing machine is what it sounds like. Here's a picture of her. It's a girl!

Brandishing a black and white sonorgram at me. You could clearly make out details like head, feet, fingers of the fetus, curled up in a gray blob. I handed the photo back to her and Jamie thumb-tacked it on her bulletin board.

—Couple more pages good to go here, I said.

—Just don't make any major changes after I lay them out, okay? Said Jamie. That's all I ask.

—Two more ads for me to pick up today: the coupon for a free muffin at Wally's Whole Wheat World and the full page ad for *River Feste '96*.

—Their slots are reserved, but anybody else will have to make their ads fit the space available. We're running out of time.

As we approached the final deadline, Jamie and I were like Cox and Box, those two fellows who shared a bed in London by working opposite shifts at a factory. The less we saw of each other, the better we got along.

—We're definitely having a total immersion birth, Jamie said. The nurse-midwife has a hot tub we can use. Candlelight and soft music, that's how babies should be born.

Jamie was checking her e-mail, peeling the grapefruit.

—Here. Vitamin C, she said, handing me a section.

That sweet-sour tang of grapefruit melting in my mouth as I stumbled out into the morning light, in pursuit of *riverrun*'s final ingredients.

•   •   •

The back door bell was binging and when I opened it, there was Stanley with the truck backed-up to the loading dock. Balky wheel squeaking, Stanley rolled the Apple II cart out of the truckbed, heading toward the computer room.

—The brain transplant was successful, Stanley gravely announced. The address list was saved.

—Good timing, I said. Because we're almost ready to go to press.

—Does that mean I can have my baby now? said Jamie, a stricken look in her eyes. I don't think I'm ready yet. Surely just a few more pages...

—No one's ever really ready, Zelda said. The most you can hope is to be alert and receptive when the time comes.

—Not me, said Merry. Just give me an epidural and wake me up when it's over.

—Is nausea a good sign? Said Jamie, closing her eyes. And feeling dizzy?

—Nausea is good! Zelda said. It's the primary sign. Dizzy is okay. Just don't try standing up.

—Then I think it's starting, said Jamie, 'cuz I'm about to throw up. And, oh crap, my water just broke.

Jamie was crying and reaching for tissues.

—This isn't anything like I thought it would be, Jamie sniffed. She's not due for two more weeks!

—Kids have no patience these days,

Zelda said. In my day it was different. Children didn't speak unless spoken to and didn't come until they were called.

—Should I call an ambulance? Merry volunteered.

—It's not an emergency, said Jamie. I'm just having a baby. I don't want her being born to the sound of sirens and alarm.

—Where's Dr. Wu when you need him? said Zelda.

—Up in the air, between here and there, said Jamie, head back, eyes closed, semi-delirious.

—He's been doing consulting work in California, I found myself explaining.

—Put her legs up on the other roller chair, Stanley said, going behind Jamie, and setting both hands on the back of her chair. We can MacGyver her out to the truck.

As Stanley pulled Jamie backwards in the roller chair, I followed closely, supporting her legs with the second chair. Rolling past Zelda, she reached out to clasp Jamie's hands for a moment.

—Just relax and try to enjoy the ride, honey, Zelda said. It's all part of the process, even the pain.

Steering Jamie out to the loading dock, Stanley and I helped Jamie up into the passenger seat of the truck.

—The keys are in the ignition, Stanley said, shaking my hand. God bless and good luck!

As we accelerated up the ramp and out of the parking lot, Jamie was giving me last minute instructions for printing.

—Is the document saved in a pee-dee-eff format? Jamie said.

—The document is good to go, I said.

—Have you performed pre-flight procedures? Loaded fonts? Ensured that all embedded graphics are anchored?

—Roger that.

—Have you loaded the ZIP disk?

—ZIP drive engaged.

—Okay then, you're clear to start the distiller, Jamie said with a nod of her head. When the distiller stops spinning, you're ready to go to press.

—Do you think there's room for one more story and an ad?

—If the ad is camera-ready. If this story ever ends...

Afterbirth

The backdoor bell was binging and when I opened it there was Gordy, backing the library shuttle truck up to the loading dock. The back hatch was open and the truckbed packed full with cases of eighty-weight ultra-bright, printed and ready for assembly. There was a moment of silence after Gordy killed the engine, then he climbed out of the truck, yawned, stretched, and said:

—Congratulations, Jeremy. It's a magazine. One copy, anyway.

Gordy reached into the truck cab and pulled out the Spring, 1996, issue of *riverrun*, with his notation in grease pencil across its face: MASTER COPY. All we had to do now was put together five thousand more.

—Soon as we get this unloaded, Gordy continued, I'll go back for the cover sheets.

That heavy paper takes forever to dry and they wouldn't all fit in the truck, anyway. Took me a week of working nights and on Sunday.

Ink-stained, hell yes, and weary, Gordy was all that in his printer's apron, paper cap, and greasy pants. But not wretched. Far from it, Gordy had the righteous demeanor of a mountain climber at the top of a peak and enjoying the view.

—You shouldn't have to work nights, I said. Maybe it is time to out-source this job.

—Gosh, I don't know if that's necessary, Gordy said. So long as they keep paying me, I'll keep printing.

We set to unloading the truck, stacking cases five high on dollies and rolling them in through the back door, past the art department, and around the corner into the dominion of Stacey Cartwright, office manager, waiting for us, arms crossed and a look in her eye.

—Good timing, Gordy, Stacey said. The volunteers all went home and we were running out of projects to keep the community service workers busy.

Opening the door to the hallway for us, Stacey said: Just keep going that way. Knute has been here since six a.m., and I think he's finally got it going.

We rolled down the long corridor through a rising din. Opening a door at the far end, we entered a den of cacaphony. *Rackety-banging* and *whap-whap-whapping*, sheets of paper were feeding into a dervish-like machine that was folding them and shooting them out onto rollers. Knute was down on his hands and knees with an oil can, attending to a long assembly of wheels,

belts, and pulleys set up on steel trestles. Then something jammed, the machine started shrieking, sheets shredding, and a sudden stench of burning rubber filled the air.

—Hit the kill switch! Gordy shouted.

Because of the noise and the ear covers he wore, Knute couldn't hear Gordy calling. When Gordy yanked the extension cord, unplugging the motor, Knute was first startled by the sudden silence and then by his discovery that Gordy and I were in the room with him.

—Dang donation envelopes! Knute said. They always jam up the works.

We soon had the truck unloaded and the boxes set up assembly-line fashion around the walls of the room. Knute ran the folding machine while Stacey directed the community service workers in moving cases of folded sheets to the ballroom where they would be assembled into sixty-page journals. I was putting together a copy for myself when Stacey said they needed me upstairs to cover lunch breaks for co-workers.

Elevator Interlude

Barney was reviewing the text for his New Users Class while waiting for the elevator. At my approach, the doors seemed to magically roll open.

—I'm investing in your stock, Barney said, on the long ride to the second floor. *River-run* is going nowhere but up.

—Sky's the limit, I said. For the first time in my life it's like I'm at the right place and right time. But really, I owe it all to Jamie.

With a sudden lurch, the elevator stopped

and the doors rolled open, revealing steel beams beneath the second floor and legs of people walking by.

—Close enough for government work, I guess, said Barney. Give me a boost, and we can climb out.

New Users Group

—You guys are in charge, said Franny, when we reported for duty at the desk. Jordy and I are going to The Acropolis to negotiate By Statements. We might be late. You can close without us.

—So much to talk about, so little time, said Jordy. Hey, you're going to love the New Users Group today, Barney.

You never knew who would show up or what they would ask. The hardest thing to get across to new users was that nobody was in charge of the internet. The world wide web wasn't organized for their convenience and there was no authority to complain to if you couldn't find what you wanted or didn't like what you found.

The great thing about the New Users Group was that, at least for the duration of the class, our department was calm and quiet. Checking my KeyMail, I found a message from an old friend.

KeyMail©.

Date: May Day, 1996

From: RachaelR@WRITE.com

To: JeremiaD@RiverBendPL.com

Re: New York Visit

Hi Jeremiah,

Congrats on getting another issue of your magazine to press. I know how trying that can be when you're dealing with paper and ink and actual people. Digital publishing and virtual meetings are all we ever have around here.

Working at home and on the road (or in the air) seems great at first. Choose your own hours and wear what you want (or not) but you kind of miss the human contact. While the world may well be your oyster, your home (and by that, I mean the place where you work) is no longer a physical place. Home (work) becomes something else, and maybe I'll write about that someday.

Yes, writing for an on-line publication is a whole new thing. No, they don't pay me in copies. Sure, it would be "swell" to see you again…if I'm in town. Got to go now (well, not literally). Where shall we meet?

Rachael and I had become friends while writing for our college paper on the green, green coast of Washington State. Rachael was the managing editor. I wrote book reviews and sold advertising, feeling like Leopold Bloom, Jr. as I made my weekly rounds among small enterprises of the old fishing port.

When it was time to go to press, we all worked together: entering text on the compositor, printing and cutting the sheets into columns, applying melted wax to the reverse side, painstakingly pasting our stories—bits and pieces of information with pictures and captions—onto the blue-line grid. What I learned in college has only been reinforced by my experience since then; publishing is a collaborative medium made up of iconoclastic introverts held together by the brute force known as a deadline.

Since then, I had followed Rachel's career as a writer for small but trend-setting magazines published in Seattle, Los Angeles, and New York, earning a national reputation as an articulate and discerning critic of popular culture. Now Rachael seemed to have hit the stratosphere, working as a columnist for an on-line publication with offices around the world.

KeyMail©.

Date: Later that day, 1996
From: JeremiaD@RiverBendPL.com
To: RachaelR@WRITE.com
Re: See you soon?

Dear Rachael,

Thanks for the tip, re: John Peery Barlow and his "Cyberspace Independence Declaration." *New Perspectives Quarterly*, rcvd. and Kardexed. Did you know he's going to be a featured speaker at ALA? You could tell him in person what you think of his new utopia.

Can you meet me on Sunday, July 6, at The Internet Cafe @ Javits Center? All of the nerdiest librarians will be hanging out there. I will be the guy passing out copies of *riverrun* and checking baseball scores on-line.

All quiet on the internet frontier at River Bend PL as Barney is teaching a New Users Group: Zack, a Unabomber look-a-like, primarily interested in *The An-*

archist's Cookbook; Andy: overweight, out of work, on-line Wheel of Fortune fan; Von: Vietnamese refugee, taking on-line classes through the University of Phoenix; and a newly retired couple who have never been on-line before, holding hands and wading out into the surf.

•   •   •

A few hours later, I went downstairs to check on the progress of *riverrun*. The printed sheets had been folded, stacked, and neatly laid out on a series of tables running the length of the ballroom. Stacey was directing workers moving in a conga line around the tables, nestling folded sheets into one another, sheet-by-sheet assembling sixty-page journals ready for stapling.

The guy manning the power stapler was doing yeoman work, efficiently shuffling sheets into order, mashing them down onto the steel saddle, and blasting-in staples, *blam-blam-blam*.

—Want a cookie? said Stacey, with a tilt of her head, offering a plastic supermarket tray of lemon-frosted sugar cookies.

—I'm not eating anything that glows in the dark, said a community service worker wearing fingerless gloves, stuffing bound copies with donation envelopes and flyers.

A swarthy fellow with a surly attitude, he was indiscriminately grabbing handfuls of flyers and haphazardly slinging finished copies into a box.

—What's that guy got in his drink?, Stacey asked me. Does his breath smell like alcohol? You better check his work.

A buffet table had been set up with a sald bar and loaves of bread, sandwich ingredients and condiments, donated by one of our advertisers. Zelda was presiding over the buffet from her rocking chair while reviewing her copy of *riverrun*, making exclamations of joy at highlights from key stories and ejaculations of despair when discovering errors, which she would immediately correct with a red pen.

Jamie was sitting on a bench by the bandstand, nursing her baby, her shawl like a shield.

—Is it okay if I steal some copies for the Rotary Club luncheon? said Helena, poking her head in from the hallway door.

—I guess so, I said. If it's okay with Stacey.

—We need fifteen hundred copies by five o'clock for the mailing list, Stacey said, and you know it.

—I'll just take a few, Helena said. She picked off a handful of copies from the assembly line and began carefully inserting bookmarks, announcements, and donation envelopes into each one.

Stacey had dismissed the inebriated community servce worker and given the box of sloppy copies to me. I was separating the good ones from the mis-assembled copies.

—Some of these are good to go, I said to Helena. Help yourself.

—So how many copies are we printing now? said Helena.

—Five thousand, I said. Two thousand for ALA. Fifteen hundred for the mailing list, fifteen hundred for general distribution.

—Two thousand copies of *riverrun* going to New York, sweetie-face, Jamie cooed to her baby. How 'bout that?

—What do you guesstimate it would cost to print, say...ten thousaand for our Fall issue? Helena said. With the bond issue coming up for the Twenty-First Century Library, we need something really special.

Helena looked to me, and I looked toward Jamie. Finished with nursing, Jamie was laying the infant into the baby carrier and covering it with the shawl,

—A single color mailer would have more impact on the voters we need to reach than any amount of *riverruns*, said Jamie. We need one great image of the Twenty-First Century Library, and whatever Jeremiah comes up with for a blurb. But you want coated stock for that and it's going to cost big-time.

—Just send any overdrafts to the Friends of the Library, said Zelda. Go big or go home. That's what they say now, isn't it? Go big?

—Let's say thirty-five thousand mailers, Helena said. You and Jeremy can put that in your By Statements. Twenty-five thousand to go out in the mail. Five thousand for handing out door-to-door. Five thousand to insert in the Fall *riverrun*.

Jamie pulled a calculator from her baby diaper bag and started entering numbers.

—So what are you planning for our Summer issue? Zelda asked me.

—It's going to be all about ALA, I said. Live from New York!

Virtually There

407: Education, research, related topics

—What is ALA? Helena said. It's five days of information overload, and this year it's being held in New York City, the information capital of the world. You'll find out for yourselves why they call it "the city that never sleeps."

Aussie campaign hat at a rakish angle over her eyes, Helena was addressing the video-cam, lounging in a deck chair behind a low table littered with books, bottles, fruity drinks and tropical flowers. A digital delay made for stacatto projection on the screen in the ballroom of Keystone Hall.

Behind Helena was surging surf, an ocean beach, palm trees swaying in the breeze. Zelda sat nearby, leaning down and *shl-uu-ur-up-ing* on a plastic straw planted in a strawberry daquiri rather too near the microphone.

—Looks like the sun is setting? Trixie said.

Trixie was with us in Iowa, sitting on stage in the library ballroom, along with Nancy and Cody, craning their necks to look up at the screen. Their were two dozen of us in the audience, all approved for an all-expenses paid trip to New York.

—Yes, we'll be jetting, said Helena, puzzled.

Zelda chuckled merrily, saying:

—Setting? Oh yes, the sun is well over the yardarm here.

—Which is…where are you guys this week? said Cody.

—Brunei, said Helena.

—If it's Tuesday, we're in Brunei, said Zelda.

—Meeting with KeyCo staff, investors, and other stakeholders, said Helena. You'll be able to talk to them when we meet in New York to make final decisions about, well, everything. Whatever you need. Just let the KeyCo sales reps know.

—Tell them about the cultural exchange programs, Zelda prompted.

—Right! Cultural Exchange! KeyCo staff will be visiting our buildings getting a hands-on feel for the needs of public libraries. They'll be working one-on-one with us, setting up systems, merging cultures, adjusting By Statements.

—While members of our staff, Zelda interjected, will be working at KeyCo facilities around the world.

—Thanks for explaining that, said Trixie. Can we get on with our meeting now?

—Why don't you get on with your meeting now? said Helena. We'll stand by, in case there's questions later.

—Pay no attention to that little man behind the curtain, said Zelda, and signaled, to an off-screen waiter, for another drink.

406: Organization & management

Turning around to face us in the audience, Trixie said:

—Thanks to KeyCo, we're all flying free to ALA this year!

—They swung a deal for us with their charter travel group, said Nancy.

—We'll have to split up when we get to New York, Trixie continued. So it's the Millennium Hilton for Helena, Zelda, and associate directors.

—Everybody else, said Cody, will be at the Howard Johnson's on Eighth Avenue.

—Sleeping two or three or four to a room, depending on what's available, said Trixie. It's all in your handouts. Guys will be rooming together, 'cuz there's only three of you: Stanley, Emerson, and Jeremiah.

—The hard part was figuring out how to match up the ladies, said Nancy. Based on your personality PROfiles?

—So I hope this works for everybody, Trixie said.

—And if not…, said Nancy.

—We'll deal with it then, Cody concluded.

—We have a schedule for every day, Trixie said. That's appendix A, the pink sheets in your handouts?

—We meet each morning in the lobby of the Millennium Broadway, said Nancy.

—Nine A.M. sharp, said Cody. Try to keep in mind that this is a business trip, not a sight-seeing tour.

—Field trips and group-building exercises are all there on the green sheets, Trixie said.

—Roll call will be taken every morning when we meet in the lobby at the Millennium, Cody emphasized, using his laser light to circle the building on a map of Manhattan.

—I think we covered that already, said Nancy.

—Bed-checks every night, said Trixie.

Leave a message with the concierge if you can't be back by midnight.

—Or just stick a note on Helena's door, said Nancy.

—That's a business suite she'll be sharing with Zelda, Cody explained.

—Her travel buddy, Nancy explained.

—You've all been assigned a travel buddy, said Trixie.

—Stay in touch with your buddy at all times, said Cody. If you don't know where your buddy is, let somebody know.

—Because of liability issues, said Nancy. Your personal freedom ends where the library's responsibility begins.

—At all times keep in mind that you are representing River Bend Library, said Trixie.

—So act appropriately, Cody warned.

—And if you can't do that, don't get caught, concluded Trixie, twinkling her eyes.

499 Miscellaneous languages

—One more thing, said Helena.

Everybody jumped, startled to be reminded of the virtual link between the library auditorium and that soothing, sunset beach scene on the projection screen. It was like being addressed by someone living in a fourth dimension.

—Whatever you do, said Helena, don't miss the KeyCo reception in the ballroom of the Algonquin Hotel, Sunday afternoon! There'll be live music and a swell spread. Just tell them you're with River Bend Library. We have reservations for everyone.

—Okay. Bye-bye, said Zelda, waving her hand dismissively. Over and out.

500s:
Science

riverrun

VOL. 130
NO. 2
SUMMER
1996

ALA:
Summer Camp for Librarians

24 staff from River Bend Library were among the 22,000 information professionals attending the 120th conference of the American Library Association recently held in New York City.

It was summer camp for librarians as they attended panel discussions and poetry readings, hobnobbing with authors, workshopping concepts, exploring new paradigms, celebrating all things library-related.

Most librarians still found time for shopping, sight-seeing, and watching shows, both on and off Broadway—a road with 350 years of history.

The street that Walt Whitman compared to life itself is alive as ever, but changed in every way, no more so than at the intersection of Broadway, 42nd Street, and Seventh Avenue; known since 1904 as Times Square. After decades of decline, Times Square is being re-born in a controversial process known as "Disneyfication."

Times Square, New York, New York. Photographs in the Carol M. Highsmith Archive, Library of Congress, Prints and Photographs Division.

The evidence was all around us, and we came to know the neighborhood well during our week in the city. Thanks to a generous donation from our new partners at KeyCo, rooms were reserved for library staff at the fabulous Hotel Millennium.

The Millennium Broadway Hotel
West 44th Street, New York City

Broadway, 1855

Thou portal—thou arena—thou of the myriad long-drawn lines and groups!... Thou, like the parti-colored world it-self—like infinite, teeming, mocking life!

—Walt Whitman

Microsoft CEO Bill Gates announces the launching of "Libraries Online," July 8, 1996. At right is New York Mayor Rudolph Giuliani.
(AP Photo/Adam Nadel)

river rafters

Editor:
Jeremiah D. Angelo

Art Director:
Jamie Petrie

Webmaster:
Barney Rubble

Unix Guru:
Stanley Livingstone

Vigilantee Coordinator:
Stacey Cartwright

Managing Manager:
Franny Andzoey

Preefrooders:
Merriam Webster

Zelda Fitzgerald

Editorial Board:
Keystone College:

Dr. Jefferson Davis

Dr. Steve Canyon

Dr. Mephistopheles

Library Director:
Helena Montana

Printer:
AVATAR Press

riverrun is published by Friends of the River Bend Public Library. All Rights Reserved. No part of this publication may be re-printed without written permission except for excerpts used for purposes of Review Articles, © 1996 River Bend Public Library.

Vol. 130   No. 2   Summer 1996
Veximus estum en riviera urbi.

4   Trip Report

6   Standing on the Verge of Getting It On

7   4th of July in NYC

8   At the KeyCo Booth

11   Pee-Dee-Effing

13   A Visit to the National Digital Library

riverrun recommends:

Wiegand, Wayne A.
*Irrepressible Reformer:
A Biography of Melvil Dewey*.
Chicago: ALA Editions, 1996.

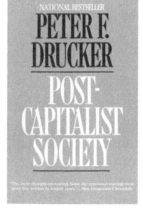

Drucker, Peter.
Post-Capitalist Society.
New York: HarperCollins,
1993.

Drucker, Peter.
*Managing in a Time of Great
Change*.
New York: Truman Talley Books /
Dutton, 1995.

KeyCo® & Your Library
River Bend Public Library was established in 1866 by a grant from
munitions manufacturer Munificent T. Keystone for the Veterans of the
Civil War and for the residents of River Bend, Iowa. Operated by the City
of River Bend and partially funded by the Keystone Trust, the library is
a wholly owned subsidiary of KeyCo®, the corporate entity now calling
the shots.

Clip'n'save.

Do-It-Yourself Bookmark

Melvil Dewey
1851—1931
Melville Dewey invented the
Dewey Decimal Classification (DDC)
system when he was 21 and working
as a student assistant in the library of
Amherst College. His work created a
revolution in library science and set
in motion a new era of librarianship.

Dewey changed librarianship
from a vocation to a modern profession. He helped establish the
American Library Association (ALA)
in 1876; he was its secretary from
1876-1890 and its president for the
1890/1891 and 1892/1893 terms. He
also co-founded and edited Library
Journal.

A pioneer in library education,
Dewey became the librarian of
Columbia College (now Columbia
University) in New York City in 1883,
and founded the world's first library
school there in 1887. In 1889, he became director of the New York State
Library in Albany, a position he held
until 1906.

All copyright rights in the Dewey Decimal
Classification system are owned by OCLC.
Dewey, Dewey Decimal Classification, DDC,
OCLC and WebDewey are registered trade-
marks of OCLC.

http://www.oclc.org

Melvil Dewey
Dictionary of American Portraits
Dover Publications, 1976

Trip Report

Wednesday, July 3rd

597 Fishes

Trapped for two hours in a machine designed to process people while waiting for our connecting flight to New York at Saint Louis International Airport, Terminal 2. There's a Pizza Hut, a Taco Time, a sandwich shop, and a bar surrounded by parking garages and empty tarmac vistas.

It takes an act of will to sit still and just be where you are. The steel ceiling beams sprayed with cheesy fireproofing, accented by lime green lighting. This is how fish must feel, trapped in an aquarium.

598 Aves

Sitting in the front row, facing backwards, watching people fly—packed together inside an aluminum tube. As we take off, half the passengers lean back, closing their eyes, as if the plane's flight might be caused by an act of their collective will.

540 Chemistry and allied sciences

Four of us shared a taxi from LaGuardia Airport. I was sitting up front with the driver, Abdul Osama from Istanbul. He was taking classes at NYU, possibly in political science. It was hard to understand because of his accent and the radio on full volume, tuned to news about the explosion at a fireworks stand:

"EIGHT PEOPLE KILLED AT A FIRE-WORKS STAND OUTSIDE CHICAGO TO-DAY," the radio news guy was announcing.

"Happy Fourth of July," said Abdul. "Boom! You're dead. Americans don't know what to do with all their freedoms."

After he unloaded our baggage at Howard Johnson's, Abdul pressed a card in my hand, saying, "You are not like the others. If you want to know more about our organization, please, take this."

The first of the dozens of business cards I was to receive that week, it said: Al Qaeda Cab. There was a 1-800 number and an e-mail address: AbdulOsama@aol.com.

534 Sound & related vibrations

We had a New York minute to drop off our bags in our rooms, then we were hustled back out onto the street, dividing into a fleet of taxis for the ride to a dinner being hosted by our new friends at KeyCo. The Typhoon Brewery lived up to its name.

Sounds from the open-air kitchen echoed off galvanized steel tables and mirrored walls while voices shouted to be heard in the rush hour atmosphere. Flames shot up from the central brazier where three cooks made performance art out of cooking over

People We Pass - Stories of Life among the Masses of New York City / Edward Penfield.
Reproduction Number: LC-DIG-ppmsca-05950

an open fire.

As we sampled the five beers brewed at Typhoon, the menu—simple yet profound—was translated for us by Sunny Yin-Yang, Technical Services Librarian at River Bend Library. Born and raised in Thailand, Sunny explained the philosophy of food from her native land.

"Five food group!" Sunny said, holding out her left hand and counting on her fingers, fairly shouting over the ringing din of the room, "Sawty! Sweet! Sour! Bittah! Hot! What you rike is who you are! Barance is key! Mix and match! Rots a ruck!"

"I'm sweet and sour."

"I rike it hot."

"I rike it hot and salty."

"You're a salty dog."

"I rike it hot and salty and sweet and sour, with bitter brewed beer."

"Try the green squishy stuff," Marian enthused. "It's great!"

522 Techniques, equipment, materials

While Stanley Livingstone, Chief Technology Officer, was at a special meeting with KeyCo technicians, I was up till midnight reviewing strategy with our bookmobile driver, Emerson Blake. A veteran of past ALAs, Emerson systematically worked through the telephone-book-thick conference program, highlighting special events in yellow, secondary events in green, and mandatory events in red. He stuck stickies marking each day and made sure he had ready a map of the city and a mass transit guide, along with a supply of business cards, pens, and paperclips. Then Emerson put on his pajamas and his black satin eyeshade and went to bed.

Too excited to sleep, I went downstairs and down the block to the drugstore to buy a pocket comb. The street action continued unabated—it's a block party every night in New York. No librarians in sight. Somehow, forgot to buy comb.

Smolan, Rick. *24 Hours in Cyberspace: Painting on the Walls of the Digital Cave*, 1996. (With CD-ROM). *Digital Wall in Singapore*, photo credit: R. Ian Lloyd. http://www.againstallodds.com/cyber24.htm

Standing On The Verge of Getting It On

"The natives there dressed in birds' feathers of various colors, and they came toward us joyfully, uttering loud cries of wonderment."

—Giovanni de Verrazzano, landing on Manhattan, 1524

That description could also apply to George Clinton and the P-Funk All-Stars headlining a 4th of July benefit concert for Central Park Summerstage.

There were up to twenty of them on-stage demonstrating "the funk," dressed in costumes of their own design. Bootsy Collins was re-united with Bernie Worrell, who kicked off the concert with a ten minute solo that ranged from gospel to jazz to funk, to psychedelic sonic nonsense and back again. Bootsy joined in for short riffs, shouting for "the whole damn building" to sing. Which was strange, because we were outside, on the lawn, the sun going down over the heartland.

The weather was dodgy with periods of partial clearing. I was dancing with Djuna, Betty, Veronica, Cody, and Marian when the rain started pouring.

I was heading for the shelter, but Djuna grabbed my wrist. Her other wrist was being held by Cody while his other arm was linked in the arm of Marian. Marian was tipsy, tilting, laughing, linking arms with Betty and Veronica. Marian seemed to whip-saw us all around her pivot point and the rain was really coming down. We just kept dancing. They were playing *Standing On the Verge of Getting It On* and the rain was coming down.

Central Park at Night by Adolf Dehn, 1934.
Ben and Beatrice Goldstein Foundation Collection. Library of Congress, Prints & Photographs Division, Reproduction Number: LC-DIG-ppmsc-00787 (digital file from original print) LC-USZC4-6576 (color film copy transparency).

World Trade Center Towers and New York skyline, New York, New York. Highsmith, Carol M., photographer. Reproduction Number: LC-DIG-highsm-12458 (digital file from original)

4th of July

577 General nature of life

Early a.m. taking the elevator down to pick up a comb from the concierge. Fully dressed, except hair looks like I have just stepped out of shower, which is the case. Elevator keeps stopping as professionally dressed fellow librarians board and depart.

"I thought I was up early," I said.

"All librarians are up early," one woman cheerfully ventured. "And we all work late. Librarians just never have any fun."

573 Physical anthropology

Walked six blocks to the Millennium Hotel where I had coffee and tiny poppy seed muffins in the lounge while waiting for the rest of the group to arrive. A public walkway passes through the building, connecting West 45th Street to West 44th Street, so the traffic is constant and diverse.

As the days pass, you get better at recognizing librarians. They are not those perfectly groomed mannequins in sleek business suits, and certainly not among those women in tight skirts, cut-off at mid-thigh or unbuttoned to the crotch and adorned with gold chains. By their canvas book bags and sensible shoes, you will know them—but there are more varieties of librarian than

you might think.

During the opening general session I was sitting next to a young woman who didn't look like any kind of librarian I had yet seen. She was wearing a short flounced skirt and high heels. When she spoke to her companion *en francais*, I began to develop a larger view of the world of librarians.

There are motherly librarians and techy librarians and Lipstick Librarians. Academic librarians dress in tweedy suits, well-used and comfortable-looking. There are all different kinds of librarians, was what I finally had to conclude. The most reliable way to recognize a librarian is by that inner glow shared among these servants at the font of knowledge. That, and the fact that 82% of librarians are women. That's a clue, for sure.

569 Fossil mammalia

We had to sign up for at least one tour before being released to our own devices for the remainder of the day. I chose the Library of Theater History tour and took the opportunity to research *The Music Man*.

It's amazing how much Meredith Willson got right about small towns and public libraries. But so much has changed since then, I can't help thinking how cool it would be to do an update with a 21st Century Library.

Board Books Are Big

"Kids are the fastest growing market for just about everything," said the Minnie Mouse lady at the Disney booth. She wore a Minnie Mouse blouse and a polka-dot skirt with a silky black tail attached that she twirled absent-mindedly as she chatted with us.

"Baby Boomers are re-living their childhoods through their kids," said Veronica Lake, Childrens Department, River Bend Library, wearing an I HEART NY tee-shirt, sensible walking shorts and red Reeboks®.

"But with way cooler toys and books," said a librarian wearing a formidable collection of buttons and badges from previvous ALA conventions attached to her dark green jumper. Like a middle-aged Girl Scout at summer camp, she wore sandals and ankle socks, short, sensible hair, and was stuffing souvenirs into an enormous bookbag.

"Indulging their kids' every whim and caprice," said Veronica, consulting the events schedule. "Well, what's next? Tea With Eloise at the Plaza Hotel? Or do you want to check out Fun With Dick & Jane at the Grande Marriott?"

"What's 'Fun with Dick and Jane?'" I said.

"It's a Smithsonian exhibition, said Veronica, "and it's coming to River Bend for six weeks in the fall."

"I don't suppose you have *Eloise* yet in a board book?", the Girl Scout librarian asked Minnie Mouse. "We could use a dozen copies."

"Board books are big!", Minnie Mouse enthused. "*Eloise* isn't available, but we've got a whole series with movie tie-ins. Sign up for the set and we'll throw in free tickets for a matinee performance of *The Lion King*."

At the KeyCo® Booth

"So where's the home office?" I asked. "Redmond, Washington? Or Silicon Valley?"

"We're from all over," Jason said. "More virtual than actual."

Jason was wearing the KeyCo golf shirt and sport coat combo over your basic beige Dockers. He had great hair, and he mentioned that he was missing his kids' AYSO soccer tournament to be in New York for this gig.

"KeyCo is an on-line presence with a back office in the outback," Jane explained.

Jane had Peter Pan hair, big red plastic frames on her glasses, and a pin-striped business suit with an apricot scarf.

"Australia. New Hebrides. Republic of Brunaire," Jason shrugged. "It changes as conditions change. That's the beauty of satellite transmission and fully networked peer to peer computing."

"I still don't get what it is that KeyCo makes." I said.

"We don't make anything," said Jane, squinching up her nose distastefully.

"We're enablers."

"Suppliers of demand."

"Brokers of information retrieval and dispersal systems."

"Whatever you want— we can get it for you wholesale, networked, and cross-platformed."

"Open U-R-L and inter-operabililty."

"Innovative interfaces are what we're all about."

"When the needs of your customers go beyond the book."

Dick

Recommended Reading

Barlow, John Perry.
    "A Declaration of
        Independence
        of Cyberspace."
Electronic Frontier Foundation, February 8, 1996.

https://projects.eff.org/~barlow/
Declaration-Final.html

Jacobs, Karrie. "Utopia Redux,"
WORD.com, April 18, 1996.
http://www.nettime.org/Lists-Archives/nettime-I-9604/
msg00024.html

Above, right: Javits Center

Above, left: Entrance Hall, SIBL.

Top: Media Wall at SIBL, Science and Business Library, New York City, formerly the B. Altman Department Store, built in 1919 and remodeled for $85 million dollars.
http://www.nypl.org/locations/sibl

"The Internet is similar to what the library was one hundred years ago. It represents who we are, how we act, transact business and engage in relationships. The Internet is about information empowerment. I think it will change world culture."

–Michael Wolff, Investors Business Daily, 9/21/95

Chase, Elaine Raco; Wingate, Anne. *Amateur Detectives: A Writer's Guide to how private citizens solve criminal cases*. New York, N.Y.: Writer's Digest Books, 1996.
Dewey Decimal: 808.3872 C4873a

LIVE! From Javits Center

544 Qualitative analysis

Q: Is content King? Or is it all about the internet portal?

"Netscape rules. In less that a year, it has achieved ubiquity."

"What else is there besides them and AOL?"

"AOL is the suckiest, and I mean that literally."

"Yahoo, Excite, Infoseek, Cnet and Prodigy…"

"Lycos and AltaVista, MetaSearch and Bigfoot, the e-mail directory."

"Don't forget e-Village, the Apple web community."

"Community from another planet is what Apple users are."

"I like the new simultaneous search engines, such as NlightN and Infonautics' Electric Light."

"Who-the-what-the?"

"Those guys down at the end of the hall? Looks like they just started up this week."

526 Mathematical geography

Q: Do you often use Pathfinder, the Times-Warner website portal?

"Oh yeah, whenever I have a tricky reference question you know I always click on Pathfinder first. NOT!"

518 Numerical analysis

Q: Have you heard of Microsoft Explorer?

"Netscape may rule now, but once Explorer takes off it's gonna be like The Empire Strikes Back."

"The Microsoft booth is thirty feet long on both sides of the aisle. They're passing out free CD-ROMs with Windows NT and Explorer."

"What I hate is all the damn banner ads on websites. I wonder if you could have the option for ads—but only if you want more info?"

"How hard would it be to create a search engine based on algorithms that track most-cited sites? You know? A reference tool of most-referenced sites? Listed in order of relevance?"

"You'd get a googol-lot of answers for each question, that's for sure."

"What's a googol?"

"A flock of geese?"

"No, it's the number one followed by a hundred zeros"

"You could call the website Googol!"

"That's a silly name."

"So is Yahoo, but they're worth three hundred million dollars now."

Pee-Dee-Effing

"Pee-dee-effing is the way to go if you want a publication with downloadable text and embedded graphics," said the first sales rep at the Adobe booth.

"That's the general idea," I said. "We want an on-line serial publication with discrete chunks of pictures and text. We'll have reports from current events mixed in with an ongoing narrative and references to our library collection."

"One picture's worth a thousand words, but they eat up megabytes like crazy," said the other sales rep. "Go ahead. Take a picture."

"Five megabytes for that photo—at least," said the other sales rep. "Five megabytes would hold the entire works of Tolstoy, because—hey—all it is is text."

"You're suggesting that one picture of the Javits Center today is worth all the works of Tolstoy?"

"No, I'm saying that if Tolstoy was here today," said the first sales rep, "he'd be pee-dee-effing his pamphlets and religious tracts on the internet. Those essays that he published in his later years, such as *My Confessions* are just the kind of stuff that PDF does best."

Free Cookie Coupon
Wally's Wheat World
1234 Waterfront Street, River Bend, Iowa

Javits Center, July 7, 1996
Photograph Copright 1996 by Jeremiah D. Angelo.

Above: Mercury, atop Grand Central Station. Right: Chrysler Bldg. Below: Rose Reading Room, New York Public Library. Photos copyright 1996 Jeremiah D. Angelo.

'Zines Scenes

About seventy of us were jammed into the room at the Marriott Marquis Hotel and we all had our own 'zines. The panel discussion was moderated by Chris Dodge, a part-time cataloger at the Hennepin County Library public library and part-time editor of the Minnesota Library Association Social Responsibilities Round Table Newsletter.

What is a 'zine? was the first question to be addressed by the panel.

"A 'zine is what you do for yourself—it becomes a magazine when you start considering what the reader wants," responded panel member Chip Rowe.

Chip is an assistant editor at Playboy magazine and publisher of *Chip's Closet Cleaner*, a 'zine of pop culture, humor, trivia, and fun. As Chip explained, "It's subsidized by a large American corporation. Hef won't mind. That's how he started."

Chip has experienced the dilemma of being too successful. After contracting to have his 'zine distributed nationally, all unsold copies were returned to him with their covers carefully ripped off to ensure they were not sold by anyone else. "Somehow, that took the fun out of the publication," said Chip.

Gradually, Chip realized that he was changing the content of his 'zine, adding items of general interest to make it more popular. He decided to quit national distribution and return to publishing only what was truly important to himself. No longer worried about making a profit, his goal now is just to break even.

"'Zines are a form of folk art," said Chip. "It's an easily learnable skill that people practice for their own amusement. Like folk art, the quality of the production is extremely variable. Very rarely, actual fine art may be the result. Most of this stuff is crap. Out of two hundred 'zines, only one is Nancy's!"

Chip was referring to *Nancy's Magazine*, published by fellow panelist Nancy Bonnell-Kangas of the Columbus, Ohio Metropolitan Library. *Nancy's Magazine* started twelve years ago in San Francisco, hotbed of underground publishing. As she recalls:

"'Zines were appearing, breeding like bunnies and roaches. But there was no publication that called my name."

So she started her own 'zine and it has changed her life.

"It's like a chain letter that works!" Nancy exclaimed.

A Visit to the National Digital Library

Our guide led us upstairs to a gallery where we could observe the scholars and credentialed visitors studying in the Writer's Room of the New York Public Library. From this inspirational vista, we crowded into an antique cargo elevator. There were about a dozen of us, and when no more of our group could fit in the elevator, our guide said, "Push the CELLAR button. We'll meet you down there!"

The elevator seemed almost as slow and old as the one back in River Bend in which all of us had spent so many meditative minutes, but after a long, creaking descent, it finally settled down to the ground floor. There was a dramatic pause, then the doors rolled back to reveal a dark, gray corridor.

"It looks like my basement," said Merriam, sounding kind of pleased to see something familiar.

"It smells like...like a fishburger," said Djuna.

"Somebody's been down here eating fishburgers," said Veronica, in a singsong voice.

We waited, and wondered if we had gotten off on the wrong floor, our group cohesion dissipating as some were ready for a lunch break and talking about where to eat, when suddenly our guide came rushing past, leading a pack of librarians, rather like the White Rabbit leading Alice into Wonderland. We had no choice but to follow her down, down into the maze of tunnels underneath the streets of Manhattan.

(Continued on page 15.)

The LIBRARY *of* CONGRESS
AMERICAN MEMORY

HOME   BROWSE   ABOUT   HELP   CONTACT

Search all collections
SEARCH

The Library of Congress > American Memory Home

High school girls learn the art of automobile mechanics. Left to right: Grace Hurd, Evelyn Harrison, and Corinna DiJiulian, with Grace Wagner (under car), at Central High, Wash. D.C., 1927. LC-USZ62-111359

100th Annual River Feste
Sept. 3-5, 1996
Down by the River Side
For more info:
Contact Marian the Librarian,
Arts Department
555-Get-Lucky

American Memory
American Memory provides free and open access through the Internet to written and spoken words, sound recordings, still and moving images, prints, maps, and sheet music that document the American experience. It is a digital record of American history and creativity.

A Visit to the National Digital Library (*Continued from page 13.*)

"Follow the fishburger trail!", said Betty, getting a big laugh.

Our tunnel soon joined a main underground thoroughfare with beige walls and ceiling, bustling with librarians, security guards, and maintenance workers. Overhead were exposed ducts and great skeins of wires and fiber optic cables.

We turned right at an exit sign for Bryant Park, passing by a cafeteria and an espresso bar. We were crossing 42nd Street underground, headed toward the general vicinity of Grand Central Terminal, being led to a building whose exact location I am not allowed to reveal. In the event of a national emergency, this secure command post will serve as America's lifeline to freely distributed online information.

No natural light intruded into the auditorium, a square room with glass walls three stories high. It was eerily like being inside an aquarium. Sound baffles, carpets and padding with aquamarine colors made for an under-water like silence. On the other side of the glass were corridors and offices and, sometimes, people passing by. We spread out across the seats, while on the small stage a woman introduced herself as Laura White, our digital tour guide

Laura stood at the side of the stage using a computer whose image was projected for the audience. She demonstrated how to navigate the National Digital Library website and then began selecting items from the American Memory collection. Using web-based "streaming technology," Laura created a multi-media production by combining an audio recording from 1912 with a film from 1903 of a dancing lady.

"In the very near future people won't need to go to the library," said Laura, "because the library will come to them."

City Hall Park panorama, circa1913, copyright; Irving Underhill, New York. No. M-48. Airplanes in sky and tall building at right spliced into negative. Photographic print: gelatin silver ; 17.5 x 33.5 in. LOT 12475, no. 9, Panoramic Photographs, Library of Congress Prints and Photographs Division. LC-USZ62-137785

Available Exclusively at
Bluesville Music Emporium

Our Back Pages
This advertisement was published in *riverrun*,
Vol. 12, No. 2, Summer, 1887. LC-USZ62-87637

Non-profit Organization
U.S. Postage Paid

River Bend, Iowa
Permit #1234

Mr. & Mrs. John Q. Public
1776 Live Free or Die Avenue
River Bend, Iowa
54123

KEYCO®
Another fine KEYCO product

e-mail The Virtual Librarian:

MadameLibrarian@RiverBendLibrary.com
24-hour
"Hotline"

South Town Center Branch Library
101 Cornets Avenue
South Town, Iowa 51233

Rolling Hills Branch Library
1010 Rolling Hills Road
River Hills, Iowa 51235

Bookmobile
Call 555-5555 for current
route information.

Law Library
2nd floor
County Courthouse
76 Trombones Lane
River Bend, Iowa 51234

Downtown Outreach Library:
River City Community
 Action Coalition
1010 Waterfront Street
River Bend, Iowa 51234

River Bend Public Library
1010 Meredith Willson Boulevard
River Bend, Iowa 51234

www.riverbendlibrary.com

600: Technology

Down on the Killing Floor

605 Serial Publications

Sunday afternoon, while waiting in a long line for a $2.95 bottle of water, I recognized a familiar form. Something about her carriage; implacable, arms crossed, head canted, observant and detached, wearing an artfully tattered t-shirt, vintage jeans, and black and white Chuck Taylor Converse high tops. I was sure it must be Rachael when she turned around and I saw the message on her shirt:

Great Northwest State College
GO Fighting Voles!

—Rachael Rabinowitz, I said. How the hell are you?

We were standing on the concourse of the Javits Center, thousands of voices bobbling in our ears, the Hudson River at our backs and skyscrapers of Manhattan arrayed before us.

—Jeremy D! Just when I was thinking this was some kind of put-on, Rachael said, laughing incredulously, looking down, away, around and back.

Laughing at me, or with me, was what I could never figure out. There had been an undeniable attraction ever since we met in a multi-medi class called Communications and Community. She, a Jewish girl from Brooklyn, and me, a Catholic boy from the midwest. Seeing Rachael on her home ground was a revelation. Tawny-skinned, broad-nosed, brown hair, brown eyes darting, assaying, judging; sometimes veiled, sometimes not. Rachel would have been as perfectly at home in a middle-eastern bazaar as she was at Javits Center.

— How did you end up working in a library? That's the part I'm still finding hard to believe.

—I'd be baking whole wheat bread and cookies if I hadn't lucked-into this job as editor, I said, pulling a copy of *riverrun* out of my shoulder bag and handing it to her. We're really big in River Bend.

—I saw one of these at the Poetry Center, Rachel said, flipping rapidly through the pages.

—I've been distributing copies around New York for three days.

—Nice paper, Rachael said, testing the texture of a page between her thumb and forefinger. Your layout is kind of busy. Old-timey?

—Well, they've been publishing it for a hundred and thirty years.

—Hey, woodcuts are back in style. But I don't want to take your last copy, she said decisively, and handed it back to me.

Casually checking her plastic Swatch with the oversize face and big goofy numbers, Rachel said:

—So…where should we go for lunch?

—I guess we could grab something to eat in the food court….

—*Euuuhhhh*…not here! Rachael shuddered. Hey, welcome to the 'hood! Brunch is what we do best in Manhattan on Sunday afternoon.

—There's one more exhibitor I have to meet, I said. If you're hungry, I hear they're got cookies at their booth.

—Never take cookies from strangers, Jeremy, especially at a trade fair. You've got to wise up, buddy! You're in New York!.

609 Historical, areas, persons treatment

Following our noses to the source of fresh-baked cookies, we easily found the Net-Con® booth, where two girls in NetCon t-shirts were working behind a counter under a sign that said: FREE COOKIES & KOOL-AID®. They were baking cookies in a tiny oven and serving drinks in paper cups to passersby, asking in sing-song voices:

—Would you like a cookie?

—Are you drinking the Kool-Aid?

—What's with the free cookies? I said, munching into a warm and chewy peanut-butter cookie.

—Yeah, what kind of business model is that? said Rachael, tasting a morsel from a tray of chocolate chip cookies.

—Cookies are what computers exchange when you're on the internet, said the girl serving cookies.

—So they can talk to each other, said the other girl, judiciously filling paper cups with brightly colored, artificially flavored, sweetened water.

—That's how Netscape works, said the cookie girl.

—If you want to know more, get a Net-Con Guide. Dad has some over there, said the girl pouring drinks, nodding toward two men sitting together under a sign that said: NetCon® Books: Internet Guides for Life Online.

There was Michael Woolfe, president of NetCon® New Media, publisher of NetCon® Guides and "internet evangelist" at WORD, the on-line magazine. Sitting next to Woolfe, wearing a cowboy hat and strumming a well-travelled acoustic guitar, was John Perry Barlow, author of *A Declaration Of Independence of Cyberspace.*

—Oh my heck, I said. It's the Benjamin Franklin and Thomas Jefferson of the World Wide Web!

They were perched on stools next to a cafe table topped with a laptop computer and a live video feed of the frenzied exhibition floor. Michael Woolfe was clapping his hands, keeping time, while John Perry Barlow was strumming and humming, improvising a song:

—*I was down, down, down, on the killing floor....*

As Rachael and I approached, Michael Woolfe smiled in mischevious recognition of Rachael, saying:

—Hey homey, how's it hanging?

—We were just on our way out, said Rachel, but Jeremiah made me come back for the cookies.

—What I'm really here for are NetCon® Books, I said. We've got ten PCs on-line at our library and we'll double that when we get our Gates Grant.

—NetCon® Books are essential, said John Perry Barlow. People need that reassuring look and feel of old media as we venture out into cyberspace.

—There's a rising tide floating all boats, said Michael Woolfe. But you have to keep churning cash just to stay afloat. You can smell the burn-rate rising!

—It's the Gold Rush of '96, said Rachael.

—You could write a book about it, I said.

—You could write a song about it, said John Perry Barlow.

—You could do a song and dance about it for that matter, said Michael Woolfe, and get five million in venture capital, if you have a website.

In the background, voices of the girls were drifting through the trade show hubbub:

—*Kool-Aid!*

—*Cookies! Fresh, hot baked!*

—It's like the Oklahoma Land Rush, said Rachael.

She wasn't smiling. With quiet, clear-eyed outrage, she pressed her point:

—What people are racing for isn't real. That "home on the range" is pie in the sky.

—This is my home, said John Perry Barlow, gently touching his portable pc. Everything important to me goes out and comes in via my PowerBook® and a T-1 line. All I need is an outlet to re-charge my batteries, which Mr. Woolfe was kind enough to provide.

—Anything for a sale, said Michael Woolfe, winningly.

—Thanks to this internet entrepreneur, my computer is re-charging, and I feel a song comin' on, said John Perry Barlow. You never know when the muse may strike.

With a dramatically descending arpeggio, John Perry Barlow strummed his guitar and sang out:

—*I was down, down, down, on the killing floor.*

And I was won-won-wonderin' what I

was there for...

In the background, the girls sang their chorus.

—*Hot cookies!*

—*Cold Kool-Aid*!

608 Invention

Handing a copy of *riverrun* to Michael Woolfe, I said: Can we get permission to use excerpts from your books in our next issue? We print five thousand copies and distribute across Iowa and the Midwest.

—Nice rag, said Michael Woolfe. For obsolete media, it's pretty cool. You should win an award or something.

—So you're from River Bend Library? said John Perry Barlow. Sounds like a sweetheart deal you guys have worked out with KeyCo. But watch your copyrights if there's anything valuable in your collection. Those guys'll eat your lunch.

—KeyCo is helping River Bend get on-line, I said. "Equity On The Information Super-highway" is the theme of this conference, and nowhere is it needed more than at small town libraries.

—What benighted committee of information professionals came up with that slogan? said Rachael. Whatever the internet is, it isn't a "Super Highway."

—The world wide web is more than just new media, said John Perry Barlow. It's a new form of life…and afterlife.

—Some people think the internet is just another way to sell widgets, said Michael Woolfe, and for the most part, that's where we're at now. But it can be so much more. Like the invention of the printing press, it changes everything. This is the start of a new Renaissance.

—A whole new world, said John Perry Barlow. A nowhere that is everywhere.

—And Utopia was its name before that, said Rachael. What you guys are selling is mass delusion on a global scale.

—Well, you know what they say, said Michael Woolfe. On the internet, nobody knows you're a dog.

—Or a wolf, said Rachel.

As we were leaving, the girls offered their wares one more time.

—Would you like a cookie? said the first little girl.

—Are you drinking the Kool-Aid? said her little sister.

—No, just water for me, said Rachael. But thanks for asking.

The Brooklyn Girl's Guide to Manhattan

641 Food & drink

Rachael and I escaped the convention center, fairly running up the escalator and down the concourse toward the Eleventh Avenue exit where we gratefully sucked in the humid and gritty air of Manhattan. Clouds were coming in over the Hudson and it looked like it might rain.

—I don't know where I want to go for lunch, I said. But I know I need fresh air.

—I feel like Lot's wife, Rachael said.

—Don't look back!

—I know. Or we'll be turned into pillars of salt.

But we both turned and stared for a moment at the main entrance to the Javits Center, bristling with librarians coming and going, lining up for shuttle buses, talking in small groups, semaphoring to friends across the way, as taxis jockeyed for position and the Eleventh Avenue traffic unrelenting.

—Is there any place in New York that's not noisy and crowded and there's not somebody trying to sell you something? I asked.

—How about Central Park?

We caught a bus to 75th Street, then got off and walked down the block to the Citarella Market at Broadway. Rachel was rolling the tiny shopping cart down narrow aisles, gathering smoked salmon ravioli, Havarti cheese, a bunch of grapes, and a twisted loaf of challa bread.

—Check it out, I said. Mahtzoh crackers and kosher Coca-Cola!

—Thanks, but how about a nice merlot and some plastic cups?

690 Buildings

Grocery bags in hand, we walked toward the green horizon and the Dakota, that great gothic structure presiding over the 72nd Street entrance to Central Park.

—Why do you suppose they wanted to live in the Dakota, of all possible buildings in the world? I said. Wouldn't a nice place in the country have made more sense?

—I suppose they wanted to be near the park and among their own kind, said Rachael. People with more money than they know what to do with.

—So, were you here when it happened? The day John Lennon died?

—No, that was when I was in Seattle, writing for *The Rocket,* said Rachael.

—I was writing for the *Humboldt High Times* in exchange for room and board. Everybody freaked when John died, but I saw it as a sign.

—You got back to where you once belonged?

—Yeah, I got back. And I've been stuck in River Bend ever since.

—We had to toss a week's worth of layout when we heard about John, said Rachael. But we cobbled together a special commemorative issue without missing a beat. And as I type-set testimonials and pasted-in the pictures, all I could think was: Am I going to be writing about rock'n'roll for the rest of my life?

—Do you think Yoko is in today? I said, craning back my head and squinting up at the top floors.

—Please don't act like such a tourist, Jeremiah. I mean, really.

624 Civil engineering

We soon found a place to sit on the great lawn among all the other Sunday afternoon people of New York. Eating, drinking, talking with Rachel; it seemed as if we were two dabs of color in a landscape by Georges Seurat. I was laying on the lawn with my head propped up on my lumpy shoulder bag, the plastic cup of merlot balanced on my chest, and the towers of Manhattan towering over the meadow. It was kind of eerie watching the blinking red beacons at the tops of the World Trade Center appearing, then disappearing, into the gray scudding clouds.

—The World Trade Center is a place I was hoping to visit sometime this week, I said. Depending on the weather.

—The World Trade Center? That perfect example of totalitarian architecture recalling nothing so much as the windswept, barren plazas of Stalinist Russia?

—It's "a colossal example of the International Style," it says in this guidebook.

—The World Trade Center is a triumph of capitalism over all that is human-scale and life-affirming. Such as Central Park. Or Times Square.

—Terrorists tried to blow it up three years ago, and failed, I raved. The World Trade Center is so strong and yet so flexible, it's like the eighteenth wonder of the modern world. Ten thousand people go to work there every day.

Holding her cup out in a toast, Rachel said:

—To the poor bastards who have to work there!

We drank, and there was a moment of silence.

—If they did succeed in blowing up the World Trade Center, the world would be a better place for it, said Rachael. I mean, the Cold War is over. They're tearing down monuments everywhere.

686 Printing & related activities

—What I really want to see is Publisher's Row, I said.

—Publisher's Row?

—You know, that street where all the publishers publish on? Where you throw your manuscript over the transom?

—They have air conditioning now, Jeremiah. Nobody has transoms anymore, except in old movies.

—Well, wherever all those publishers went to. That's what I want to see.

—Book publishing is over, Jeremy, didn't you get the e-mail on that? They gobbled each other up. The ones that didn't move fast enough are extinct. Publishing is metamorphosing into all media, and no place more so than in Times Square.

—Okay, let's start there, I said, unfolding the map out of my day planner. But I don't get why they call it a square, cuz' it looks more like an X to me.

—It's not an X, it's a nexus, said Rachael. Broadway, Seventh Avenue, and Forty-second Street intersect in three-hundred-fifty years of history. Times Square is the omphalos of New York. That's why the Disneyfication of Times Square is such a, literally, gut-wrenching experience for people who live here. Times Square is where you rise up out of the subway and into the belly of the beast.

—Excuse me, but what's "Disneyfication?" Sounds like a disease.

—Exactly! Don't even get me started on Disneyfication. It's too horrible to even talk about what they're doing to Times Square.

Crossing-Off Brooklyn Ferry

623 Nautical engineering

—Okay, forget the World Trade Center, I said. And I've already seen Times Square. What I really want to do is ride the ferry while reading aloud from *Crossing Brooklyn Ferry*.

—There hasn't been a ferry to Brooklyn in a hundred years, said Rachael.

—Oh well, I said, crossing-off Brooklyn Ferry.

—How 'bout we walk across the Brooklyn Bridge while reading *The Bridge* by Stephen Crane? I should get home before dark for a change.

Rachael was giving me that familiar look again, wondering why we always ended up in these impossible situations together. It was a mystery to me, too, but it had something to do with both being solitary observers of society. It certainly wasn't a sexual attraction, because we had been over that long ago.

—Love the bridge, I said. Hated the poem. Besides, I just crossed it this morning with five thousand librarians in the Fun Run. What I'd really like are some up-close and personal pictures of the Statue of Liberty.

—Surely you jest, said Rachael. Nobody who lives here ever goes there.

—Pretend you're from Iowa, I said. This is what our readers want to know.

—The weather looks kinda iffy, Rachael whined. What if a squall blows up, the ferry capsizes, and everybody drowns? Like what happened in Turkey. How embarrassing would it be to die in a boat full of tourists?

To the Lighthouse

620 Engineering & allied operations

How would you describe the bland complacency of these sheep-like tourists? More people in jeans and windbreakers than people in shorts with sweaters wrapped around their waists. More trucker caps than tennis visors. More sneakers than sandals. More cameras than people, all here to take home our snapshot of Liberty.

—Talk about your huddled masses yearning to breathe free, said Rachael.

—My grandpa saw the Statue of Liberty when he was seven years old and just off the boat from Italy, I said. It meant nothing to him. It looked like statues he had grown up with in the old country, but giant-sized, like everything else in America. He was in quarantine for a week, then they put him on a train to Chicago. He and his family got jobs working in a cannery.

—Every day was "Take Your Child to Work Day," said Rachel.

—People used to work more, is all Grandpa ever had to say about it. And he never got to come back and visit New York. I guess that's partly why I'm here. I feel like I owe it to him.

—I don't think the Statue of Liberty was even built when the Rabinowitzes came over, in, like, 1882. We've been living in that shtetl over there, ever since, said Rachael, gesturing vaguely toward Brooklyn.

659 Advertising & public relations

We stood at the rail on the second floor deck enjoying the rush of air, that strange brew of industrial waste and sea breeze, watching Manhattan receding and the great gray-green lady looming ever larger. All around us; land, sea, and air, seethed with life.

—If all the world is becoming American, I said, then New York must be what Rome once was.

—Rome is the eternal city, said Rachael. I don't think New York is quite there yet.

—Okay, compared to Rome, New York City is up to like what? Two-hundred-fifty B.C.? Not exactly an empire. Ruling the world with media instead of armies. Sounds like America, circa 1996.

—That's what they'll call this era we're on the cusp of now, Rachael said, giving me that Sibylline look she had when she was thinking big.

—Circa 1996?

—Circa '96: the Twentieth Century is over and the Twenty-first Century is well under way. People just don't get it yet.

—Circa '96, I said. Sounds like a scent that if you could bottle it and sell it on the internet you'd make a hundred million dollars.

—Circa '96, said Rachael. The fragrance that makes you smart, young, good-looking, and rich! Smells like….

—Smells like Teen Spirit, I said.

—Smells like the tide going out, Rachael said.

—That "high tide of civilization," I said. I suppose it's still receding. But what I always thought was, you never know what you'll find washed-up on the beach.

643 Housing

—Rome isn't what it used to be anymore, either, said Rachael. I was there last week at a home design show and it was the same shiny dreck you see in Paris, Tokyo, and L-fucking-A.

—I didn't realize you felt so strongly about design. I mean, it's just fashion, right?

—Bad design is what's killing the world, one passive consumer at a time.

—So you're a consumer advocate?

—I'm an advocate of better living through human design. As opposed to anti-human design like you see in *Architectural Digest* and *House Beautiful*. Notice there's never any people in those double-page spreads, and nothing about what it all costs? What if there was a magazine about design for real people, with kids, and pets, and limited budgets?

—That idea, and a good website, is all you need to get started. But you need a catchy one-word name like *Slate, Concrete, Wallpaper*, or *Word*. And you might have to move to San Francisco.

—Stranger things have happened, Rachael said with that enigmatic smile, turning her head down and away.

Classified Information

607 Education, Research

Return to Ellis Island said the sign on the wall, and we did. Throngs of citizens milling about, looking for a clue. This motley stew of humans taking pictures of one other. Crying babies and old men breaking down. Hyped-up kids on roller blades cutting across the plaza, flags of many nations flapping in the wind, and Rachael sitting in the cafeteria across from me, sipping coffee from a styrofoam cup. I was working on my trip report. Rachael was working on a manifesto for her new magazine. Both of us alone together and writing again, just like old times. Feeling so free and easy is what made me suddenly realize that I wasn't.

—How long do you think it would take to get from Ellis Island to the Algonquin Hotel? I said.

—You mean literally, or metaphorically? said Rachael.

Now that Rachael had a place to write, a cup of coffee, and a great view, she didn't want to leave. Being able to write anywhere was a point of pride for her as a professional journalist, and if Ellis Island was where inspiration struck, then that's where it would be written down.

—I'm supposed to be at a big KeyCo wingding, I said. It's all hands on deck at the hotel from six until midnight. Dining, dancing, and an open bar. You could come as my guest but I know you'd despise them.

—Even if you did manage to board that ferry loading now, said Rachael, and can find a taxi when you get off the boat, he'd have to be the demon-driven, high-on-hashish, Turkistani cab driver from hell to get you there in time.

—I think I know that guy, I said, and I've got his card!

There was Abdul Osama's business card still in my wallet…and that was the last I saw of

Rachael. She stood up for one of our typically awkward public embraces, then Rachael sat down again to her coffee and note pad. That's where I saw her last: writing down tiny facts and observations, adding up to startling conclusions.

Using the pay phone in the lobby, I called Abdul Osama and he agreed to have his taxi waiting for me at the pier. And we might well have arrived at the Algonquin on time, but what happened after Abdul went through the first red light is better left unsaid. Much was lost in translation. Under advice of legal counsel I am leaving out what happened after we crashed into the shrubbery near the Columbia University School of Library Service, where Abdul made good his escape. All you need to know is that a security guard named Roxanne first saved my life, and then indoctrinated me into mysteries of library science.

And then it was Monday morning, and the Gale Shuttle Bus revving-up on the parking strip in front of Howard Johnson's collecting librarians for another day of meetings. Most of them had that zombie look you get after five days of information overload, like refugees from an industrial accident of the knowledge worker kind.

That's why I avoided the bus, walking whenever possible, meeting natives, reading the writing on the wall. Lost in the meatpacking district that evening, I wondered into a cabaret where Martha Grahm was performing live. If you can picture Martha Grahm as a six-foot-four man dancing *Appalachian Spring* while delivering a monologue in that breathy, clipped alto.

So it must have been Tuesday night

when all of us from River Bend and our new friends at KeyCo took over the Hard Rock Café for a farewell dinner. Afterwards, some few of us made an impromptu visit to the White Horse Tavern. I knew I'd had enough to drink, but sleep seemed impossible.

Computers with internet access were available for members of the press at Javits Center, so that's where I wandered next, just as it was getting light and the cleaning crew going home. After presenting my press pass to the security guard, I was soon on-line, checking my e-mail, and sending my Trip Report as an attached document. After a week of excessive everything except sleep, it's easy to see how I attached the wrong document and e-mailed it to ALL STAFF. It wasn't my intent, but what everybody received was a note to myself; a dream about me and Marian the Librarian.

A tremendous relief came over me when I hit SEND and I felt that now I could sleep. As I stumbled toward my trundlebed at Howard Johnson's, Helena's triumphant voice came back to me in the early morning light: something she had said on Redevelopment Day seemed imbued with sinister new meaning. *Best of all*, she had said, *Keymail is forever.*

(See Attached: Appendix A: *KeyMai/DreamReport.doc)*

Part Two

700: The Arts
Meetings, Dreams, and Hidden Agendas

710 Civic & Landscape Art

The next day I was back in River Bend, crapped-out on the sleeping porch of my second floor walk-up. Consciousness dimly returned with the dawn and swallows dive-bombing insects outside the screened windows. Rooster-tailing motor boats zipping among fishing trawlers. Oil tankers, freighters, and tugboats trailing barges in lazy, winding chains. Then a picture from the past hove into view; a paddle-wheel riverboat, saluting River Bend with its shrill steam whistle blast. Attached to the railing on the Texas deck, a hand-painted sign fluttered in the breeze:

Vote for Initiative #2
Save the Magnolia!

A public service message paid for by:
Derrick the Dude

743.414 Artisan Bread

Slinging my messenger bag over my shoulder, I set off on my bike rounding-up ads and stories for the FALL issue of *riverrun*. My first stop was down on the waterfront among warehouses and stevedore shacks along a street of mostly empty old brick buildings at Wally's Whole Wheat World. A rich mix of bakery scents poured through the screen door. A ghetto blaster encrusted in years of flour dust was cranked to full volume as workers kneaded loaves of whole wheat bread while standing around the sides of a long wooden table.

—Hey, it's the deserter, said Bourkely Tarbett III.

Bourke had been working since three a.m. His eyelashes, eyebrows, and military-cut hair were dusted with fine flour, as was his apron, camouflage t-shirt, and cargo pants.

—So you finally came dragging your sorry ass back, just like we always knew you would, said Justina. A scarf covered her hair, worn pirate-style, and gold hoop earrings gleamed in her ears. When not working at the bakery, Justina was working on her doctorate in Women's Studies at Keystone College.

—I'm here about an ad for the bakery, I said. Where's Wally? We need it soon or he'll miss the Fall issue.

—Wally is out scouting new locations, said Bourke. And he says the offer still stands, if you want to manage the southwest branch out to Hooperville.

—You know how much I liked working here, I said. What I can't handle is golfing with Wally after work.

—Or working under close supervision, interjected Justina, with a winning smile.

The oven timer went off with its industrial *BUZZZZZ*, over-riding all conversation. Bourke pulled on his rasty old oven mitts and raised the lever opening the oven door.

—Break's over, said Bourke. Back on your heads.

A burst of heat from the oven and a view of shelves jammed with bread pans rotating over flames like a Ferris wheel in hell. With a flick of the control stick, Bourke slowed the rotating shelves, stopping them level with the deck. Pulling out a strap of four bread pans, he banged them against the steel shelf to loosen the loaves and dumped them out, steaming and rolling across the cooling rack.

—Tell Wally I'll be back, I said.

—Thanks for the warning, said Bourke.

727 Buildings for education and research

Then it was uphill all the way to Key-stone College, where the biggest issue on campus was adequate parking. The college had grown in fits and starts outside town, up on the bluff, as River Bend's core had deteriorated. I was heading for the Communications Building, but I stopped first at the English department, an old farm house behind the Agriculture Department, next to the barn and stables.

There was a handwritten note thumb-tacked to the front door:

Steve:

GET OUT NOW!

It's my room and you know it.

Jeff

Walking around to the rear of the house, I quietly let myself in to the community kitchen shared by faculty. There were flowers in a vase on the table and a teapot gently simmering on the stove, but apparently no one in the building at the moment. Either that or they were all working on their books behind respective closed doors.

I put the folder marked FICTION in Jeff's mail box, and the folder of NON-FICTION in Steve's mailbox, with notes attached about the deadline for the next issue of *riverrun*, and thank you very much for your time. After filling the other mail boxes with copies of *riverrun*, I exited by the screen door— careful not to let it slam—and got back on my bike.

742: Perspective

Gearing down, I started pedalling up to Dr. Mephistopheles' aerie, high among the architectural statements clinging to the bluffs overlooking the river. What a view. From that perspective it seemed anything was possible. The Communications Building was itself a kind of statement, bunkered into the hillside, camouflaged and self-effacing. If not for the satellite dish tower on its roof, you'd never guess anything was up there.

Dr. Mephistopheles was up on the roof among the shrubbery, setting up a web-cam.

—Check it out, he said, typing com-mands onto his laptop keyboard: It zooms and pans. Imagine what kind of surveillance KeyCo could do with this.

—Jeez, Frank, that is so cool, I said. How the heck do you get to be Professor of Cyber-netics, anyway?

—I've just always been good with my hands, I guess, said the professor, holding out both hands and turning them over. It's a gift. That, and being in the right place at the right time.

—Like with this KeyCo deal.

—Mmm-huh, the professor absently agreed.

He was panning the camera across River Bend, pausing over the old downtown, inching along the modest brick buildings until he found the newest, shiniest, glass and steel edifice, and at its gleaming pinacle, Mayor Matt's office. Then he started zooming-in.

707 Education, research, and related topics

Keystone College was going to host a community website for River Bend. What I needed from Dr. Mephistopheles was information about when it was going to be up and on-line. All the technical stuff about linking the library to their site and up-loading *riverrun* in .pdf format was over my head. But to people like Jamie, Barney, and Stanley, it was a game, and a competition among them to stay ahead of the curve. In all this, I was merely the messenger.

Then it was a long coasting ride downhill back to the library basement and my usual routine, sorting bins of magazines and newspapers. I got a hand-truck from the loading dock, wheeled the stack of bins to the elevator, and began the long, slow ascent while sifting through the mail. Buried among press releases, advertising, and manuscript submissions for *riverrun*, was a registered letter from Mayor Matt addressed to me. Inside it was an invitation to participate in a meeting of the River Bend Redevelopment Agency. There were also letters from two non-profit groups inviting me to serve on their boards of directors: a "not-for-profit" organization called Mississippi River Writers, and an arts advocacy group so new that they didn't yet have a name.

The elevator doors rolled open onto the second floor scene like a curtain raising on a stage with scenery that had been changed during intermission. Everything was beige, modular, and vinyl, with padded, sound-absorbing surfaces. Everything was interchangeable, but the people were the same. There were twenty PCs set out in cubicles for general use and ten more in the Computer Lab where the Listening Center used to be.

Barney and Franny were sitting side by side in plush swivel chairs at a command post with matching PCs. Everyone was wearing polo shirts in a variety of shades emblazoned with the KeyCo logo.

—Hold the door! said Evelyn, rolling a cart full of *Saturday Evening Posts* around the corner as the alarm buzzed its feeble warning, the doors rolled shut.

One thing unchanged was the Kardex, squatting toad-like in the middle of all that new office furniture. Next to it were piles of periodicals awaiting my return.

—Welcome back, Jeremiah, said Evelyn. Sorry, we got behind with the magazines while you were gone, what with setting up the new PCs.

—And she's no longer an Assistant Librarian, said Franny.

Evelyn buffed her nails on her sleeve, then lifted her lapel so I could read her badge:

Evelyn Wood
Information Broker

—The pay is the same, said Evelyn, but now I'm working with Barney. It's a full time job keeping these pcs running, updating programs, and staying on-line.

—Magician's Apprentice is what we wanted on her badge, said Barney. But they said that's not a real KeyCo job title.

Rolling the truckload of mail bins over to the Kardex, I sat down and set to work.

—Why are we still using the Kardex? I asked the world at large. Surely if KeyCo can do everything else in the world, they can come up with a reliable serials module.

—I doubt it'll ever happen, said Franny. Serials are by their very nature inconsistent. They skip issues and create special issues, merge with other publications, go out of business, then start up again with new owners and a new publishing schedule.

—You'd need a program that allows for random behavior on a regular basis, said Barney.

—You mean on an irregular basis, Evelyn pointed out. She was leaning against the wall in that philosophical mood you get while waiting for the elevator.

—Bottom line is we need the Kardex as insurance, said Franny, in case KeyCo doesn't pan out.

That was when I became aware of an odd noise emanating from the next cubicle; a mechanical-whirring and then the sound of crunching like dry leaves. When I peeked over the side, there was Jordy, patiently feeding a stack of documents into the slot at the top of a tall black box.

—It's a KeyCo thing, Jordy said with a shrug. All departments must have paper shredders.

—How's it go? I asked.

—Put your paper in here and it falls out in strips into the bin, said Bill.

—Don't you have to turn it on?

—It's always on.

—Funny, said Evelyn, libraries used to be about preserving information.

—Libraries are about preserving knowledge and wisdom, said Jordy. But you can't save everything.

—I think there's a difference between discarding…I said.

—De-acquisitioning, you mean, said Jordy.

—Whatever, I said. There's a difference between tossing out the trash and shredding it.

—We're not shredding everything, said Jordy. Just financial records and personnel reports. Certain classified documents you don't need to know about. And patron records—for confidentiality.

—Dang!, said Evelyn. We're gonna need a bigger wastebasket!

—Probably we could mount it on a fifty-five gallon drum, Barney said.

—Hey, where's my bulletin board? I said, suddenly noticing a bare rectangular space on the wall with a lighter shade of paint just above where my desk used to be.

More than mere messages, my bulletin board had been an organizing principle, a three-foot by five-foot refuge of free associations among words, ideas, images, and thoughts for the day: all the raw ingredients that went into creating *riverrun*.

—I think I saw it out by the dumpster, said Franny.

—Didn't you get the e-mail on that?

said Jordy.

—Everybody got *your* e-mail! said Evelyn.

755.5454: *trompe-l'oeil*

Later in the day, I managed to catch Helena alone in her office for a quick meeting.

—If you're here about that e-mail, forget it, Helena said, hand on her telephone. It's all up to the lawyers. It's not an issue for me, I know we all make mistakes. But you might have to meet with the county attorney. Hey—don't let this distract you from the fine job you and Jamie are doing with *riverrun*. Donations for the 21st Century Library keep pouring in. I can't wait to see what you guys come up with next.

She smiled tightly, hand still on the telephone.

—Something else? she said.

—Here, I said, thrusting the letters at her. I don't know if this is in my By Statements, but I've got two invitations to serve on community boards.

Helena sat down, took her hand off the phone, and motioned for me to close the door. She didn't want to make decisions for me, and was reluctant to reveal what she knew, but I got her to name names and be specific.

—It would be a very good thing for the library to have you at that RDA meeting, Jeremy, said Helena. I'd go myself, but I've got too many other meetings already. Tell Jordy you'll be representing the library and paid on library time. We can pass the bill on to KeyCo as research for the 21st Century Library. This community art group sounds like a good deal, too.

—Because of the internet, it's finally happening. We're building an on-line calendar of community events. Jamie can post library events on it with links to our website and to *riverrun*.

—Sounds like a great opportunity for the library, Helena said. Do whatever you think is best, Jeremy. I'll make sure you're compensated for your time. Now, what is this about the Mississippi River Writers?

Helena was curiously turning over the glossy, tri-fold pamphlet.

—It's an honor to even be asked, I said. But attending meetings could be a problem. They have them up and down the river, Minnesota to New Orleans. Plus, there's that annual Confluence in Oxford, Mississippi. What do you think?

—Why don't you become an associate member? Helena said. Maybe trade the membership fee for an ad in *riverrun*? Arrange a soiree at our library? You guys could all meet in the Eight-hundreds.

It's these kind of meetings and decisions that are affecting my dreams.

755 Religion & religious symbolism

I was in a mass of people outside in a field in a vast space and we all felt something come over the crowd. Looking up, we discovered that it was Jesus, flying over us like a float in a Macey's Thanksgiving Day Parade.

Then I went back to running all over town. There was this woman I met, a writer /poet /journalist. She says something smart, then runs off toward the street and jumps into the front seat of a taxi/bus heading uptown.

I jump into the back of the vehicle,

among the immigrants and lower class. There are these dark-skinned natives speaking strange dialects and sharing drugs. Gradually I work my way up to the front of the taxi/bus just as the woman gets off at some kind of educational institution in a nice neighborhood. She goes inside and I follow.

It's a newspaper/university. The woman is one of the writer/teachers here and I'm wandering the halls after hours meeting people coming in and out of offices.

She leaves messages for me, but when I come back to her office, she's never there. So I'm writing a message for her on an old scarf, a gift from another woman, long ago. I'm dubious about my motivations, and I'm running out of room to write on this scarf.

Then it's daytime again and everybody's back in their offices as I'm running around town and it's on the news and official:

Jesus Christ appeared to a large mass of people recently. His presence was first felt, then seen, floating over the people in a vast and peaceful space, floating horizontally, arms stretched out, white garments drifting up cloud-like into the atmosphere.

We're all watching this on television and in the papers and on the internet. Everybody everywhere is talking about it. It's the greatest story in the history of the world. People find it hard to believe, but it's in all the news media, so it must be true.

—*Oh yeah,* I say. *It's true. I was there.*

Then I wake up, late for my next meeting.

Social Capitalists @ Work

765.4321: Beaux Arts
     July 19, 1996
     Board Room, River Bend Art Society
     Sibyl Seraphim, publisher/editor **Nexxus**
     Argentina Robinofsky, writer/publicist
     Jeremiah D. Angelo, editor of *riverrun*
     Juliana: fabric artist
     Fiona Finneas: Keystone College Arts Dept.
     Mrs. Vanderplast, River Bend Art Society
     Adam Zand, R. B. Chamber of Commerce.

—First item of business is still the problem of a name for our group, said Sibyl, with a chiding look around the conference table. We've had several meetings, and there's still no consensus on what we should call ourselves.

—That's the only thing there is consensus on, said Adam.

—When we adjourned last month, we got to what was it? What's it say in your notes, Jeremiah?

—Beaux Arts.

—Right. And that's so last century, you know? said Sibyl. Which is what River Bend needs to get over. The Twenty-first Century is happening here and now. We've got to get on-board or be left behind, and by the way, deadline for our August is today. So don't leave here without giving me your stuff.

Sibyl was a woman of parts, earth-tone outfits, and long, straggly, prematurely white hair. Retiring in River Bend after twenty years with the U.S. Coast Guard after serving on the east coast, the west coast, and the Mississipp River. Sibyl was now bringing a new age vibe to our little town by publishing and editing *Nexxus: News, Notes, & Nightlife.*

—How about Beaux Esprits?, said Argentina, marking the place with her finger in a dictionary. A *bel esprit* is a wit or genius, and two or more together would be *beaux esprits*.

This suggestion was well received. Argentina, a special events coordinator, always had the noblest goals for our nascent group. She was a dark-skinned latino with a shock of hair died firey-red.

—*B... E...*, Sibyl said, trying out the sound of it.

—We could have *BE-ins*, said Argentina. Spontaneous art happenings.

—Meetings would become BE-ings? Juliana wondered aloud. Juliana was an artist with only one name: Juliana. (*Hoo-li-ah-na*, she would say. *Zhat is my name.*)

—Beaux Esprit Group? said Fiona. Fiona was keeping to the agenda and watching the clock She was multi-tasking before there was a word for it.

—The acronym would be B-E-G, said Adam. I'm guessing that's not the image we want to project.

Adam carried the biggest day planner of all, bound in leather. He always wore a suit and tie and scuffed, brown wingtips. Adam's office was located in the otherwise vacant Ferry Building, next door to the River Bend Mall. Nobody was more invested in redeveloping River Bend than Adam Zand.

—What about Arts Alliance? I suggested.

—AA? Are you kidding? said Adam.

—We'd be first in the phone book, Gloria pointed out.

—Think of the calls we'll be getting if people get us mixed up with the other AA, Fiona sighed.

—We'd double our membership instantly, I said.

—Probably a lot of membership overlap already, Jeremiah, said Jim, with a meaningful glance at Sybil.

—Can we table the discussion until our next meeting? Sybil suggested. And get on to our next item of business, which is the website.

—I had a meeting with Dr. Mephistopheles a few days ago, I said. He showed me a beta-version of the site and it should be good to go for our next meeting.

—We'll have to meet on campus, said Fiona. At least until KeyCo connects the rest of River Bend.

—What would it cost to get our art collection on-line? Mrs. Vanderplast wondered. They have grants for that kind of thing?

—That's what I want to know, said Sybil. How do you non-profit groups get that groovy grant gravy?

—First of all honey, said Fiona, you need to file your five-oh-one-cee-three, establishing that you are, indeed, non-profit.

—All they'd have to do is look at my bank account, said Sybil. I've done nothing but lose money since our first issue.

—What you do have is social capital, said Argentina, giving Sybil a quick hug and a laugh. That's one thing we all have plenty of.

—*Vhee are a zhocial capital zhociety*, said Juliana.

Juliana could be relied upon for grand statements like that, speaking half to herself, trying out new ideas like shades of colors for one of her constructions.

—Social Capital Society? Adam incredulously replied. Scary sounding name, don't you think?

—Social Capitalists @ Work? I suggested.

—Sure, said Argentina. Anything with an @ sign is cool this year.

Sybil started banging her little gavel on the podium, saying:

—People, people, people! Forget the name! It's not important. What's important is that it's happening.

Once again, we ran out of time before reaching consensus on what to call our merry band. It didn't seem to matter. We knew we'd run into one another again in River Bend. There was a common feeling that our time was now and Sybil was our leader. It wouldn't be fair to say that what went down during the Deep River Blues Festival was all Sybil's fault. In the subsequent events that transpired, she was merely the catalyst.

The meeting adjourned. We all checked our dayplanners, exchanged press releases, flyers, and business cards, and dashed off to our next scheduled meetings.

713 Landscape architecture of traffic ways

—River Faire is all about the seven hundreds, said Marian, the fine art librarian. And the more you know about the seven hundreds the more you'll understand what River Faire means for the future of our fair city.

She blushed, catching her breath. There were maybe twenty of us milling at the Park & Ride, and a guy from the *Forward-Progress* taking pictures. An old railroad spur had been donated by Union Pacific as part of a rails-to-trail program. Whether or not the land could it be restored in time for River Faire '96 was the question.

—You see how I get about the seven-hundreds, Marian resumed. They're vital. Art is life. Where's there's life, there's hope. Instead of this, she said with a dismissive wave at the defoliation and ruin along the Mississippi shoreline.

Some arrived late, others left early. It was a hot day and a long hike. Those same few people who showed up at art openings, public hearings, and city council meetings. Mayor Matt was there with his crew. Sybil was signing up volunteers for the Deep River Blues Festival. Derrick the Dude was talking up his campaign to *Raise the Magnolia*. Most of the art advocates showed up, along with Steve and Jeff from the college, and some U.S. Forest Service guys, one of whom was a lady.

It had been Marian's idea to meet here and have our planning session *en plein aire*. She led the way in designer jeans, jogging shoes, and an old River Faire t-shirt, striding out along the rough trail paralleling the railroad track.

—We want a landscaped pathway along the river, said Marian. We want views and we want fresh air. We want benches along the way to sit and rest and smell the flowers.

—Your basic covered shelters, said Adam Zand. What would it cost for materials?

How would you design something like that?

—Learn all about it in the seven-seven-teens, said Marian. Look under Structures.

—How about a gazebo? Said Mayor Matt.

—Landscape architecture? said Marian. That's your seven-twelves. Seven-thirteen is the riparian landscape we're walking through now. Look around. You see nothing but seven-four-teens and seven-fifteens: your water features, your woody plants. A little further down the path and we come to the seven-sixteens: herbaceous plants, such as kudzu, violets, woody nightshade.

719 Natural landscapes

We crossed a narrow isthmus of natural landscape. The railroad tracks continued north, while the land extended out in a peninsula, the Mississippi River wrapping around this point and the ruins of what must have once been a lighthouse. It was wild. Half of it was swamp. But there was definitely a shelf of usable land that could conceivably be cleared to make space for an audience. And there was that promontory where you could almost picture musicians tuning up.

Thus was born the *Deep River Blues Project*. It was Sybil's idea, but we were all deeply, bluely, implicated in what went down. Sybil said it was all about on-line advertising and links to River Bend's website. The deal was sealed when she told us about the video crew that would produce a documentary of the three-day festival, timed to coincide with *River Feste '96*.

After poking around and generally agreeing that it would be totally cool to have a music festival, we agreed to meet again at Mayor Matt's office to finalize plans. Then we split up and went our separate ways. Some people continued on up the tracks. Some turned around and headed back to town. Some wandered around out to the point, skipping rocks across the river. And there were some few who had brought along food and drink for a picnic in the tall grass.

753: Symbolism, allegory, mythology, legend

—So who are you? said Derrick the Dude.

—I'm Marian, the fine art librarian.

—Yeah, I know you're fine, said Derrick the Dude, but who are you?

—Marian Madley, she said, reaching out to shake hands with the Dude. Fine Art Department, River Bend Library.

—Jeez, I love your vision, said Derrick. I want to be part of that.

—Well, what's your vision, honey? Said Marian, pushing back a lock of hair that seemed somehow animate with its own determination to drift around her head, penumbra-like, in the golden light of the setting sun.

—My vision is to save the *Magnolia*. Re-float the boat. Bring back them good old days of riverboats and freedom. "The awful Sunday afternoon lonesomeness of the Mississippi River," as Huck Finn describes it.

—God, I love a man who quotes Mark Twain, said Marian, heaving a sigh and laughing at herself, for her own stupid vulnerability, or at the smooth moves of Derrick the Dude, it was impossible to say.

—Perhaps we could continue this conversation elsewhere?

—Let's not, and say we did.

751 Techniques, equipment, materials and forms

Jamie was holding up translucent, sky-blue sheets, with rippling text flowing like water.

—Check it out Jeremy! She said, letting the sheets float on the breeze like a cape on the wind, like the sheets on my bed.

I woke up with a start. There was a song in my head and it sounded like Deep River Blues. At work that day, I told Jamie about my dream, and I asked if she could embed a link in the virtual edition of *riverrun* to a feature story about the music festival.

—Good idea! she said with that laughing, daring, look in her eye. You guys could make a CD and sell it online.

—Do you suppose we could publish a commemorative book about the festival? With a CD inside?

—Ride the wave, Jeremy!

763 Lithographic processes

—Where's Jordy? I said, noticing that everybody was present for our monthly staff meeting, except the head of our department.

—Didn't you get the e-mail? Evelyn asked.

—Welcome back, Jeremy, said Franny. While you were out, there's been some changes.

—Jordy no longer works here, said Barney. He got a better offer.

—Franny's the new department head, said Evelyn.

—Congratulations, I said. But what happened to Jordy?

—I guess Jordy was de-acquisitioning what he should have been saving, said Franny.

—Oh crap, I said. Did he throw away the old *riverruns*?

—No, not those, said Franny. Jordy said they could be the most valuable items in the collection. And what do you suppose he meant by that?

—Beats me, Evelyn said, but whatever you do, don't throw away old *Life* magazines.

—They were duplicate copies! Franny said, rolling her eyes.

—They're like money in the bank, according to Helena, Barney coolly observed.

—Other libraries will pay top dollar for those, said Evelyn.

—People on e-Bay will pay money for anything, said Barney.

—The library is not about losing money anymore, Franny concluded. And Helena said that until further notice, I'm in charge.

—Jordy has moved on to a better world, said Barney. He's chief librarian, plus he gets room and board.

—Jordy's directing the digitization program at the monastery now, said Franny. He was researching his doctoral thesis and ended up volunteering. When the Abbot found out he was available, well…they got a grant from *Opus Dei* and put him on the payroll.

—I don't think Jordy was working out so well *vis-a-vie* the matriarchy here anyway, said Evelyn. Present company excluded, but most guys don't.

—I believe the correct term is gynocracy,

said Barney. Rule by women. You don't have that problem living in a monastery. Only downside is, there's no sex.

—Oh, I think Jordy's got that department covered, said Evelyn, touching her pearls, discretely tilting her head toward Franny.

Hostile Work Environment?

791.4372 B176: Batman feature film

The less we saw of Cody the better was the policy in our department. No point in alarming him about those junior gangsters, Esteven, Leonardo, and Carlos #1 selling pornography they had printed-out from library computers. Most of us admired their entrepeneurial spirit. Banishing the boys from the internet for a week was all it took to reform them into model netizens.

Cody was preoccupied, anyway, with construction of the 21ˢᵗ Century Library. He was always flying off somewhere like Batman to clandestine meetings or rescuing damsels in distress at branch libraries. When Cody was gone, life went on much more smoothly, and what he didn't know about was probably for the best.

I doubt he even noticed when I retrieved my bulletin board from the dumpster and attached it to the only space in the building not made-over by KeyCo: hanging on a nail in the staff elevator. It was a way for co-workers to stay in touch, I was thinking. Encourage frank and open discussion while generating story ideas for *riverrun*. But that's not how KeyCo saw it. An escalating volley of e-mails flew back and forth between me and various associate directors. One day, in the middle of checking-in magazines, the phone rang and Franny said they needed me for a meeting in the Board Room with Cody, Trixie, and a representative from KeyCo.

—Hostile Work Environment is what we're talking about here, said Trixie. Your bulletin board undermines the authority of the managers.

—*Hostile Work Environment?* I dumbly repeated. That's exactly what it's been like here since KeyCo took over. I thought libraries were supposed to support intellectual freedom.

—Intellectual freedom is intended for library users, not for staff! Cody snapped.

—What about my First Amendment right of freedom of expression?

—Hanging an effigy of Cody in the elevator is not a First Amendment right, the KeyCo rep explained in that serious tone she used, wearing those serious black rectangular glasses, black pageboy framing her pale, round face. I think her name was Jennifer and she didn't last long—an information professional with no experience working in a public library. She had assumed Nancy's job downstairs. Whatever happened to Nancy? is what I was wondering. Maybe she transferred to that KeyCo facility with an ocean beach where Helena and Zelda held their virtual teleconference? It seemed entirely plausible, and I couldn't think of anyone more deserving. With these tangential thoughts racheting through my head, I made an attempt to explain what had happened.

—It was a Batman action figure some kid left in the Computer Center, I said, in a calm and rational voice. All I did was put Cody's nametag on him and pin him to the bulletin board.

—That's not funny, Jeremy, said Cody.

—That's sad, said Trixie.

—See, this is what we mean, said Jennifer.

—That's your passive-aggressive way to get back at authority figures, Jeremy, said Trixie.

—Hostile-Work-Environment, said Jennifer, tsk-tsk-tsking.

—What it comes down to is Anger Management for you, buddy, said Cody.

—You'll thank us for this later. Believe me, Jeremy, said Trixie.

—It's for your own good, said Jennifer.

—Being an angry white man is nothing to be ashamed of, Jeremy, said Cody.

—Sure, I said. And I'm sure the library gets group rates.

754 Genre paintings

Elevatored upstairs to the electronic din of the Computer Center. Talked to Gordy about scheduling the next issue of *rivverun* and negotiated printing expenses. He can only get enough of the good paper stock for one more issue and we'll have to cut it down to sixteen pages.

Checked my e-mail and found the memo from Cody, re: the memo from Trixie, re: the memo from Jennifer about chatlines, and what is our policy for dealing with patrons speaking to each other over their partitions? Is that a privacy violation, or what?

I printed out a copy of my By Statements with the new KeyCo standards attached and then it was my turn for a quarterly performance review with Cody and Franny in Cody's office where I noticed there were no pictures on the wall. Everything was very beige and impersonal as we negotiated my By Statements: reviewing the past six months, scheduling and planning everything to be accomplished through the end of the year.

—I got your e-mail, I said.

And it went downhill from there. Franny sat quietly on the side, not saying anything, clutching her stomach. Unless Cody or I asked her directly, she kept out of it.

—Another thing that's going to have to change, said Cody, is your working habits. Jeez, Jeremy, you're out of the building more than you're in. You need to manage your time more effectively. Learn to use the phone and e-mail like a normal person. Come to work on time and go home after work like everybody else does. There are liability issues.

—Lie-ability issues? I said. Yeah, I've got plenty of issues with people who lie.

—Bottom line is, Cody grimly smiled, no more working on your own time. Just get your job done in the time that's available. Work smarter, not harder.

790 Recreational & performing arts
KeyMail©
August 15, 1996
From: Stacey Cartwright
To: ALL Library Staff
Re: River Faire
Clear the decks and man your stations! The Planning Posse is heading out to the river parkway, PDQ. We will survey

the site so everything runs good and not like last year, about which the less said, the better. Fortunately, there was no loss of life and minimal property damage. But what a mess to clean up. Anyway,

:(

So PLAN AHEAD!! Wear APPRO-PRIATE ATTIRE for weather CONDITONS and if you can find a parking spot which is always a factor. Please arrive at YOUR SCHEDULED BOOTH at YOUR SCHED-ULED TIME!!! See you there!!!!

;> Stacey C.

800: Literature & Rhetoric

Storyville

813 Fiction

There were fifteen of us sitting around a long table in the conference room adjacent to Mayor Matt's office. Walls made of glass on three sides afforded views of the river, Main Street, and high along the bluffs, the campus of Keystone College. Somewhere up there Dr. Mephistopheles's webcam was zooming and panning, and I wondered if it could see through tinted glass. Then I realized if he really wanted to watch this meeting, he would probably hack into those security cams in the corners of the room. By that time, KeyCo had webs of fiber optic cable everywhere.

—What a great view, said Sibyl Seraphim.

—I'm enjoying it while I can, said Mayor Matt. 'Cuz we're unloading this property soon as we get the right offer. There's more important projects, like this new community we're discussing today.

—The neighborhood formerly known as Bluesville, said Adam Zand.

—Bluesville was legendary, said Sybil. Billie Holliday sang there, back in the day. Robert Johnson, Muddy Waters, Big Bill Bronzy, all the greats.

—Bluesville is history, said Eleanor. That's what we're here for is to create a new model, a new brand, we can all get behind.

Eleanor was Mayor Matt's PR flack, so we all saw rather a lot of her. She kept us well supplied with press releases, planning documents, and artist renditions of a bright, watercolor future for River Bend.

—Darky Town was what they called it before that, said Dr. Cornelius, president of the River Bend Community Action Coalition.

—Great, said Mayor Matt, boyishly blowing hair out of his face and rolling his eyes.

The youngest mayor in River Bend's history, Mayor Matt was still working on his MBA, but it was plain to see he was destined for greatness.

—Darky Town is what they called it when I was born there, said Dr. Cornelius. Now you can call it whatever you want, but it was sure enough Darky Town then.

—Can we start the presentation now? said Mayor Matt with a tight little smile.

The computer-projected presentation began with a schematic view of the gridwork streets and urban blight that we all recognized as old River Bend.

—First step is demolition, said Mayor Matt. Check this out.

Zooming in on a blighted block of the grid, Mayor Matt clicked on the DEMOLITION button. A digital bulldozer appeared and with a pleasant rumbling sound trundled back and forth, clearing away old buildings with little puffs of dust, bricks tumbling down.

—Now, here's where we add mass transit systems, said Mayor Matt, and he pushed the button for light rail.

On screen, digital train tracks were laid down: *thwack, thwack, thwack.*

—Then we choose the right mix of Retail, Industrial, and Residential, said Mayor Matt. That's critical. For now, we'll set the controls on auto, set the budget for twenty mil per year, and voila, watch what happens!

Digital trains started tootling around the tracks. A factory appeared at one end of the rail line. At the other end of the line little houses started popping up, one by one. Retail shops began appearing at nodes of the train tracks, and then tiny figures began coming out of houses, getting onto trains, going to their jobs, and going shopping at the mall.

—Is there a name for this ideal community? said Adam Zand.

—Sim City®, said Mayor Matt. This is just a beta-version, but you get the idea. You can't start building the future until you demolish the past. It's tough to get that across to citizens in a positive way.

—There's resistance to the RDA, said Eleanor, is what Mayor Matt's talking about. Recriminations and mis-understandings among stake holders. That's why we asked you here today, to help shape our message.

—God forbid that an act of God should wipe out the waterfront like the floods we used to have in the old days, said Mayor Matt. Long, long ago, before the Corps of Engineers tamed the river.

—Some kind of natural disaster might not be all bad, Eleanor agreed.

—Plus, and, said Mayor Matt, there's

your insurance money, and there's FEMA. That's like money in the bank.

—In short, until we know results of the bond election this fall, our plan remains an evolving design, said Eleanor.

—With three initiatives on the ballot, said Mayor Matt, anything can happen.

—So there's three bond initiatives now? I said. What-the-hey?

—Haven't you heard about the Panopticon? Adam Zand said. There's some serious out of town capital behind that proposal.

—I'm not taking sides and I'm not against anything that gets River Bend moving again, said Mayor Matt. But that's not what we're here to talk about.

—What we need is for you guys to brainstorm, said Eleanor. As stakeholders and community influencers, your input is critical. Now, what do you envision as your ideal community?

—A pleasant, pleasing kind of place.

—Pleasantville?

—Great name for a movie, but who'd want to live there?

—A secure environment.

—A gated community. Twenty-four-hour surveillance cameras.

—Would a guard come with that, like, in a watchtower?

—It could be arranged, said Mayor Matt.

—Securityville?

—Sounds safe, but, I dunno…kind of bland?

—How about Celebration?

—They're using that one already in Florida.

—Dang, all the good names are already taken.

—You need to start thinking outside the box, people, said Eleanor.

—Storyville?

—Isn't that part of New Orleans?

—Really? I thought it was where stories come from. You know, American stories about Americans doing American things.

—What a great place to live that would be.

—Storyville was where the prostitutes lived in New Orleans. So that's out.

—Dang, all the best names are already taken.

—You already said that.

—Outside the box, people!

—How about Happy Place?

—I can't believe you seriously mean that.

—Oh, touch me in my Happy Place.

—Get your minds out of the gutter, people!

—A Clean, Well-Lighted Place?

—Exactly. Order. Calm. Rational. Think of a name for that.

—Orderville?

—You've got to be kidding.

—No, it's a real place in Utah. Just a ghost town now.

—See? All the good names got taken long ago.

—What about...Dewey...Decimalville? I wondered aloud.

—That is either the dumbest idea I've ever heard, or a stroke of genius, said Sybil,

giving me her cool, appraising look.

—The Dewey Decimal system can accomodate anything, I said, feeling inspired. Besides planning for industrial, retail, and residential growth, shouldn't we plan for expanding the life of the mind? To me, that means a community built around a Twenty First Century Library.

—If the bond for your new library is approved by the citizens? Mayor Matt mused. And if your HUD grant ever comes through? Sure. I can see that.

—I thought the HUD grant was "in the bag?" said Sybil. That's what Helena Montana said to the city council.

—It was in the bag and on that plane with Ron Brown when they went down over Croatia, said Adam Zand, somberly reminding us of another great stroke of bad luck for River Bend during a year of catastrophes.

—Might be others with HUD grants was in that bag, too, said Dr. Cornelius, smiling sadly. Ron Brown was a brother.

—Oh my gosh, Dr. Cornelius, I said, blushing in embarrassment. I had no idea you were related.

—Fool! Not my actual brother, said Dr. Cornelius. I mean, he was working for The Man, but he was still a brother.

814 Essays

To essay comes from the French, *assay*, meaning: *to try*. Try imagining River Bend on a late summer afternoon at the library. Nobody who didn't have to be there wouldn't be in the library that time of day at that time of year. It was a totally dead, calm, Horse Latitudes afternoon.

—Open the window, for gosh sake, said Evelyn Wood. Give a body some fresh air.

Evelyn was surfing on-line dating services. Trying out on-line personas like trying on new outfits. There was a man in Idaho, a widower, with two teenage sons; a part-time farmer and part-time computer nerd who liked to build PCs and chat about it. Anyway, that's what he felt safest chatting about with Evelyn.

Taking a deep breath of fresh air flowing in the now-opened bay window, Evelyn hunkered down to the keyboard and started furiously typing.

The Mississippi River Writers Confluence

801 Philosophy & theory

The Mississippi River Writers Confluence was cancelled due to lack of anybody showing up at the same place at the same time. They were all in their cubicles, writing. Okay, sometimes they went out to the Zippee Mart for beer and fried chicken or milk and coffee, depending on whether it was p.m. or a.m. and if they were going to or coming from their night jobs or their day jobs. So scheduling was definitely a factor.

Nevertheless, meetings did occur and words were exchanged. I clearly recall early one morning setting out my goods on a table in the corridor on the second floor of the student union building at Keystone College. Other tables around the atrium were rapidly filling with sales reps from graduate writing programs, publishing companies, and bookstores.

Jeff was passing by and stopped to pick up our latest issue of *riverrun*. Oh what a feeling it was as something in it made him stop, then ever so slowly pivot on his heel, and sit down on the table, reading all the while.

I'll never know what it was that so caught his attention because the auditorium doors burst open just then, releasing students, teachers, hangers-on, and camp followers of Mississippi River writing. For the next ten minutes I was distributing copies of *riverrun* to passersby, along with our writer's guidelines, publishing schedule, and advertising rate sheets. Sales reps were distributing pre-publication copies of books, students were buttonholing authors, and everybody was exchanging business cards.

In the midst of the ruckus, Jeff was quietly reading at the end of my table. Then Steve, Jeff's associate in the English department, eddied out of the crowd, picked up a *riverrun* and began flipping through the pages. People were coming back from the cafeteria now, cradling Styrofoam cups of coffee, merging with traffic exiting the lavatories, toilets flushing in their wake, scurrying back to the auditorium and to various meeting rooms for the next session.

—Great turn-out this year, I said, to Steve.

—We were lucky to get some big names this year, Steve said, wiping a light perspiration from his shaven dome and glancing around appreciatively at the festive scene.

Steve was short and might have been stout except for his devotion to mountain-climbing. He was bagging mountains and writing books about them.

—Somehow, we always do, said Jeff.

Great stuff in here, Jeremiah. Keep up the good work.

Jeff tucked the magazine into his weathered, leather, over-stuffed briefcase. It was a medical bag inherited from his grandfather, a horse and buggy doctor, which I happen to know because that's the kind of thing we usally ended up talking about when it was finally time for Jeff to pick the winners: cornered, in his office, after hours.

Jeff was tall and had a ragged head of hair for which he had only provisionally accepted responsibility. He liked to write about rivers and had a manuscript in progress. It might become a project for a university press, but you never know with that kind of thing. Maybe if he was teamed with a good photographer, that might work. A good photographer would help the sales of Steve's books, too.

—You know, there's worse places to run a writers conference, Steve said.

Now Steve was leaning back against the table and Jeff was looking at his watch and peering at the schedule.

—Worse places to end up teaching for the rest of your life, too, Jeff agreed.

—Sure, there's more prestigious places, Steve continued. But then you'd have to live there, you know? You lose your quality of life.

—They say that wherever you're teaching when you turn forty, that's where you'll always be, said Jeff.

The final stragglers were entering the auditorium, doors were closing, it was suddenly calm again.

—Well, I gotta run, said Jeff, looks like I'm on a panel.

—I better get over to the reception room, Steve said. They should be back from the airport soon with our keynote speaker. It cost ten thousand dollars to get E.L. Doctorow, can you believe it? For twelve hours of his time—a layover on his way to Chicago. We were just lucky they could fit us into his schedule.

Inappropriate Behavior?

812 Drama

The e-mails were flying hot and cold when Jamie announced that she was marrying Dr. Wu and moving to Silicon Valley. Jamie and I had a moment alone together in the art department on her last day as I was arriving and she was leaving. No longer a stick-figure girl, Jamie had blossomed into a woman, wife, and mother. Something she said, or left unsaid, stayed with me. She was giving me advice on layout and design for the Fall *riverrun* and then, because I had asked her, she shared her ideas on what to do with my hair and what I should wear.

—Ow, she said, cupping her breasts. They're full again. My baby needs me now.

Then she was gone, leaving so much left unsaid between us that I was inspired to write Jamie a letter. Somehow the peace and quiet of the library after-hours seemed like the perfect place to tell Jamie I loved her and that she had changed my life. I worked on the letter until the cleaning crew came in at midnight, then I left it under her keyboard to find in the morning.

The next day, when I reported to work, I was immediately summoned downstairs to the now all too familiar boardroom, for "Inappropriate Behavior".

—What's that supposed to mean? I said. Inappropriate Behavior?

—Well, not swooning around the library falling in love with co-workers, for example, said Jamie, rolling her eyes and looking away.

—Jeez, Jeremy, said Marian. To most of us, the library is just a job, and we'd like to keep it that way.

—Eight hours a day, forty hours a week, and get the heck out of the building when your shift is over, said Jennifer. Professional attitude. That's the KeyCo way.

We were seated around a long, glass-topped table, in a beige room with soundproof walls and subdued lighting.

—Nobody cares what you do at home, Helena said. On your own time.

—That's your own beeswax, said Marian.

—But at work, certain behaviors are expected, said the county attorney. Sexuality should *never* be an issue.

Her name was Mignon, and she was a little minx, with a head of cunningly cut jet black hair, wearing a black, silk lady lawyer suit with big lapels.

—Funny that I'm the only guy in the room, I said, looking around at the faces of the five women.

—It's not funny, Jeremy, Helena said. That's what you've got to get over.

—It's that passive-aggressive attitude, hiding behind a mask of humor, that gets you in trouble, said Jamie.

—We're here to help you, said Marian, carefully folding her hands on the table in an attitude of compassionate resolve.

—Help is maybe something you're not used to getting? In your lonely-guy lifestyle? said Helena. Accepting help from others is the feminine advantage. We stick together not by choice, but because we have to. That's the genetic hand we were dealt. That's what women have always done.

—It takes a village, said Jamie, Marian, and Jennifer in chorus.

—And it takes the law to back it up, said Mignon. That's why we're meeting here today. Although there are grounds for sexual harassment charges, and there certainly is evidence, she said, cheerfully tapping the folder on the table, neither Jamie nor Marian are bringing suit against you.

—We're not going to fire you for making a mistake, said Helena. But we sure as heck are going to have sexual harassment training on a regular basis from now on.

—What concerns us all, said Marian, is these are repeated incidents. First, you had a dream about me and told everybody about it by e-mail. Then you wrote a letter to Jamie.

—Who will be next? Is how I would put it to the jury, said Mignon. Then you hit 'em with stalking.

—Stalking? I said, incredulously. I admit to writing letters to Jamie and to Marian. Those were meant to be personal and private.

—How private is it when you e-mail everybody in the library? said Marian.

—I attached the wrong document!

—Ignorance of operating instructions is no excuse in the eyes of the law, said Mignon.

—You had KeyMail training along with everybody else in the library, Jerry, Helena cooly pointed out.

—I admit it, I said, my voice getting all shakey. I love my co-workers. Jamie. Marian. You, too, Helena. You've all changed my life.

—You've changed our lives too, Jeremy, Helena said with that steely blue gaze.

—Goodness, yes, said Marian, eyes watering with appropriate emotion.

—It is fun working with you Jeremy, said Jamie, carefully. But…but…

—But that's no reason to project your emotional needs onto others, said Mignon. A Hallmark card would have been sufficient. Instead of these effusions of…of, how would you characterize these writings?

—Tokens of my esteem? I said. Love? Respect?

Taking out a sheet of paper from her legal folder, Mignon read aloud:

—In the matter of the first offense, the accused writes to Marian, quote: *I love you madly, madly, Madame Librarian*, unquote.

—Those are lyrics from a song! Not meant to be taken literally!

—What about this KeyMail you sent from Javits Center, New York City, on July ninth, ninety-ninety-six, that you contend you inadvertently sent to ALL STAFF? *"Waking up at three a.m. with a hard-on for Marian? Her vagina had scalloped edges?"*

—It was only a dream!

—Your right to dream ends where your co-workers right to feel safe begins, buster, said Helena.

—Why on earth you thought it appropriate to share your dream is something I'll never understand, said Marian.

—We had been talking about dreams the night before! Remember? That there are messages in dreams. And you said that you kept a dream journal, too.

—Sure, I'd had a few drinks, Marian laughed. It was after hours. We were two adults. Or so I thought.

—We all know you mean well, Jeremy, said Helena, attempting to steer the meeting toward an amicable conclusion. And we've come here prepared to help.

—So just relax, said Jamie, standing up, wrapping a black silk apron around me, and picking up a pair of shears. We're here to help you.

—First of all, with your hair, said Marian. Because, honey, it needs work.

The walls seemed to be closing in and glowing as the women moved in around me, brushing, combing, and cutting my hair. I woke up tangled in the sheets, naked, sweating, and panting for breath.

It was a new day outside and there was a change in the weather. Hot and humid summer was yielding to the cool breath of fall. And I don't know why, but the first thing that came to mind was a memory of Djuna, at work the day before. Small and vivacious, Djuna once described herself as "a freelance dancer." She was wearing a simple crop top and blue jean mini-skirt, tipping forward on those wedgie heels she likes to wear, leaning into the counter, and flirting with a good-looking guy. Her shapely brown legs pretzeling around each other as she chatted, laughing lightly, squeezing and flexing her thighs.

Recalling that vision in the fresh air and cool morning light, it was suddenly clear to me what I really wanted. W hat I really wanted was to go to the Gender Blender Ball at the Fabulous Cafe Mauve. But first, I would have to buy a wig.

The Late Great Age of Café Mauve

813.813813: Erotica

"...Mr. Whistler said: 'Mauve? Mauve is just pink trying to be purple...'"

—*The Mauve Decade: American Life at the end of the Nineteenth Century* by Thomas Beer, published 1926, Alfred A. Knopf, New York.

The first thing you should know is that a good wig costs at least a hundred dollars and it's not returnable. It said so right there on the hand-lettered sign on the far wall of the closet-sized shop in a corner of the mall. Because I did try to take it back, after trying it on in the privacy of my apartment and realizing that this could be the worst mistake of my life. When I returned to the shop, an hour later, waving the receipt, the saleslady said:

—Sorry, there's no returns. And there's nothing wrong with this wig, the color matches your natural hair real good. Now just sit down, honey. Try it on, and maybe I can help.

It was an Audrey Hepburn look I was going for, sophisticated as *Roman Holiday* but tousled and bohemian as *Breakfast at Tiffany's*. I'm tall, thin, mysterious; right?

Carrying the wig on its polystyrene head in a box in a plain, brown bag, I went directly to Victoria's Secret. Holding up those wisps of fabric, coolly appraising the infinite accoutrements of desire; it was all part of what I wanted to know.

—For my wife, I said to the salesgirl, when she asked if I needed help. Something for her birthday. She's kind of large. About my size.

I ended up with a sampler of zippy thongs, lacey panties, and a simple negligee of creamy satin.

Will you be wanting these...gift wrapped? said the girl, giving me the oddest look.

—I guess that won't be necessary.

As for a brassiere, I had no idea they cost that much money. I ended up buying one on sale at WalMart. It was silk, with black straps and leopard spots. It turned out to be way too generous in the cups, but there was no way I was taking it back.

I still had no idea about what kind of dress I was going to wear. There's so much stuff out there, and it's not like I had any prior experience or training in how to dress like a girl. So it was an authentic Audrey Hepburn moment when I noticed those designer sheets on sale. A little light went on over my head, and I had a vision: leopard skin toga!

But finding a pair of size twelve high heels proved impossible. I ended up at the Shoe Barn where they had a size eleven wedgie I could squeeze my foot into. I found I could walk, if not very far.

To think that women do this every day. I used to wonder why, if it's so impractical and uncomfortable, do women dress like that? Now I felt like I was beginning to understand, as I teetered back and forth in front of a wall of mirrors.

It was Halloween, have I mentioned that? Employees were all wearing costumes and last-minute shoppers were rushing through the aisles, laughing at their own outrageous outfits. People seemed feverish in anticipation of this one night of the year when anything goes, even in River Bend.

Café Mauve was a new club that had recently opened in the old Ferry Building. Its name was the first of many reasons why Café Mauve wasn't destined to last long. People thought it was a coffee shop, not catching connotations of decadence, elegance, and fancy drinks. Grits and eggs were never on the menu at Café Mauve. No, what you got instead was a quiet, cool place where you could be who you want to be, maybe even get real.

That it was located in the long-vacant Ferry Building was another thing about Café Mauve ensuring its demise. Sure, the neighborhood was dangerous after dark, the building was funky, and the plumbing unreliable. That was part of the charm for people who value an authentic experience of the really real. Café Mauve was like some rare orchid that rarely blooms, and then not for long.

•   •   •

While shaving in the bathtub one day you notice your stomach hair for the first time, and it's easy to start shaving across the smooth surface at the water line. Then you start moving up, and suddenly your chest looks like an adolescent's again. You're back at the age before sexual differentiation, on that threshold between becoming a man or becoming a woman, when anything was still possible. Shorn of hair, your breasts are suddenly sensitive to the slightest breeze from the open window and it seems like your nipples want to stand up and shout.

Fatally, then, you stretch out your leg and start shaving an ankle. This entails much more time that you'd ever imagined you could possibly spend on making yourself look desirable. You want to have some good music on, a glass of wine, and the sun going down in a blaze of mauve sky. You want to feel beautiful inside, desirable from the inside out, working your way up the calves. The backs of the knees are the worst, just impossible between those stringy tendons.

When you get to your thighs you're wondering: how short of a toga are we looking at here, anyway? You keep inching up well past the point of anything realistically possible. You know that. But it gets easier, the higher you go. Funny how your skin gets darker, too, shaving around the pubis. Pour yourself another glass of pinot noir. Light some candles and oh-so-carefully finish the job. What about those hairy arms? What the hell, you drunkenly decide, sweeping the razor back and forth.

It's like being re-born. Naked. Hairless. Of indeterminate sex. Only then did I start putting on the pieces I had assembled of a new identity.

•   •   •

Stuffing the wig and my costume into a gym bag, I walked to the Ferry Building, where

RETURN TO CIRCA '96

I changed clothes in the Men's room. One of those grand old tiled places with high ceilings, marble fixtures, and furtive sounds emanating from the stalls. When I finally dared to come out, there was a line of people waiting to get in and somebody in a gorilla suit at the door checking IDs and taking admission. Scanning my driver's license , then looking me up and down, the gorilla said:

—You go, girl!

Café Mauve was jammed like it would never be again. Everyone had come to see the freak show, but the few people in street clothes were the ones who looked strange. People were shouting to be heard over the music, pointing, vamping, laughing. After a few drinks, strangers who had never met before were flirting outrageously, safe in the knowledge that after all, it's only Halloween. Partnered or not, everybody was dancing.

•   •   •

But what I liked most about Café Mauve were those quiet hours after work, sitting at a little table by the window, sipping a Bloody Mary. Very, very slowly, while watching the sun go down. Then I would have another. Once or twice I played pool. Kind of awkward with heels and fake boobs and bending over. So much better just to sit by the window and practice breathing like a girl would breathe. Rich full breathes that lift up your breasts, even if they are only napkins stuffed in a bra.

I had a couple outfits by then; delicate, high-collared, Judy Garland chemises you could unbutton down to there, and a little black skirt with a slit up the side. After a while and a

few drinks you can get dizzy and start to feel, I dunno, pretty, maybe. Just hanging out with the gay bartender, the lesbian waitress, and the handful of regulars during the late great days of Café Mauve.

Being a wallflower was all I aspired to. One of those quiet, thoughtful girls you see reading a good book or the *New York Times Sunday Magazine*. An extra you can count on, providing nothing but quiet smiles, solidarity, and a tasteful background for the main players; those outrageous drag queens that made Café Mauve infamous in its day.

So this is what Tippi feels like, I realized, as I sipped my drink, stretching out my nylon-stockinged toes, free of those hateful, tight shoes. Tippi, the transvestite, whose chosen place to step out in the night was the public library.

It surprised me at first that I never saw Tippi at Café Mauve. That's how I realized my kind of difference was different than hers. What Tippi wanted was to be desired from afar. What I wanted was something more real.

One night I was sitting by the window, zoning-out on twinkling lights of ships passing by on the river. The song on the juke box was *Spooky*, by Junior Williams and the All Stars, when a man in a suit came over to my table. Loosening the knot of his tie, he said:

—Would you mind if I sat down?

—It's a free country, I said. Be my guest.

Sitting down opposite me, and after close examination, he said:

—So. Is this some kind of gay bar?

—It's not just for gays. There's all kindsa

people in the world.

 —So what kind are you?

 —Well, I'm not gay.

 —But you dress like a woman and you smell like a woman and the way you sit there like that… Say, what are you drinking?

 —They make a jolly good Bloody Mary here.

 —I'll have one of those, then. You want another?

 —A drink? You're buying me a drink?

 —Sure. Why not? You're… You're different.

 —And you're sweet. I don't even know your name.

 —Harry. I'm Harry Hill, a traveling salesman.

 —I'm Robin. Rockin' Robin. Welcome to Café Mauve.

 •   •   •

 As Harry signaled the waitress, I momentarily put on my glasses and scanned the scene. He was a middle-aged guy, clean-shaven, not in bad shape, his hair carefully combed in a pompadour, and he was doused in cologne.

 After our drinks were served, Harry got up to cross over and sit on my side of the table. Sliding in close, Harry said he was staying at the Hilton and would be leaving town tomorrow, and then he got to the point.

 —So. You like sex with guys?

 —I like sex.

 He had his hand on my knee. It felt so strange through the nylons, not really real.

 But you've had sex with guys? Like sucking somebody off? Or jerking somebody

off?

 —Yeah…I guess so. I'm kind of exploring.

 His hand was moving up, up, my thigh, and I had to remind myself again about breathing naturally.

 —So. If I invited you to my room at the hotel for a party. Would you like that?

 —What kinda party?

 —Oh, you know. Just you and me. And you suck me off, would you do it?

 —No, I wouldn't do that! I hardly know you.

 —But you like sex with guys.

 —Maybe I do, maybe I don't.

 —What if I paid you twenty bucks?

 —I'm not that kind of girl!

 What a jerk. Buys a girl a drink and thinks he can make advances. I put a hand on his wandering hand, and said:

 —You know, really, I'm just here for a drink after work. It's been a long day.

 —Long day for me, too, honey, he said, instantly crestfallen. Sorry if I was outtaline.

 After that, Harry relaxed, and told traveling salesman jokes. He showed me pictures of his kids and talked about what went wrong with his ex-wife. Good old Harry. Made me feel like a woman for the first time in my life.

 •   •   •

 The second time I felt like a woman was a few weeks later, after the Kareoke Queen Competition. Most everybody else had gone home and I met a guy named Willie. He had come with a friend, one of the lesbians sitting around the big table in the back where I forget why I was there, but we were taking turns buying pitchers of beer. People were pairing up, getting up to dance, leaving Willie and me alone at the table.

—I'm not gay, you know, Willie said.

—I know, I said. Me neither.

Then they played *Spooky*, and when I said it was my favorite song, Willie said:

—Would you like to dance?

—I'd adore to dance, I said.

I was taller than Willard, so it was awkward, but he put his right arm around my waist, held my left hand in his, and we were off. I followed his lead, head on his shoulder, watching the room spinning around backwards. His hand was exploring, and as I pressed in closer I could feel his dick straining through layers of fabric.

—You're a funny girl, Willard said.

—Thanks, I guess, I said.

—No, I mean, really. You're different.

—Maybe we could go somewhere, I said. Get to know each other better.

I didn't want him to know where I lived, so I was relieved when he said:

—How about my place?

Willie had a Volkswagen Bug, and all I remember about that ride is shivering from the breeze blowing in the window, or maybe in anticipation, as Willie's hand came exploring, between shifting gears, and the stars spinning. He was living, if you call it that, in a beige apartment in a beige complex out by the freeway with a sign out front that said:

If You Lived Here, You'd Be Home By Now

It was a temporary assignment, Willie explained. He was a computer consultant based in Silicon Valley, and at any time could be re-assigned to other consulting jobs around the world. He showed me the bedroom, then turned on the stereo.

—So what kind of music do you like? said Willie.

—*Spooky*.

—Anything else?

—You know, sometimes just silence is good.

I was composing myself carefully on the bed, leaning back against the wall, watching Willie fussing in the kitchen

—Do you want a drink? he said.

—I've had plenty already. Just water, please.

—Ice with that?

—No ice. Just a big tall glass of water. About a quart of it, I think.

Willie sat down awkwardly next to me on the bed. Drinking the water, I started feeling better immediately.

—I've never done this kind of thing before, Willie said.

—Me neither, I said. It's all new to me.

We got horizontal, and he started undressing me, apologizing for being so clumsy with buttons and straps.

—Take as long as you like, I said. I've been waiting all my life for this.

—Wow, he said. Jeez. You're hot.

—I am, I said. Do you mind if I take off my wig? You have no idea how hot these things are.

—How do you want to do this? he said.

—This is good, I said. Keep doing that.

With my free hand I reached up and

pulled off the wig. Willie was looking me in the eyes.

—You don't even need a damn wig, he said, kissing me like I've never been kissed before.

Too drunk to climax, Willie and I grappled on the bed without resolution, and then we passed out. Birds were chirping and a new day dawning when I woke up to find Willie getting dressed to go be a computer consultant again. I still didn't want to reveal where I lived, so he dropped me off at the Ferry Building, and we agreed to meet me there in the evening.

·   ·   ·

The third and final time I really felt like a woman was that night. Working till nine at the library, I was worried I might miss Willie by the time I could run to the Ferry Building, change into my Robin persona, and order my first Bloody Mary. But when I finally made my entrance, the place was empty, except for two employees.

—The kitchen is closed, you know, said the gay bartender.

He was one of those old fat gay guys who have seen everything.

—On account of our paychecks bounced, said the lesbian waitress with the mermaid tattoo, crew cut, biceps, the whole nine yards.

—So the cook quits, says the bartender. And takes the slicer and microwave with him as collateral!

—What an asshole! said the waitress.

—The owner or the cook?

—Both, I guess.

—So are you guys closed, now? I asked.

'Cuz I'm supposed to meet somebody here.

—We're still open for drinks, said the bartender. Want the usual?

—Sure, I said. Extra celery, V-8 Juice, and Tabasco?

—Fucking health drink is what it is, said the gay bartender, cheerfully setting to work.

—How about you, Ruby? He said to the waitress. Fix you one, too? It's on the house tonight.

—Or until we get paid.

—Was there a guy here earlier? I asked. Kinda nerdy looking? Big glasses and a pocket protector kinda guy?

—Nobody matching that description, said the bartender decisively. You're the only customer we've had all night.

·   ·   ·

For the next three hours, Café Mauve consisted of the gay bartender, the lesbian waitress, and me; and by then we were old friends.

—Need a ride, Robin? said the bartender. Me and Ruby are going to close early and have drinks at my place.

—At least we can fix up some food there, Ruby said. I make a pretty good omelet, if you've got any eggs.

—You're welcome to come, too, if you want, said the bartender.

—I guess not tonight, but thanks, I said.

—Sorry your date didn't show, said Ruby. Now you know how it feels to be stood up by a guy.

·   ·   ·

Café Mauve was back in business the next week, when the payroll finally cleared the bank and the cook brought back the kitchen equipment. But the place was constantly under police observation, and when they were caught serving alcohol to minors it was the end of Café Mauve. The Ferry Building went back to being vacant again, and Café Mauve a minor footnote in River Bend history.

It was shortly after that when the freighter drifted loose down the Mississippi, ramming into the pier on a Saturday afternoon during the height of the Christmas shopping season on Re-Election Day. The Ferry Building was demolished, along with parts of the Hilton and most of the mall. It was the end of River Bend as we knew it, and the birth pains of our 21st Century Library.

—The Mauve Decade? said a voice at the bar. *In River Bend, The Mauve Decade lasted about fifteen minutes.*

900: History & Geography

The Gambler, the Sheriff, and the Library Director

978.9789: Shoot-Out at the OK Corral

A line of citizens waiting their turn to comment and ask questions was snaking out the door, down the hall, past the overflow room where video monitors had been set up for late-comers to the great debate at Keystone Hall. Mayor Matt was at the podium, introducing three groups presenting municipal bond proposals. It was the final showdown for the Gambler, the Sheriff, and the Library Director.

Library volunteers were distributing flyers for *Initiative #1: The 21st Century Library*. It was sobering to realize everything depended on its message motivating enough of these yahoos to vote. Our opposition was represented by colorfully attired riverboat gamblers and dance-hall dames promoting *Initiative # 2: Raise the Magnolia!*, along with tickets for free riverboat rides and bags of wooden nickels for on-board casino gambling.

Then came the sound of a marching band approaching, a detachment from the River Bend Jobs Corps. Wearing dress uniforms and bearing arms, the para-military, green-beret-clad troop passed-out pamphlets for *Initiative #3: Build The Panopticon*.

Details of the plan for a new prison were finally revealed, and a mighty nice poster they had for it, too. Bold graphics, a compelling argument, a proven design, and a catchy slogan for their non-profit, fund-raising arm, *Magna Dolorum*.

Crowd control was not an issue in that over-heated, standing-room-only ballroom with cherubs smiling down upon us from their niches in the coffered ceiling. Ranks of uniformed police officers had come to show their support for the new prison. They were the first to give up their chairs and soon all of them were standing in solidarity around the walls of the room. We were literally surrounded, and our chances looked nil.

As the representative for Initiative #1, Helena spoke first. Sitting next to her was Zelda, who had recently suffered a nasty spill, breaking her hip, and then caught pneumonia while recuperating in the hospital but had insisted on attending in her wheelchair, with a laprobe and a box of tissues close to hand. She said not a word, but sat staring out at her fellow citizens like the personification of stricken, hollow-eyed conscience itself.

Representing Initiative #2, Derrick the Dude spoke next, wielding a PowerPoint Presentation with knock-your-socks-off visuals and an emotional appeal to citizens about why River Bend must "*Raise the Magnolia!*" You could see how Marian could fall in love with a guy like that, and he had ready answers for any questions. It was all about restoring River Bend's faded glory, creating jobs with a riverboat casino and a new revenue stream for schools, roads, and "whatnot," as Derrick liked to say.

—You'll have a floating museum of river boat history with a real-time casino, Derrick concluded. It's a Win-Win deal for River Bend.

Then it was time for Initiative #3, presented by the Sheriff, a stout, sweating, bald dude in regulation uniform, topped by a white Stetson.

—I'm not a talker, I'm a do-er, he said. To me, it's a simple, bottom-line business proposition. Build the Panopticon. Create new jobs in a growing field. Ensure public safety and secure a tidy profit by renting out extra rooms at a higher rate to the Federal Penal System. This is a plan guaranteed to succeed.

Then the people had their chance to comment and ask questions, each for three minutes. Mayor Matt adroitly avoided taking sides and kept a close eye on the clock, happily bonging the gong when a citizen went over-time. Eleanor, his aide, helped out, keeping track on a whiteboard of key points for and against each bond proposal in three tidy colums.

The hearing ground on for hours through heat, humidity, and enneui; democracy in action. Under peristent questioning, Helena admitted that the library was a non-profit organization and that the enabling legislation allowing Key-Co's control was being held back in committee. Though they never made her cry, I think that's when she realized our ship was going down.

—The library belongs to the people, Helena said. Making a profit can never be part of our mission. But with KeyCo's support and the passage of this bond, we'll build a free, public library that will be a flagship for the next century and a beacon unto the world.

Even the Sheriff and Derrick the Dude had to applaud when Helena said that. She was a great speaker, no doubt about it, and all admired her fighting spirit.

At the stroke of midnight Mayor Matt cut off any further debate. There would be no conclusion until the election on November 8, but there seemed to be a general consensus of opinion. The Panopticon was seen as a "need." The Library of the Future was seen as a "want." And the riverboat casino was seen as a "must have." So there were plenty of warning signs of imminent disaster.

What no one expected was the invalidation of the first election because of a misprint on the ballot. And when the make-up election was scheduled to be held at the River Bend Mall on Saturday, December 14, our disaster was compounded.

Where's Wally?

Part 1.

915: China

—Where's Wally?

—Today, Wally is out looking at properties and meeting with lawyers, said Bourke.

—Poor bastard, said Justina.

—We're still holding space for his ad in the Fall issue, I said. I need to know if he wants it or not, and if so, what size does he want? I'll just leave our rate sheet in his office.

—Thanks, said Bourke. Just pile it on top of the others.

Justina was kneading two half-loaves at a time, one with each hand. She set them onto a flat sheet of rounded loaves and with a few expert slashes of a scoring knife, incised a design suggesting rye grass. Two large loaves received extra attention, as she inscribed something special.

—The hell are you doing? said Bourke, annoyed that Justina was taking so long. The clock was ticking and the next batch of bread was rising.

Bent over her work, Justina puffed hair out of her face with the side of her mouth, and said:

—It's Chinese. This one is *River*. And this guy is *City*. Don't you think they'd make cool tatoos? You know, one on each arm?

Justina struck a pose, flexing her biceps, then painted the loaves with eggwash and set them to rise.

Where's Wally?

914: Switzerland

Part 2.

—Where's Wally today?

—Wally is at a Cistercian monastery in Zurich this week, said Justina.

—He's studying old world baking methods, said Bourke.

—Tell him it's a sponsorship opportunity for a book and CD.

—Sponsorship opportunity? Bourke said, dubiously.

—But we need to know by the end of the week.

—How much is a sponsorship opportu-

nity going for these days? said Justina.

—Depends on how much Wally wants to chip in for, starting at a thousand dollars a page. The same rate as an ad in *riverrun*, only this is a special commemorative issue.

—Special commemorative issue of what? said Justina.

—Of all the shit that didn't fit into the other issues. Plus, you get the CD from the Deep River Blues Festival.

—Which was cancelled on account of rain, as I recall, said Bourke.

—No, the show went on, but it became an all-acoustic festival after the power went out. The whole sordid, story will be in this special issue, along with complete election coverage.

Where's Wally?

917: Iowa description and travel

Part 3.

Woke up from a nightmare and couldn't get back to sleep so I went for a long walk around River Bend. At that early hour, the only place with lights on and people inside doing things was the bakery. I went around to the back door, let myself in, and there was Bourke with the great wooden blade, stirring yeast, honey, and water into a giant steel bowl on casters. Justina was standing by the mixer, hefting the giant aluminum beater up onto its spindle. She pushed the ON button, and it began its familiar rhythmic clunking sound, creaming fifty pounds of brown sugar and ten pounds of butter.

—Horse walks into a bar, said Bourke. Bartender says: Why the long face?

—And why are you here at three a.m? said Justina. Not that we're not always glad to see you, Jeremiah. Want to help me scoop cookies?

—Why not, I said. I'll probably end up working for Wally again, anyway. Tomorrow's my annual performance review, and it doesn't bode well.

—My performance review was pretty typical, said Bourke. Wally and I went bowling and he won, as usual, but I got two strikes in a row. Wally said if I could do that again, he'd give me a twenty-five cent raise. They set 'em up and I knocked 'em down. Then he wanted to go double or nothing: another strike for a fifty cent raise. And I made it! Too bad you guys don't bowl.

—Wally and I just go out to lunch when it's time to talk about a raise, said Justina. And not at a bowling alley.

KeyMail©
November 9, 1996
From: JeremiaD@RiverBendPL.com
To: RachaeR@WRITE.com
Re: Bridge to the Future
Dear Rachael,

I've been meaning to write to you for months now, but other stuff seems to always come up. Did you vote yesterday, and how was the weather?

It was warn and sunny here, and then it clouded over. I was walking to my polling station when I noticed something small and white swooping down over the power lines, and then a sudden burst of feathers. There was a fat pigeon held fast in the talons of an snowy owl, winging away into the clouds. What an omen to see on the way to vote. A light mist started falling and passing cars turned on their headlights and windshield wipers.

This year, my precinct is voting at the Special Ed. School. Out on the lawn, a touch football game was in progress with a cheerful crew of kids sliding and rolling in the muck.

I went inside to the gym to vote, then I walked to the Bangkok Chef for the lunch special, only $3.95. The Bangkok Chef is one of those little enterprises you see springing up in former 7-11s, the modern equivalent of a railroad car diner. It's all white and red inside, with pictures on the wall of the King and Queen of Thailand. A family from Bangkok who barely speak English run the place.

The waitress was wearing traditional dress of embroidered silk. Her daughter—a toddler in silk pajamas—greets customers, visits tables, and climbs up onto the cash register. It's a complete, 5-star dining experience.

When I walked home it was starting to snow. Kids were getting out of school and wandering homeward.

"This snow doesn't look real," I overheard one boy say to another as they biked past.

He was right. The tiny pellets looked like Styrofoam, like inside one of those glass globes you pick up and shake to see the flakes swirlling around.

Yes, I did get your e-mail at the library. We were monitoring election results all day on the internet, and by the time the library closed at nine o'clock, Bill Clinton was on television in the lobby, making his acceptance speech, "building a bridge to the future."

Walking in the silence and falling snow, I thought about what a useful metaphor that is is for those kids playing football in the rain, on their bikes after school, and that Thai toddler at the Bangkok Chef. These days will seem like the old world to them. There's no going back once you cross that bridge.

Re: Your 1996 Performance Review

920 history of groups of individuals

I met with Jennifer and Cody in Cody's office, with that new cubicle smell, hotel room art on the wall, and no personal affects anywhere. In the middle of the table between us was a copy of my By Statements. Jennifer and Cody were shuffling through a thick file documenting everything I had done at the library that year, along with quarterly reports from three different managers. There were flyers, brochures, and advertisements I had designed, along with stories about the library I had published in *Nexxus* and the *Forward-Progress*.

Riverrun is looking good, said Cody, holding up the Summer issue and flipping through the pages. Great publicity for the library and making us all look good. Nobody denies that.

—Other than being chronically late in publishing each issue, said Jennifer, KeyCo has no objections. So when is your next issue coming out, anyway?

—Two more pages and we can go to press, I said. Jamie is working with me from her home office in California. I send her text and graphics as KeyMail attachments and she's sending the magazine back as a PDF. Then Gordy prints and assembles it with our corps of volunteers.

—I guess it's cheaper that way, said Jennifer. But you should look into sending the PDFs straight to Kinkos. Cut Gordy out of the loop and you'll get your product to market a lot faster.

—All bullshit aside, said Cody, what's your lead story?

—The bond election is the story. Duh! I said. But we can't go to press until we find out who wins.

—You're aces in spades for drama, said Cody, with that tight little smile. But what you lose points for is bad behavior, bad judgment, bad decision-making, is what it is.

—Like photocopying Lilly Eskelson's picture onto this computer sign-up sheet, Jennifer said. Too bad about that, otherwise you'd be four-point-oh for the past quarter.

—Yeah, this is just weird, Jeremy, said Cody, waving a lined sheet of paper decorated with a campaign photo and the slogan: *Vote for Lilly Eskelson, River Bend School Board!*

—It's from the League of Women's Voter's pamphlet, I said. Remember? And they left out her picture?

—Yeah. Right. Lilly Eskelson lost again, and this year, she got her picture left out, said

Jennifer. So what?

—Right, I said. And we were supposed to fix the voter information pamphlet? By pasting this picture into five hundred copies? So I started pasting her picture onto everything. Why not put her picture on the computer sign-up sheet? She never wins, anyway.

—It was *wrong* to use the resources of a public library for your personal beliefs, no matter how absurd, said Jennifer. Don't you get that?

—Also, it was *wrong* to post this *Muscle and Fitness* calendar in the staff elevator, said Cody. Lucky you didn't get hit with Sexual Harassment for that little episode.

—Why does the library subscribe to that magazine if we can't display their calendar?

—It's just too bad you keep shooting yourself in the foot, Jeremy, said Jennifer. And you keep asking all the wrong questions.

—What it seems like is you're not really with the team concept, said Cody. Like you're out in left field. Like you think you scored a touchdown and that's not even the game we're playing.

—You probably wouldn't have gotten into such trouble, said Jennifer, if Franny had done a better job managing you.

—She approved everything I did, I said. I always let her know where I was going and when I'd be back. And why isn't she present at this meeting?

—Franny's not going to be with us much longer, said Jennifer. But really, Jeremy, what on earth were you thinking with that so-called *Deep River Blues Project*? When did writing a grant for a music festival become part of your By Statements?

—And you thought you could publish a book about it, with a CD enclosed?

At this, Cody snorted, Jennifer couldn't keep a straight face, and then I was laughing with them, tears coming to my eyes.

—But seriously, said Jennifer. What happened to those old newsletters you discovered?

—What old newsletters? I said, ingenuously.

—That box with back issues of *riverrun* you told Jordy your were going to index, said Cody. Back, like, in February, when you were cleaning out the storage room?

—Jordy doesn't work here anymore, I said.

—But your By Statements are still here, said Cody, tapping a finger on the list of duties I had signed on for and agreed to perform. Until you complete that job, you're still on probation.

—KeyCo is keen to see the results of that project, said Jennifer.

—They're in a secure location, I said.

—You're suggesting you took library property without authorization? said Jennifer, incredulous, shocked, appalled, etc., with mustard on top and a side of fried onions.

—That's a terminal offense, said Cody.

—Criminal charges could be brought against you, said Jennifer.

—Jordy was about to toss them in the dumpster!

—Jordy was going to de-acquisition them, said Cody. That's different.

— They want them back, said Jennifer. No questions asked. Just return the documents.

Full page ad

River Feste '96

(Check with Sybil ASAP!)

COMMEMORATIVE DISASTER ISSUE

RAMMED!
Runaway freighter demolishes Mall

First came the emergency siren wailing the distress alarm of the *Bright Day*, a 78,000-ton freighter laden with Christmas goods from China, as its engines lost power and it began drifting toward the River Bend waterfront.

Then came a "terrifying" sound of grating concrete and shrieking metal as the ship made contact. Fifteen shops and restaurants were all but eliminated, along with portions of the Hilton Hotel, as the ship plowed into the River Bend Mall, injuring scores of holiday shoppers and sending hundreds more into pandemonium while cutting a 160-foot swath through wharf, stores, and restaurants, including the late, great, Café Mauve.

In the grand ballroom of the hotel, citizens had gathered to view models of the three proposed tax initiatives: the 21st Century Library, the *Magnolia*, and the Panopticon. Voting had already begun and bursting ballot boxes provided no small part of the cloud of white fragments swirling in the drifting snow and white powder that engulfed the scene.

By dropping two anchors, the *Bright Day*'s captain narrowly avoided the cruise ships docked along the wharf. But the leviathan's momentum carried its other end in a wide arc like a slow-motion movie as the freighter's bow slammed into the mall, shearing off buildings like that scene in *Airport*

(Continued on page 4.)

VOL. 130
NO. 3
FALL / WINTER
1996

riverrun

November 8, 1996: River Bend, Iowa
Tugboats stabilize the *Bright Day* against what remains of the River Bend Mall.
Photograph copyright © 1996 by by Lafcadio Hearn, for *riverrun*, c/o RiverBendPL.com.

Liberty Enlightening the World
An artillery salute welcomed President Cleveland to Bedloe's
Island, inadvertantly setting fire to the *S.S. Magnolia*. Realizing that
"the only way to save her was to sink her," Captain Rex T. Keystone
pulled the plugs, allowing the ferry to go down, putting out the fire.
Re-floated and towed to River Bend, Iowa, the *Magnolia* has been
rotting ever since. Photograph by H. O. Neil, October 28, 1886. Library of Congress. LC-DIG-ds-04491

river rafters

Editor:
Jeremiah D. Angelo

Art Director:
Jamie Petrie

Webmaster:
Barney Rubble

Unix Guru:
Stanley Livingstone

Vigilantee Coordinator:
Stacey Cartwright

Managing Manager:
Franny Andzoey

Preefrooders:
Merriam Webster

Zelda Fitzgerald

Editorial Board:
Keystone College:

Dr. Jefferson Davis

Dr. Steve Canyon

Dr. Mephistopheles

Library Director:
Helena Montana

Printer:
AVATAR Press

riverrun is published by Friends of the
River Bend Public Library. All Rights Reserved. No part of this publication may be
re-printed without written permission except
for excerpts used for purposes of Review
Articles, © 1996 River Bend Public Library.

"Autobiography is only to be trusted when it reveals something disgraceful. A man who gives a good account of himself is probably lying, since any life when viewed from the inside is simply a series of defeats."

-Salvador Dali

KeyCo®
& Your Library
River Bend Public Library
was established in 1866 by a
grant from munitions manufacturer Munificent T. Keystone for
the Veterans of the Civil War and
for the residents of River Bend,
Iowa. Operated by City of River
Bend and partially funded by
the Keystone Trust, the library
is a wholly owned subsidiary of
KeyCo® the corporate entity now
calling the shots.

Vol. 130   No. 3   Fall/Winter   1996

Sublimimus per terribilis hiatus!

4.   RAMMED!! Special Report
     Library Staff C.E.R.T.-ified Heroes

8.   Oh, Dem Deep Shit River Blues
     Intrepid reporter survives music festival.

14. Riverrun No. 1, 1866
     1st Edition found in Library archives!

riverrun recommends

Editors, The. *Disaster Preparedness Coloring Book.* Published by the American Red Cross, 1996.
Dewey Decimal: 332.421D

Watkins, T.H. *Mark Twain's Mississippi: A Pictorial History of America's Greatest River.* Published by Weathervane Books, distributed by Crown Publishers, 1971.
Dewey Decimal: 977 W3357

Awful conflagration of the steam boat Lexington
on Monday eveg., Jany. 13th 1840, by which melancholy occurence; over 100 persons perished.
Published 1840 by Currier & Ives. Reproduction Number: LC-USZC4-3102 (color film copy transparency)

RAMMED! Special Report!

Continued from Page 1.

where the 747 takes out the terminal—but way worse than that—because it was real. "I saw it plow through cement like a tractor plowing through dirt," said Lafcadio Hearn, a River Bend resident shopping for a Christmas present for his niece, who had hinted that anything less than *Tickle Me Elmo* would be unacceptable.

"It just plowed through Cafe du Monde like there wasn't even a restaurant here," he said, referring to the popular grits and eggs coffee shop.

In the ballroom, librarians watched in horror as their detailed model of the 21st Century Library, made of glass and lighted up like Christmas, burst into a shower of flying shards upon impact with the *Bright Day*. The good news is that the model of the Panopticon—a solid hunk of reinforced concrete—was hardly damaged, except

for the watchtowers got bent out of shape. Anyway, it sunk, and was later recovered. On a positive note, the model of the *Magnolia*—jarred loose from its pedestal—landed upright in the water, and was last seen floating downstream. A fifty thousand dollar reward has been offered for its return by Derrick the Dude, C.F.O. of the "Raise the Magnolia!" tax initiative.

"It was like slow motion."

After destroying most of the pier in front of the Mall, the *Bright Day* ricocheted toward the *Flamingo,* prompting at least a dozen panic-stricken gamblers to jump from the boat's upper decks into the river.

"It hit the wharf and started veering off and it was like slow motion," said Derrick the Dude, who was holding "a pretty good hand" at the time on board the casino boat's second deck as the freighter's relentless path of destruction approached the *Flamingo's* stern.

"We only had six or seven seconds to sit there and wonder, 'Is it coming or not?' and then we had to jump."

As the Dude leaped from the *Flamingo's* second deck, a woman who had jumped from the top deck plunged past him. "I didn't get to meet that little lady, but I'd sure like the chance to sometime," commented Mr. Dude. "Pier 31 is my current address, where we are working to restore the *Magnolia.* Come on down anytime."

Meanwhile, in the hotel ballroom, C.E.R.T.-trained librarians leaped into action. Assessing damage and forming response teams, the newly minted rescuers

More injuries were caused by the panic than by the crash.

said they found employees unconscious under clumps of rubble and dazed shoppers wandering aimlessly.

"It's like a movie."

The shopping center's internal fire-fighting system went off, shooting geysers of water through the mall and turning its floors into a slippery, glass-strewn surface. The stench of gas pervaded the wreckage, as pipes broke apart.

Another of the first responders was Sybil Seraphim, editor/publisher of *Nexxus* magazine. Spotting a cook from the Corn-dogateria under crumpled slabs of concrete and smashed wooden chairs, she helped him to safety.

"It was an unbelievable mess down there, with a cloud of white powder drifting around like a massive explosion," Seraphim said. "Fortunately, the librarians all had C.E.R.T. training, and knew exactly what to do."

River Bend librarians set up a triage center in a mall service entrance, slapping on neck braces and taping the injured to backboards. At least 121 victims were rushed to downtown hospitals.

"How many people down that need stretchers?" Cody Calhoun called out in the dust, debris, and swirling snow.

"Too many!" a colleague shouted back.

"No problem," said Cody. "Knute—take the truck and requisition two-by-fours from Home Depot!"

"You betcha, Cody," Knute replied. "We'll build our own stretchers!"

"Stanley—get over to Bed, Bath & Beyond and round up blankets," Cody commanded. "We're gonna need uh, let's see…"

He broke off, counting on his fingers, gazing toward the river through the drifting powder and falling snow where the wall used to be.

We were all in shock, that dreamlike slow-motion hyper-awareness you get when an ocean freighter crashes through walls, floors and ceilings. It's not the end of the world, it's just the end of an illusion. "It's like a movie," everybody kept saying.

More injuries were caused by the panic than by the crash itself. People injuring themselves running over other people escaping from they knew not what. Police and firefighters flocked to the mall, and by 6:00 p.m. dogs were being used to sniff through the rubble for survivors.

Less than an hour after impact, River Bend Mayor Matt arrived at the scene and surveyed the disaster from beneath the dented bow of the *Bright Day*. Mayor Matt said he had no idea how the mall could recover from this blow.

"This is bad, this is really bad," said the recently re-elected Mayor. "This has been a year of disasters, you know? First there was the Wal-Mart fire—our biggest employer—up in smoke, and then the rampant crime, the bankruptcies, and now this…" Mayor Matt said as his voice trailed off in despair.

"But on the plus side—hey, disaster relief funds are in the bag. This is a well-documented event of maritime negligence. We'll sue—and we'll win! River Bend will re-build from this tragedy."

Bond Election Results

Due to the recent disaster, results of the Bond Election have been declared Invalid.

"We'll have a do-over soon as we clean up this mess," said Mayor Matt, "and get that FEMA app in the mail."

Oh, Dem Deep Shit River Blues

"Here's your t-shirt," Sybil said, taking one from the basket of t-shirts bungee-corded onto the back of the ATV. "We got a break on the price by ordering all Extra Large. Hop on, and I'll drop you off at the staging area."

Pulling on that simple white shirt—plastered with corporate logos and names of local business sponsors—made the Deep River Blues Festival seem real at last after all those months of planning, scheming, and seemingly endless meetings. It all depended upon community support, like this ATV donated by a local sporting goods store. As I climbed onto the seat behind her, Sybil said:

"Thanks again for volunteering, Jeremiah. Hold on!"

With nothing else to hold on to but Sybil, I wrapped my arms around her waist as she gunned the engine and we were off, roaring down the trail. Sybil's hair was tangled and greasy, her smell was funky, her clothes looked like she'd been wearing them for three days.

"I haven't slept in three days!" Sybil yelled over her shoulder above the roar of the ATV. "Can you believe it?"

From her breath I could tell Sybil had also been drinking, and using whatever else was required from her pharmacopia during that long weekend. We were soon careening on the ATV among River Faire re-enactors, road crews for rock bands, clumps of volunteers, and early-ar-

The *America*, Courtesy of
River Bend Historical Society.
Reproduction Number: LC-DIG-det-4a17928

riving blues fans straggling along in our dust.

Then a walkie-talkie voice started squawking from the holster on Sybil's belt:

"Rouge Warrior One—do you copy? Rouge Warrior One."

Through the static and garbled sound, I recognized the voice of Argentina Robinofsky.

"Can you get that, Jeremiah?" said Sybil. "I'm fully engaged at the moment."

Taking the unit out of its holster, I punched the button and said:

"Yo. Rouge Warrior One here."

"What's your position, Rouge Warrior One? Is that you, Jeremiah?"

"This is Jeremiah," I said. "Sybil's fully engaged. We're enroute to the staging area."

"We need you at Dead Head Point!" Argen-tina squawked. "We have a situation."

Then we lost contact.

Then we rolled the ATV and we ended up in the borrow pit.

Then we ran out of gas. The engine started cutting out and then you know how it just stops? And there's that sudden silence, except for the chain whizzing around the axle and the wheels coasting for the longest time down a dusty trail in the middle of nowhere? The whole day was kind of like that with unexpected pockets of peace and quiet all along the river.

Continued on next page.

Mississippi River in Natchez, Mississippi
Highsmith, Carol M., 2008 October 10.
Reproduction Number: LC-DIG-highsm-04385

Mississippi River at Keokuk, Iowa.
Copyright, F. J. Bandholtz; 1907, photographic print: gelatin silver; 9.5 x 42 in.
Reproduction Number: LC-DIG-ds-04517 (digital file from original item)

Then Sybil slumped forward on the handle-bars, resting her head on her arms and began softly crying.

"We are fucked," she sobbed. "We are so fucking fucked."

There were scratches on her arms and legs from when we had rolled. Mosquitoes were starting to find us and the walkie-talkie voice of Argentina was squawking again:

"Rouge Warrior One! Where the fuck are you? We have a situation…"

Then a slow-moving flatbed railcar came trundling down the tracks. Musicians were picturesquely posed on bales of hay, bags of grain, and upturned casks of whiskey. A film crew was positioned at mid-deck, camera mounted on a tri-pod.

An Actor.

That had been Sybil's idea, too. The railcar was on loan from Union Pacific and the tractor pulling it was borrowed from the John Deere dealer. Trundling back and forth all day along the route between River Faire and the Blues Festival, the train was the one thing that went as planned. And when the levee broke, the train crew responded heroically during the emergency evacuation. Who could have imagined it would rain for three straight days in the middle of a River Bend summer?

Grabbing armfuls of t-shirts from the basket, Sybil and I abandoned the ATV and scrambled

for the railcar. Tossing the t-shirts up to the crew, Sybil loped along-side, then leaped up and rolled onto the deck. Reaching out a hand, she pulled me on board. We were gasping for breath, flat on our backs on the rough rumbling deck, watching tempest clouds lowering ever more near.

"Can you do that again?" said the fat guy with his hat on backwards who appeared to be directing. "Because I think we missed most of it."

"No do-overs Danny," Sybil said tersely. "Life is not a dress rehearsal—you know what I'm saying?"

Danny's documentary of the Deep River Blues Festival was the linchpin in Sybil's plan that had convinced us all to buy-in. Leveraging profits from the documentary against losses from the festival—it had seemed like a good idea at the time. That, and the website, and scheduling it to coincide with River Bend's 100th Annual River Faire. It was circa '96, and anything seemed possible.

Punching in the walkie-talkie button, Sybil said:

"Red Lady One, Red Lady One," do you read me?

"Rouge Warrior One! Yes, Rouge Warrior One. You are coming in loud and clear. Where are you guys?"

"We're on the Express, said Sybil. Heading upriver. What's your situation, Red Lady One?"

"Situation normal—all fucked up. People are sneaking into the concert on rafts and boats and swimming across the freaking Mississippi River."

"That's crazy," said Sybil. "Make them stop!"

Continued on next page.

This valuable coupon will get you one of Justina's famous

Cistercian Muffin's at

Wally's Wheat World

1234 Waterfront Street, River Bend, Iowa

"Like what should we do—arrest them?

"Call the Coast Guard!"

"Roger that, Rouge Warrior One! Good news is we'll be on the six o'clock news. The Channel Four News chopper is already here."

"Make sure those guys all get backstage passes," Sybil said.

"I can't believe people would swim such a polluted river!" I said.

"I knew we should have put in showers," Sybil said. "It was on my list…..Oh crap oh crap

Keystone Security Co.

1501
12 Main Street, River Bend

UP THE MISSISSIPPI RIVER.

TERRITORY OF MINNESOTA,

CITY OF NININGER,

NOTICES.

Above: This ad appeared in the 1887 Fall/Winter *riverrun*.

Left: Emigrants to America received a harsh welcome when they discovered that Nininger, Minnesota, didn't exist. It was a well-planned scam with maps, deeds, pictures showing a busy levee lined with steamboats, and this full-page ad in the 1887 Summer *riverrun*.
Emigration Up the Missippi, Minnesota Historical Society.

oh crap…"

"Don't even mention the Porta-Potties," Argentina's voice crackled.

"What about the Porta-Potties?"

"They're leaking."

"Holy shit!" said Sybil. "They were donated, too."

The train was really rolling now, approaching River Faire. Sybil and I were sitting on the edge of the deck, legs dangling, watching the passing scene. Booths were being erected. Characters in historic costumes were circulating. People were waving and calling to us as we rolled by, their voices obscured by the tractor's dieseling engine and musicians playing little riffs, repeating phrases again and again and then leaving off just when you start to think you know where they're going.

There was Tom Sawyer painting his fence and Huck Finn fishing. There was Mike Fink shooting a glass of whiskey off your head for ten bucks a shot, all proceeds going to the Riverboatmen's Retirement Association. There was Marian the librarian at the library booth. I noticed that this year, at least, the tents were well staked down.

We passed by booths for political parties and presidential candidates. People wearing plastic masks of Bill Clinton, Bob Dole, Ross Perot, and Malcom Forbes were walking around shaking each other's hands and slapping each other on the back. The Ross Perot masks, it seemed, were winning.

We passed by the booth for *Raise the Magnolia!* and the booth for the Panopticon. People were thronging and milling. The commingled smells of popcorn, cotton candy, corndogs, cow shit, horses, pigs, and the sounds of chickens and those roosters crowing and that echoing voice in the distance of the demolition derby announcer, then the engines revving, the smell of tires burning, followed by random crashes and the gentle tinkling of breaking glass.

Continued on next page.

Mississippi Riverboat by E. A. Banks, oil on canvas, 1870.
Minnesota Historical Society, ID Number: AV1984.21.2
Negative Number: 41245

Then came another one of those quiet spots along the river, where people were all whittling, alone and in groups, a team of guys whittling Chartres Cathedral. A little further on, and guys were drifting along the mudbanks, Okie Noodling for catfish.

"Last stop! Deep River Blues!" the conductor called.

The train came to a stop and people going to the music festival got off and headed out to join the long scraggly line of blues fans heading toward Dead Head point on foot. Carrying packs, pillows, blankets, and sleeping bags, they seemed like a column of refugees. In the distance, helicopters were hovering out on the point and along both banks of the river.

We could hear musicians jamming long before we arrived at the natural amphitheater, where all the best spots were rapidly being claimed. At one end of the meadow, a village of tents providing food, water, and emergency health care was established. Up on the hill and along the bluffs, smaller tents were popping up, along with teepees, lean-tos, cardboard shacks, and shelters made from sheets of plastic.

Down by the riverside, Humvees were humming, choppers chopping, and Coast Guard klaxons wailing. It was a full-scale military operation, with ground, water, and air participants; and there was Argentina Robinofsky directing traffic.

"Glad you guys finally showed up," Argentina said in greeting. "The volunteers are all quitting if they don't get their t-shirts!"

Argentina was semaphoring the Coast Guard chopper to a landing in the tall grass. Sybil ran out to meet it as it touched down, briefly. Two guys in uniform reached out and

pulled her onboard. The chopper immediately started lifting off again, pausing directly over my head, revolving its chassis around to face the opposite direction.

"They need me at the front," Sybil shouted.

"You never said what I'm supposed to do today!" I yelled back.

"You're on the clean-up crew," said Sybil. "Just work your way back to the

start. I'll meet you there!"

Kicking a bundle out the cargo door, Sybil blew a kiss and waved bye-bye as the helicopter headed out, her white hair wildly whipping. Dropping faster than you'd think possible, the bundle burst open upon hitting the ground, plastic garbage bags whirling up in the prop wash and scattering to the winds.

Your Advertisement Here
inquire:
Jeremiah D. Angelo

View of River Bend, Iowa, 1857
Lithograph after H. Lewis; published by Arnz and Co. Illus. in: Das illustrirte Mississippithal. Düsseldorf : Arnz & comp, 1857. LC-USZ62-3413 (b&w film copy neg.)

RIVERRUN

Volume 1, No. 1   High Lights of 1866

January

I, Miss Mary Ann Madley, being an indentured servant to Master Keystone as cook, second floor chamber maid and custodian of the library and the conservatory with all their myriad mysteries while river-walking today having recovered these items:

A box of wooden printing blocks found floating down the river.

Until the rightful Owner claims the blocks, Master Keystone says I may keep them as my own.

February

Being found after the floodwaters receded: a box of lower case type and numerals washed up in the cattail reeds. Master Keystone says to call him Father.

March

Being F*O*U*N*D today after the floodwaters further receded: a large case of CAPITAL LETTERS, numerals, ornaments, and soggy circus posters advertising things strange and wonderful.

Farther downstream than I have heretofore been and only after much arduous toil in Father's hipwaders did I discover ((nestled within a swallows nest)(encased in a cunning red enamel box)) underneath the railroad bridge: punctuation,;: all kinds! Henceforth, shall I, Miss Mariann Madlye, General Delivery, River Bend, Iowa, publish ("proclaim to the world") this news-letter being named RIVERRUN from the occasion of its founding.

Father says he sees no harm in the project so long as it doesn't interfere with my duties.

April

A is for Advertising & America as I would still be living in the Cottswolds if not for that NOTICE in the Cottswold Courier advertising emigration to fabled Iowa, heartland of the New World.

Father says that half of the money spent on advertising is lost, but they cannot tell which half.

Here is another Joke I heard from that drummer on the ferry to Keokuk last week:

Question: What do you get if you don't Advertise?
Answer: Nothing.

That is why this month I am advertising some of my own designs, from the PAST and from the FUTURE:

May

Resuming work on *The Encyclopedia Empiricana* with Volume #6: F, for Fashion, I fear I have fallen, am falling, into a vale of infinite finery. Fashions change by the season, by what's plentiful and what's rare, and by exiguencies of nature. Nature and fashion never cease changing. What people wear, and what they do with their hair—that's what our Readers want to know.

June

Imagine me making muffins for Mr. McGuffin's bakery down in the village and working as a common serving wench. "But where would I live?" I asked, ingenuously. Somewhat ingenuously.

July

Father says, "Come along now, Missy. For your own good and you know it."

It was a long, long, long boatride upriver to Cincinatti, where the Doctor was waiting for us and instructed Father on how to administer the laudunum. "Take as often as necessary," he prescribed.

August

Ever since then I've been mad for Art, all kinds. I could be a portrait painter, I know it, if people would just hold still.

September

What to wear to River Feste? A musical theater boat is steaming up from New Orleans and every farmer's son will be there. I shall perish if there's not one among them won't ask me to dance.

October

Heard the banjos playing late last night out by Darkytown. When I crept out to see for myself, there was Father, dancing with a negress, his face shining red in the fire glow.

November

"Don't worry your pretty little head about it," Father says to me about the elections and Why Women Can't Vote?

Clearance Sale:
Flags, Bunting & Liberty Caps!!!

 Please redeem this Valuable Coupon at McGuffin's Bakery for a FREE Muffin.

December

I, Miss Mary Ann Madlye, proprietess of the *Encyclopedia Empiricana* and of this Holy Bible, King James-edition, left behind by that nice fellow that drowned in the flood when the levee broke not knowing how to swim imagine that and his wife that died in child-birthing leaving behind this helpless infant whom I christen **Jeremiah D. Angelo** in honor of this other fellow with the new model steamship for which we all have such great hopes as in the illustration below:

Miss America steams back to port for off-loading and re-fitting during winter. "We lost control halfway across the river," said a dejected Captain Jeremiah D. Angelo. "But at least we didn't sink, and there was no loss of life. We look forward to re-launching in the spring, with less baggage, a more simplified design, and all new bells and whistles."

Reproduction Number: LC-USZ62-52135

Letter to the Editor

K is for KIND- HEARTED Mr. Keystone, Munificent T. Well-dressed older fellow, watch-fob, spats, Bowler hat, bookkeeper at the ironworks. Spied him at it again with his toy cannon lobbing shells over the river.

–A Faithful Reader of RIVERRUN

Alexander's Ready Reference

LOCOMOTIVE ENGINEERS and FIREMEN.
Broke Down--What To Do

This ad for a mail-order book was published in *riverrun* Vol. 2, Issue No. 3, Fall/Winter 1867.

Non-profit Organization
U.S. Postage Paid

River Bend, Iowa
Permit #1234

Mr. & Mrs. John Q. Public
1776 Live Free or Die Avenue
River Bend, Iowa
54123

KEYCO®

Another fine KEYCO product

Try our new "Virtual Librarian!"

MadameLibrarian@riverbendlibrary.com

South Town Center Branch Library
101 Cornets Avenue
South Town, Iowa 54321

Rolling Hills Branch Library
1010 Rolling Hills Road
River Hills, Iowa

Law Library
2nd floor
County Courthouse
76 Trombones Lane
River Bend, Iowa 54321

Downtown Outreach Library:
River Bend Community
 Action Coalition
River Bend, Iowa 54322
1010 Waterfront Street

Bookmobile
Call 555-5555 for current
route information.

River Bend Main Library
1010 Meredith Willson Boulevard
River Bend, Iowa 51234

www.riverbendlibrary.com

Where's Wally?

Conclusion

970 General History of North America

—Wally! I exclaimed. The hell are you doing here?

—Manual labor, like everybody else, Wally growled, with that familiar peeved tone and narrowing of his clear, bronze eyes. Give me a hand up with this, will ya?

—Yeah, sure, I said, grabbing onto the handles of the steel bowl and setting my feet for the lift.

—*Uno, dos, tres!* Wally counted, then we heaved the bowl up and crashed it down onto the kneading table as loudly as possible. Two hundred pounds of whole wheat bread dough spilled out across the kneading table. A man of few words, Wally enjoyed expressing his feelings through his actions.

It was five a.m., Christmas Eve. The bakery was in full attack mode with extra staff on hand, grinding out whole wheat bread, cookies, muffins, and dinner rolls for the holidays. Customers were already arriving to pick up their orders, and as I well knew from years of experience, all the work had to be done and the bakery cleaned and closed by noon so the staff could have a full week of vacation.

Slamming the bowl back down onto the casters so hard that the thing bounced, Wally grabbed one handle and sent it spinning down the narrow hall to another worker, who caught it and hustled toward the back room, apron strings flying.

—Fill 'er up! Wally called. Turning to-ward his wife, a buff blonde with butch haircut, he said: Honey? Take over the cash register?

Scooping up the chopper, Wally started hacking off hunks of dough, in one fluid motion cutting, weighing them on the scale, and flinging them to workers stationed around the table. It was like watching John Stockton directing traffic on a fast break in the final moments of an NBA play-off game. Michael Jordan and the Chicago Bulls may have been winning so far, but the game wasn't over yet. If you can picture John Stockton in white sneakers, white t-shirt, white painter pants and apron, dusted with flour head to foot, a hundred and seventy-five pounds of determination and skill; Wally was all that.

—Justina, whip up another full batch of blueberry muffins and a three-quarter batch of chocolate chip cookies, said Wally, with a nod toward the back room. Bourke, is something burning? We're really going to have to clean the ovens out good after today.

Turning his attention to me, Wally said:

—Another thing I don't appreciate is you going around saying I don't work here anymore. Is that supposed to be funny?

—Good timing, said Bourke, sweating and smiling while keeping up with Wally's pace. We're baking a thousand loaves today, and you show up asking for a donation.

—It's Christmas Eve, for Christ's sake, said Justina. The least you can do is listen to his bullshit story.

—Why don't you put on an apron and wash your hands, Jerry? Suggested Honey, over her shoulder from the front counter. You know you're on the payroll anytime you want to come back. Can't we talk about it while we work?

Soon it was just like old times, shaking and baking, whole wheat and rock'n'roll. Every time the front door opened, gusts of freezing air and crystals of snow blew in along with the customers, blinking in the bright light, sound, and warm wash of aromas. Bourke was loading and unloading oven shelves, jabbing color-coded pins into the clock's dial and taking them out as the buzzer sounded for whatever was done baking: red for cookies, blue for muffins, yellow for bread, brown for…

—The hell are these *brown* pins in here for, Wally? Said Bourke. Loaves you want me to burn?

—Those are brownies, said Justina. That new recipe Wally brought back from Switzerland?

—Based on a traditional Cistercian recipe full of dried fruits, nuts, and berries, said Wally, rapturously.

—Seven secret herbs and spices, said Justina. Of course, we adapted it to local tastes and what was available.

—What is that, chicory?, said Honey.

—Among other things, sure, said Wally.

—And…cardamom? said Bourke.

—I could tell you, said Justina, except then I'd have to kill you.

—You and what army? said Bourke.

Alarms were sounding, buzzers going off.

—Something *is* burning, said Wally. It's the brownies!

Dropping the chopper, pulling on oven mitts, Wally ran to the oven, slammed open the door, and started whipping out pans of smoking brownies onto the cooling rack, already jammed with loaves of cooling bread.

—Let's just roll this outside, whadyasay Jerry? You lead, I'll follow.

The rack was already rolling toward me. I had no choice but to get a hold on the grab bars and start moving backwards toward the door, opening just then, as more customers arrived. Outside, it was suddenly silent. Stars were fading out in the clear, cold, dawn.

—They'll cool-off out here in a jiff, said Wally. I definitely think these brownies are salvageable. Here, try some.

Smoking hot and indescribably delicious, Wally and I stood there scarfing down brownies. He appeared to be in no hurry to go back inside.

—Just say the word, said Wally, and you could be manager of the southwest branch bakery.

—But I don't want to manage a bakery, Wally.

—Well I doubt your future is in library science, he said, laughing giddily.

—What *did* you put in these brownies? I said, starting to laugh despite my best intentions otherwise.

—Maybe you don't need the library, Jeremy, said Wally. Did it ever occur to you that they need you more than you need them?

92: Biography

Angelo, Jeremiah D. Assigned a new identity under the Federal Witness Protection Program, he is working at a public library somewhere in America .

Andzoey, Franny. Quit her job and married Jordy soon after the events described above. Discovered a new vocation as an award-winning travel writer after publishing an article about their "spontaneous marriage event" in Tuscany.

Austen, Jordy. After helping the Cistercian Monastery get their collection on-line, Jordy transferred to the Abbey in Muenster, Switzerland, for further studies toward writing his doctoral thesis. Post-doctoral studies have taken Jordy and Franny to Venice, Milan, Rome, and Alexandria.

Belden, Trixie. After a nation-wide candidate search, Trixie was appointed the new director of the River Bend Library System.

Canyon, Steve. Steve has "bagged more mountains than I can count, really," and written books about most of them. Still director of the best damn small college writers' conference in the world, Steve is also still one helluva guy.

Cordova, Cody. After overseeing construction of the 21st Century Library & Convention Center, Cody retired. Selling out his KeyCo stock just before the bubble burst, Cody was able to retire while young and still-good looking. Tabbed to serve on the board of the Humanitas Project, Cody hangs with Ex-President Jimmy Carter, traveling the world, overseeing construction of affordable and ecologically-responsible housing.

Davis, Jefferson. Jeff quit teaching, cold turkey, and went off to write that novel he had so often spoken of at so many writers' conferences. Jeez, it's almost twenty years now, and no word from him yet.

Drew, Nancy. Soon after the events described above, Nancy moved to the hill country of Virginia, where she is director of a library designed by Frank Loyd Wright and heads the Roseola Support Foundation.

Dude, Derrick the. Living large on the fully restored *S.S. Magnolia*, a floating museum of riverboat history and fully operational casino cruising up and down the Mississippi, partially funded by the NEA, NPR, the National Historic Trust, donations from the Phew Charitable Fund, and from people like you.

Fitzgerald, Zelda. Died in her sleep of natural causes incident to old age soon after the events described above. Family and friends request that in lieu of flowers, please send a donation to the ALTAFF, Association of Library Trustees, Advocates, Friends and Foundations, a division of the American Library Association. www.ala.org

Livingstone, Stanley. Retired. Bought his own damn island with proceeds from sales of his KeyCo stock, dumping all of it at the historic high point for a company that no longer exists. Talk about your flash in the pan dot-com bubble. Just an instant in the stream of things, and yet it irrevocably changed so many lives.

Madley, Marian. Quit the library and opened an art gallery with proceeds from sales of her KeyCo stock.

Matt, Mayor. Dedicated to a life of public service, Mayor Matt was recently re-elected to his fourth consective term. "Why risk your capital in the private sector, when public RDAs are so much more lucrative, return-for-investment-wise, if you get my drift," he said with a wink and a nudge.

Mephistopheles, Dr. Frank. Linchpin of the KeyCo deal for the 21st Century Library / Convention Center, the whereabouts of Dr. Mephistopheles are not known. He's gone and left no trace. It's as if he never existed.

Montana, Helena. Retired the day after the opening of the 21st Century Library. After cashing in her KeyCo stock, Helena bought a forest preserve on the coast of Oregon where she runs a non-profit shelter for homeless women and children.

Petrie, Jamie. Married Reverend Dr. Wu. Moved to Silicon Valley with their baby, named, apparently, Digit. "It rhymes with Gidget," said Jamie during a brief phone conversation, "and that's the kinda girl she is."

Rabinowitz, Rachael. After successfully founding a new home design magazine in San Francisco and editing it for eight years, Rachael quit and moved back to Brooklyn. She teaches, writes, and travels the world in search of innovative architecture and humane design.

Robinofsky, Argentina. Currently managing the Farmer's Market for Mayor Matt, Argentina Robinofsky still hasn't given up her dream of organizing River Bend artists into a unified group.

Rockne, Knute. At age 75, Knute still comes in to keep the boiler going at Old Main, reincarnated as The Museum of Library Science, and home of the Mississippi River Folklore Society.

Rubble, Barney. Director of Information Services for the River Bend Library System. Barney is still happily married and the father of three children, "all of them perfectly healthy and normal with ten fingers and toes, thank you."

Seraphim, Sybil. Anyone knowing the whereabouts of Sybil is requested to contact the River Bend Police, Dept. of Fraud & Vice, concerning the notorious Deep River Blues Festival.

Tippi, Miss. Can reliably be found performing nightly at the 21st Century Library, an aging trouper in a bad wig.

Thompson, Tom. Tom is Chief Maintenance Engineer of the 21st Century Library / Convention Center.

Vernmeister, Vern. Still working two jobs and sleeping through staff meetings.

Walters, Wally. Wally is franchasing his rock'n'roll bakery outlets across North America and China, adapting to local tastes and what's available.

Wood, Evelyn. Married that nice man in Idaho with two teenage sons from a previous marriage. They started a computer repair business together, The Byte Shack, which Evelyn reports, has a new location opening soon in Boise.

Zand, Adam. Adam Zand was a big winner when the barge demolished the old Ferry Building where now stands the AZ Business Conference Center, hosting global travelers from around the world.

Acknowledgements

I acknowledge being deeply implicated as everyone else in this chronicle of events which took place circa 1996 concerning River Bend Public Library and I'm only sorry that I had to leave so many people out. I acknowledge using names from popular fiction to protect the innocent, the guilty, and myself; writing as I am, under the Federal Witness Protection Program.

I acknowledge falling in love with Marian the Librarian while watching *The Music Man* on television more times than perhaps may have been healthy for an impressionable boy surrounded by singing, dancing sisters. I acknowledge singing along with the songs on the red vinyl *Music Man* LP as we did chores, washing dishes, windows, walls, and vacuuming carpets with the big brown Kirby, expertly wielding every one of its attachments. Without adult supervision, working together, and singing along is how I remember it.

Mom was out running errands and Dad was at the office or on the road or at a sales convention. Dad was a traveling salesman, much like those carpet baggers on the train in the movie. "That's what it's all about," Dad would sagely nod his head while the actors sang and danced. "You've got to know the territory!" It was all about knowing your customer base and staying in touch. Sitting around the Christmas tree stuffing envelopes with calendars advertising the company Dad worked for was another of our family traditions.

I acknowledge no conscious memory of prior imprinting when I started working at the library. Only after completing this manuscript did I recover my memory of an early infatuation with lady librarians.

I acknowledge taking detailed notes during meetings in the library, at public hearings, in boardrooms and in backrooms, at bars, and during parties; and I recall more than once looking around and wondering why nobody else was writing this stuff down, because something was definitely happening. The internet was changing everything and it was all happening at once. All we had to do was hold on and hope to survive the voyage, just like the narrator of *Two Years Before the Mast*, which I acknowledge using as my model with this goal: to write a book about the impact of the internet as an epic ocean voyage. An adventure story told from the perspective of a common seaman, "learning the ropes," traveling to distant lands, meeting all kinds of people on the shores of a new world.

I acknowledge delusions of grandeur. I acknowledge failing to live up to expectations and promising more than I can deliver.

I acknowledge starting out on a Tanget 486© with Windows 95© using Microsoft WORD©. Everything was perfectly linear until I until I started moving files back and forth between it and the computers at the library running Windows Millenium©. Incompatibiliy problems developed, the mouse stopped responding, the cursor froze on the monitor. Then the screen went green and all all it would show is FATAL ERROR : <u>A</u>bort? <u>F</u>ail? <u>Re</u>-try?

I acknowledge Pat and Jake at The Bookshelf taking the dead pc off my hands in exchange for a 1996 Macintosh Performa©. It was like being re-born when the Mac powered up and I saw the folder on the desktap labelled DESKTOP FOLDERS which Jake had rescued from the old pc. Last I saw of the Tangent 486, it was still in service, running MS-DOS Space Invaders© in the game room at The Bookshelf. All retired computers should have such a happy afterlife.

I acknowledge that half of the manuscript was written before it even ocurred to me that I could create a facsimile of *riverrun*, the library newsletter that plays so central a part of this story. I acknowledge e-Bay as the place where I got WORD for Mac, Pagemaker© 6.5, and a flatbed scanner from a guy in Seattle. A wealth of old woodcuts were easily available from the library, and I used their T-1 internet lines to download historic photos from the American Memory section of the Library of Congresss.

When the Mac's monitor died, I bought a 22-inch AMD at Computerworld, and I acknowledge sending flamemail to them, demanding my rebate. Why do *you* think it would take them *six months* to mail a fifty dollar check??!!

I acknowledge that none of this would be possible if not for the Mac guy at Keystone College Bookstore when I came in bearing my Macintosh, looking for a twenty-two pin cable so I could output the newsletter issues for printing as PDF documents. We're talking 35-megabyte files on a computer equipped with only a floppy drive. It was exactly as if a gestating infant was trapped inside its mother's womb.

—They don't make 'em anymore, said the student-tech, backing away in horror, recognizing me from previous tech-support nightmares, such as making the AMD monitor compatible with the Macintosh.

—Wait a minute, he said, in sudden inspiration, I have something that might work for you, instead.

Darting into the backroom, he triumphantly returned with a ZIP drive, cables, and a 100 megabyte ZIP disk.

—It works, he said, but it's got a squeaky wheel. Take it. Please.

—How much? I said, reaching for my wallet. I'll pay.

—It's obsolete. You can have it, he said, thrusting the unit into my hands as if pushing me away along with it and everything else not made for life in the 21st Century.

Appendix A

KeyMail©

Date: July 9, 1996

From: JeremiaD@RiverBendLibrary.com

To: All Staff@RiverBendLibrary.com

Re: Trip Report

Hi Guys,

ALA in NYC is the best of all possible conferences. Wish you were here, glad that you're not, having the times of our lives. See attached Trip Report for more info.

See you soon,

Jeremiah D.

Attachment: DreamReport.doc

618 Gynecology

Getting a good start on the day by waking up at three in the morning with a hard-on for Marian. In my dream, Marian and I were laying on the front lawn of the River Bend library, making love in the dark. After five days in New York City, I was so tired I couldn't even lift my eyelids. Blind and vulnerable is how I was feeling. Marian's vagina had scalloped edges, like one of those ceramic plates from Judy Chicago's *Dinner Party*, but warm and soft, moist and inviting. I was inside, but couldn't come. That didn't seem to bother Marian, she was spread out like a natural extension of the landscape, head back and tits up.

Worried about being so exposed, I was gasping for breath and whimpering as if being tortured. It made Marian laugh. I just couldn't relax enough to have an orgasm with my eyes closed. To climax, I would have to open my eyes.

Willing my eyes open, I discovered myself in a roll-away bed at the Howard Johnson's Hotel in New York City. Emerson was snoring lustily. Stanley was crapped out in the bed at the other end of the room. The air conditioner was gently throbbing.

Here's the thing about Marian and last night. All this conference I've been looking people in the eye; the right eye, the eye of logic and business. Last night, at the bar of the Hard Rock Café, while Betty was off paying homage to the artifacts, Marian and I were alone for a few minutes. We were talking eye to eye. She was sitting on my left and turned all the way around on her stool, elbow resting on the bar, cupping the side of her head in her hand, to let me drink from her left eye; the eye of dreams and of love.

Appendix B
Ropes Course Training Memo
KeyMail©

Date: September 15, 1996
From: TrixieB@RBLibrary.com
To: All Staff
Re: Ropes Course Training

Disaster Preparedness is the theme for this year's Special Training Event. All staff will meet at 08:00 a.m. out by the swamp, down there along the railroad spur by the river. Appropriate attire required.

River Bend Search and Rescue Team members will facilitate the training on the course which they have laid out there on this site of a future county park. We're hoping for good weather but be prepared for whatever.

Employees will be issued Ropes Course Passports. Make sure you get your passport stamped at each station. You can Pass or have Do-Overs until you get it right. Failure is not an option!!

Stations are as follows:
1. Swamp Walk (Cross the board walk without falling into the swamp. Promotes basic balance and coordination skills.)
2. Wilderness Survival Discussion (Mr. Mike Fink, celebrated river boatman, will share some of his own personal survival experiences with us.)
3. Treehouse Club (Join the Club by climbing up to the treehouse, then sliding down a cable on that dealie with the wheels that you hang onto it.)
4. Trail Maintenance (Teamwork and community service skills. Good exercise for those lower back and shoulder muscles.)
5. Basic Rafting Skills (Teamwork and ingenuity are fostered as staff build their own rafts from driftwood and what have you, then float back down the river to the starting point where we will break for lunch.)

Lunch Break

Lunch will be prepared by library staff under instruction of Jose Quervo from Outrageous Taco Mobile Food Service. After preparing, serving, eating, and washing dishes, all staff will qualify for Food Handlers Permits upon completion of a multiple-choice test. Failure to pass will result in taking the test over again as many times as necessary.

Emergency Disaster Preparedness

Emergency Disaster Preparedness is the theme for the rest of the day. Staff will be issued C.E.R.T. (Community Emergency Response Team) gear which includes:
 • green gym bag with C.E.R.T. insignia
 • flashlight
 • sanitary gloves and masks

- plastic hardhat
- reflective vest
- flares
- waterproof matches
- plastic throat stent
- bandages, tape, aspirins, antisceptics, and emullients

Volunteer members of River Bend C.E.R.T. will train library staff in the following procedures:

- Disaster Awareness
- Forming survival teams and putting on survival gear.
- Triage
- "Breath of Life"
- Contusions, fractures, and splints
- Tracheotomy skills
- Restarting the heart:
    - manually (i.e., "hands-on" training)
    - using that electric shock treatment dealie
- Evacuation Options:
    - "Fireman's carry"
    - using pallets
    - using ropes

C.E.R.T. certification will be issued upon completion of disaster survival training. Failure to complete disaster survival training will result in having to stay late and maybe walk back to town.

References

Books

Alger, Horatio, Jr. *Adrift In New York*. Cleveland, Ohio: The Goldsmith Publishing Co., circa 1905.
Dewey Decimal: F Alger

Andrews, Paul. *How the Web Was Won: Microsoft From Windows to the Web. The Inside Story of How Bill Gates and His Band of Internet Idealists Transformed a Software Empire*. New York, N.Y.: Broadway Books, a division of Random House, Inc., 1999.
Dewey Decimal: 338.761005 A5685h

Baker, Nicholson. *Double Fold: Libraries and the Assault on Paper*. New York, N.Y.: Random House, 2001
Dewey Decimal: 025.283 B1683d

Basbanes, Nicholas A. *Patience & Fortitude: A Roving Chronicle of Book People, Book Places, and Book Culture*. New York, NY.: HarperCollins, 2001.
Dewey Decimal: 002.09 B2972p

Beatty, Jack. *The World According to Peter Drucker*. New York, London, Toronto, Sydney, Singapore: The Free Press, 1998.
Dewey Decimal: 658.4 B3698w

Bianco, Anthony. *Ghosts of 42nd Street: A History of America's Most Infamous Block*. New York, N.Y.: William Morrow, an imprint of HarperCollins Publishers Inc., 2004.
Dewey Decimal: 929.2 B578r

Blanchet, Christian; Bertrand Dard. *Statue of Liberty: The First Hundred Years*; English language version by Bernard A. Weisberger. New York, N.Y.: American Heritage Press, Inc., 1985. Translation of: Statue de la Liberte.
Dewey Decimal: 974.71 B6392
CAPTIONS
October 28, 1886, the day of the official unveiling.
An artillery salute welcomed President Cleveland to Bedloe's Island, and the resulting smoke nearly hid the statue from view. Photograph by H. O. Neil, October 28, 1868. Library of Congress. (MAGNOLIA sidewheeler in foreground)

Bornstein, Kate. *Gender Outlaw: On Men, Women and the Rest of Us*. New York, N.Y.: First Vintage Books, 1995.
_____, Bergman, S. Bear. *Gender Outlaws: the Next Generation*. Publishers Group West, 2010.
Dewey Decimal: 306.768 G3254 2010
_____. *My New Gender Workbook : a step-by-step guide to achieving world peace through gender anarchy and sex positivity*. Routledge, 2013.

Burrows, Edwin G., Wallace, Mike. *Gotham: A History of New York City to 1898*. New York, Oxford: Oxford University Press, 1999.
Dewey Decimal: 974.71 B9727g
Page 681: By 1860 seventeen book-printing firms were manufacturing over three million dollars' worth of volumes for the national marketplace. New York City, with 2 percent of the country's population, produced over 37 percent of its total publishing revenue. Harper and Brothers retained its preeminence. By 1853, when its workforce of five hundred issued more than four and a half million volumes, it had become the largest employer in New York City...By 1857 there were at least 112 publishers in New York City.

Capote, Truman. *Breakfast at Tiffany's: A Short Novel and Three Stories*. New York: Random House, 1958.
Dewey Decimal: F Capote

Chase, Elaine Raco; Wingate, Anne. *Amateur Detectives: A Writer's Guide to how private citizens solve criminal cases*. New York, N.Y.: Writer's Digest Books, 1996.
Dewey Decimal: 808.3872 C4873a
Who's On The Internet?
• 37 million people in the United States and Canada–17% of the total population
•24 million are adults
• 33 percent are women
• 50 percent are between ages 16 and 34
• They spend 5 1/2 hours a week surfing the Net
World Wide Web
     The Web is a collection of more than fifty thousand sites or pages that have been set up by anyone about everything imaginable. Universities, archives, museums and the private sector upload volumes of previously obscure or new information daily.

Claybourne, Anna. *The Usbourne Computer Dictionary for Beginners*. London, England: Usbourne Publishing Ltd., 1995.
Dewey Decimal: YP 004.03 C6221u

Donovan, Frank. *River Boats of America*. New York: Thomas Y. Crowell Company, 1966.
Dewey Decimal: 386.309 Do

Drucker, Peter F. *Managing in a Time of Great Change*. Truman Talley Books / Dutton, 1995
_____. *Post-Capitalist Society*. New York, N.Y.: HarperCollins, 1993.
Dewey Decimal: 330.9049 D7945p
_____. *The Essential Drucker*. New York, N.Y.: HarperCollins Publishers, 2001.
Dewey Decimal: 658 D7945e

Dunlap, David W. *On Broadway: A Journey Uptown Over Time*. New York, N.Y.: Rizzoli International Publications, Inc., 1990.
Dewey Decimal: 974.71 D9212o

Dyer, Joel. *The Perpetual Prisoner Machine*. Boulder, Colorado, Oxford, England: Westview Press, a member of the Perseus Books Group, 2000.
Dewey Decimal: 364.973 D9966p
The United States now incarcerates between 1.8 and 2 million of its citizens in its prisons and jails on any given day, and over 5 million people are currently under the supervision of America's criminal justice system. That's more prisoners than any country in the world.

Edmiston, Susan and Cirino, Linda D. *Literary New York: A History and Guide, Maps and Walking Tours*. Layton, Ut.: Peregrine Smith Books.
Dewey Decimal: 810.997471 E2413L

Epstein, Jason. *Book Business: Publishing Past Present and Future*. New York, London: W. W. Norton & Company, Ltd., 2001.
Dewey Decimal: 070.5 S3334b
The United States, with few writers of its own to protect and a printing industry to nurture, ignored international copyright throughout most of the nineteenth century. By 1853, Harper Bros., with a staff of five hundred, had become New York City's largest employer and the world's leading book publisher, having added Bibles and schoolbooks as well as books by American writers to its line of pirated works by Dickens, Thackeray, the Brontes, and others.
According to Edwin G. Burrows and Mike Wallace in *Gotham*, their magisterial history of New York to 1898, surely the greatest and at nearly five pounds the most unwieldy history of a city ever written, Thamas Babbington Macaulay was the most successful of Harper's pirated authors.

Foucalt, Michel. *Discipline & Punish: The Birth of the Prison*. New York: Vintage Books, a division of Random House, 1995. Translation copyright © 1977 by Alan Sheridan.
Dewey Decimal: 365.643 F7625d
Page 205: The Panopticon...must be understood as a generalizable model of functioning; a way of defining power relations in terms of the everyday life of men... The fact that it should have given rise, even in our own time, to so many variations, projected or realized, is evidence of the imaginary intensity that it has possessed for almost two hundred years. But the Panopticon must not be understood as a dream building: it is the diagram of a mechanism of power reduced to its ideal form; its functioning, abstracted from any obstacle, resistance or friction, must be represented as a pure architectural and optical system: it is in fact a figure of political technology that may and must be detached from any specific use.

French, Laura. *Internet Pioneers: The Cyber Elite*. Berkeley Heights, N.J., Aldershot, U.K.: Enslow Publishers, Inc., 2001.
Dewey Decimal: YP 004.0922 F8744
In August of 1995, Yahoo sold advertising to five businesses. It charged them $60,000 apiece for a three-month trial. Some users accused Yahoo of selling out. Before long, however, other companies were selling advertising, too. By 1996, 350 companies advertised on Yahoo.
On April 12, 1996, Yahoo became a public company. Shares of the company's stock were sold to investors. In one day, the price of the stock went from $13 to $43. At the end of the day, the stock was worth $33 a share. Jerry Yang made $132 million that day.

Gorsline, Douglas. *What People Wore: A Visual History of Dress from Ancient Times to 20th Century America*. New York, N.Y.: Viking Press, 1952.
Dewey Decimal: 391 G6745w

Griffith, Jim "Griff." *The Official eBay Bible: The Most Up-to-Date, Comprehensive How-to Manual for Everyone from First-Time Users to People Who Want to Run Their Own Business*. New York, N.Y.: Gotham Books, a division of Penguin Group (USA) Inc, 2003.
Dewey Decimal: 381.17 G8537o.

Hallinan, Joseph T. *Going Up the River: Travels in a Prison Nation*. New York: Random House, 2001.
Dewey Decimal: 395.973 H1895g

Henderson, Amy; Bowers, Dwight Blocker. *Red, Hot, & Blue: A Smithsonian Salute to the American Musical*. Washington and London: Smithsonian Institution Press, 1996.
Dewey Decimal: 782.1 H4961r

Jacobs, Jane. *The Death and Life of Great American Cities*. Modern Library, New York, N.Y.: Random House, 1961.
Dewey Decimal: 307.76 J176d

Kazinsky, Ted. *The Unabomber Manifesto*. Self-published, Lincoln, Montana, 1995-ish
166. Therefore two tasks confront those who hate the servitude to which the industrial system is reducing the human race. First, we must work to heighten the social stresses within the system so as to increase the likelihood that it will break down or be weakened sufficiently so that a revolution against it becomes possible. Second, it is necessary to develop and propagate an ideology that opposes technology and the industrial society if and when the system becomes sufficiently weakened.

Kouwenhoven, John. *The Columbia Historical Portrait of New York: An essay in graphic history in honor of the Tricentennial of New York City and the Bicentennial of Columbia University*. New York, N.Y.: Doubleday & Co., 1953.
Dewey Decimal: 974.71 K84c

Lears, Jackson. *Something for Nothing: Luck in America*. New York: Viking Penguin, 2003.
Dewey Decimal: 363.42 L4386s
PHOTO CREDIT Page 116: George Caleb Bingham, *Raftsmen Playing Cards* (1847). Oil on canvas. Courtesy, St. Louis Art Museum. Ezra H. Linley Fund.

Lerner, Fred. *The Story of Libraries: From the Invention of Writing to the Computer Age*. New York, N.Y.: The Continuum Publishing Company, 1999.
Dewey Decimal: 027.009 L6165s

Lessig, Lawrence. *Free Culture: How Big Media Uses Technology and the Law to Lock Down Culture and Control Creativity*. 2004.
Dewey Decimal: 343.73099 L6395f

Loving, Jerome. *Walt Whitman: The Song of Himself*. Berkeley, Los Angeles, London: University of California Press, 1999.
Dewey Decimal: 92 Whitman

McCloskey, Deidre. *Crossing: A Memoir*. Chicago, Il.: University of Chicago Press, 1999.

McGrath, John E. *Loving Big Brother: Performance, Privacy and Surveillance Space*. London and New York: Routledge, an imprint of the Taylor & Francis Group, 2004.
Dewey Decimal: 303.483 M14721

Melder, Keith. *Hail to the Candidate: Presidential Campaigns from Banners to Broadcasts*. Washington: Smithsonian Institution Press, 1992.
Dewey Decimal: 324.973 M5185

O'Neil, Paul, the editors of Time-Life Books. *The Rivermen*. New York: Time-Life Books, 1975.
Dewey Decimal: 386.0973 O5835
PICTURE CREDIT: Courtesy Missouri Historical Society. *By cordelling, poling and sailing all at once—an unusual combination—lower Missouri keelboatmen of the 18th Century make excellent progress.*

Postman, Neil. *The End of Education: Redefining the Value of School*. New York, NY.: Alfred A. Knopf, 1995.
Dewey Decimal: 370.973 P8585e

Quick, Herbert, Quick, Edward. *Mississippi Steamboatin': A History of Steamboating on the Mississippi and Its Tributaries*. New York. Henry Holt and Co., 1926.
Dewey Decimal: 387 Qu
Page 169: The "Charles P. Chouteau"—a sternwheeler of the seventies carrying a record cargo of cotton. (Stanton's "American Steam Vessels")

Raymond, Janice. *The Transsexual Empire: the Creation of the She-Male*. Boston: Beacon Press, 1979. New York: Teacher's College Press, 1994.
Dewey Decimal: 306.76

Reynolds, David S. *Walt Whitman's America: A Cultural Biography*. New York: Alfred A. Knopf, 1995.
Dewey Decimal: 92 Whitman

Register, Woody. *The Kid of Coney Island: Fred Thompson and the Rise of American Amusements*. Oxford, New York: Oxford University Press, 2001.
Dewey Decimal: 338.761791 R3374k

Rosenzweig, Roy, Blackmar, Elizabeth. *The Park and the People: A History of Central Park*. Ithaca and London: Cornell University Press, 1992.

Dewey Decimal: 974.71 R8164
Page 232: On the Fourth of July, 1865, a huge crowd of close to a hundred thousand New Yorkers gathered, and "the people reigned supreme," said the Herald. It was "the People's Day in the Park," when "many of those present now saw our urban gardens of delight for the first time." The Fourth of July was "the only day in the year on which the working classes can enjoy the liberty of the Common, stretch themselves on the grass and listen to music on the Mall." Newspapers stressed the working-class character and style of these Independence Day crowds, the lively presence of "the artisan, the laborer, the shop girl, the kitchen deities, and the rest of the working classes" and the conspicuous absence of "the elegantly appointed carriages."

Rybczynski, Witold. *A Clearing in the Distance: Frederick Law Olmsted and America in the Nineteenth Century*. New York, N.Y.: Scribner, 1999.
Dewey Decimal: 712.092 R9895c

Salinger, J. D. *Raise High the Roof Beam, Carpenters*. The New Yorker, 1955.
Dewey Decimal: F Salinger

Schiffrin, Andre. *The Business of Books: How International Conglomerates Took Over Publishing and Changed the Way We Read*. London, New York: Verso Books, 2000.
Dewey Decimal: 070.5 S3334b

Simkin, Colin. *Currier and Ives' America: A Panorama of the Mid-Nineteenth Century Scene, Eighty Choice Prints IN FULL COLOR With Extended Commentary on the Prints and the Times They Portray*. New York: Bonanza Books, 1952.
Dewey Decimal: 763.084 C9765s
...by 1835, then twenty-two years of age, he had his own establishment. Up to that time the lithographic business consisted chiefly of printing letterheads, commercial forms, music, maps and other items involving lettering and a limited amount of design. Although some other lithographers may have experimented with the reproduction of portraits or other art work, it is generally conceded that it was Currier who first saw the possibilities of publishing newsworthy subjects.

Smolan, Rick. *24 Hours in Cyberspace: Painting on the Walls of the Digital Cave, 1996*. (With CD-ROM)
Dewey Decimal: 003.50115 T9715

Taylor, William R., editor. *Inventing Times Square: Commerce and Culture at the Crossroads of the World*. Prologue by Jean-Christophe Agnew, Afterword by Ada Louise Huxtable. New York, N.Y.:

Russell Sage Foundation, 1991.
Dewey Decimal: 974.71 I6235

Thompson, Kay. Kay Thompson's *Eloise: A Book for Precocious Grownups*; Drawings by Hilary Knight. New York, N.Y.: Simon & Schuster, 1955.
Dewey Decimal: JP Thompson

Traub, James. *The Devil's Playground: A Century of Pleasure and Profit in Times Square*. New York, N.Y.: Random House Publishing, 2004.
Dewey Decimal: 974.71 T7772d
Basil March, the hero of William Dean Howell's 1890 novel, *A Hazard of New Fortunes*, lives with his wife in the dignified precincts of Washington Square, but communtes by "el" to his office at the raffish magazine he edits in the East Forties....By Howell's time, the East Side had been developed up to 125th Street, though the West Side remained largely pastoral.

Twain, Mark. *The Adventures of Huckleberry Finn, The Only Comprehensive Edition*. New York: Random House, 1996. (Originally published in different form in 1885 by Charles L. Webster and Co.)
Dewey Decimal: F Twain

Wallace, David Foster. *Infinite Jest*. Little, Brown, and Co. 1996.
Dewey Decimal: F Wallace

Warburton, Lois. *Prisons*. San Diego: Lucent Books, 1993.
Dewey Decimal 365.973 W2546p
"The Rising Prison Population" graphic.

Watkins, T.H. *Mark Twain's Mississippi: A Pictorial History of America's Greatest River*. Also Selected Excerpts from Mark Twin's *Life On the Mississippi*. © American West Publishing, published by Weathervane Books, distributed by Crown Publishing, 1974.
Dewey Decimal: 977 W3357

Wayman, Norbury L. *Life on the Mississippi: A Pictorial History of the Mississippi, the Missouri, and the Western River System*. New York: Crown Publishers, 1971.
Dewey Decimal: 977 W3584L

Western Writers of America (anthology). *Water Trails West*. New York: Doubleday and Co., 1978.
Dewey Decimal: 386 We
The legendary Mike Fink performing his favorite stunt of shooting a hole in a whiskey-filled tin cup perched

on a friend's head. New York Public Library Keelboat with Sail. From the painting by Karl Bodmer. Courtesy Nebraska State Historical Society.

Wiegand, Wayne A. *Irrepressible Reformer: A Biography of Melvil Dewey.* Chicago and London: American Library Association, 1996.
Dewey Decimal: 92 Dewey

Witheridge, Annette. *New York Then And Now.* San Diego, Ca.: Thunder Bay Press, 2001.
Dewey Decimal: 974.71 W8233n
Longacre Square was renamed Times Square in 1904, the year this photograph was taken, in honor of the New York Times Building. © Collection of the New-York Historical Society, negative number 67730.

White, E.B. *Here is New York.* New York, N.Y.: Harper and Bros., 1949.
Dewey Decimal: 974.71 W5835h

Wolff, Michael. *Burn Rate: How I Survived The Gold Rush Years On The Internet.* New York, N.Y.: Simon & Schuster, 1998.
Dewey Decimal: 338.761 W8555b
With this perception–seeing the Web as some kind of direct marketing solution, a medium that can cut the cost of a response–the scramble began. Suddenly there was a sense of what people were doing here, of what the pot of gold was going to be, of how the geeks would be moved out and America moved in.

Editors, The. *WORLD BOOK—1996 YEAR IN REVIEW.*
Internet.
In 1996 the Internet (often called the Net) grew far beyond its origins as a computer network connecting a few dozen government and university scientists. E-mail (electronic mail), once considered a novelty, became a common way for businesses and individuals to exchange messages, documents, and computer files. Businesses rushed to take advantage of the new medium, pouring millions of dollars into colorful "home pages" on the World Wide Web, the graphics-based portion of the Net, to showcase products and services…
Web software.
New versions of the two most popular web browsers (applications that access the World Wide Web) came on the market in 1996. In August, Netscape Communications Corporation of Mountain View, California, began promoting its Navigator 3.0, an updated version of the browser used by 85 percent of Internet users. Seeking to challenge Netscape's huge market share, Microsoft Corporation of Redmond, Washington, released its own web browser, Internet Explorer, in the spring and an updated version, Internet Explorer 3.0, in August.

Providing equal access.
The most important social issue regarding the Internet was how to ensure that its resources became accessible to everyone, especially to those who could not afford expensive computers and access fees. This desire to create equal access sparked a variety of plans aimed at connecting school to the Internet. Some communities organized "Net Days," at which volunteers strung cables, set up computers, and installed the software needed for schools to access the Net. These festive events were compared to prairie barn raisings. Many communities also set up computers at libraries and other public buildings, so that people without a computer could explore the net.

Newspapers, Magazines, and Journals

Adler, Jerry. "Goodbye, Damon Runyon, Hello Mickey Mouse," Newsweek, May 13, 1996.

Ambrose, Stephen E. "Liberty's Vast Empire," New York Times, July 4, 1996.

Baldringer, Scott. "Marketing Broadway as a Cool Spot / Marketing Broadway As a With-It Place." New York Times, April 14, 1996.

Beals, Gregory. "The World of 'Rent,'" Newsweek, May 13, 1996.

Bianco, Anthony. "A Star Is Reborn: Investors hustle to land parts in Times Square's Transformation," Business Week, July 8, 1996.

Belluck, Pam. "Celebrating July 4 Spirit, Undaunted But Damp," New York, N.Y.: New York Times, July 5, 1996.
PHOTO CAPTION: Any Awning Will Do: A muggy day yesterday was punctuated by thunderstorms, forcing some pedestrians on Broadway in Times Square to seek shelter.
Some Fourth of July.
A spasmodic sun, narcissistic gray clouds and a thoughtlessly headstrong wind teased and tormented people's holiday plans. Rain flashed its own independent streak, spitting, dousing, drying up, then drenching again….
The somber skies and intermittent sprinkles didn't deter people…nor did they prevent tens of thousands of New Yorkers and tourists from staking out space along the East Side of Manhattan last night to view the annual fireworks display.
Starting around 7:30 P.M., spectators began laying blankets on sidewalks along Franklin D. Roosevelt Drive while others sat on stoops or garbage Dumpsters. Many simply stood outside, or watched from apartment windows…The light rain that had been falling for much of the evening stopped shortly after the fireworks began

around 9:30 P.M.

Chepesiuk, Ron. "Librarians as Cyberspace Guerillas: An Interview with John Perry Barlow. THE COFOUNDER OF THE ELECTRONIC FRONTIER FOUNDATION PREDICTS LIBRARIANS WILL BE ON THE FRONT LINES OF THE BATTLE TO CONTROL INFORMATION TECHNOLOGY," American Libraries, September 1996.

Cutter, C.A. "Good Reading for the Public Library." The Nation, Vol. 33, page 448.

Cutter, C.A. "The Coming Public Library in New York." The Nation: Volume 34, page 420.

Cutter, C.A. "A Librarian on Public Libraries." The Nation: Vol. 9, page 233.

Dewey, Melvil, "The Profession," American Library Journal, Vol. 1, No. 1, September 30, 1876.

Dorman, David. "Technically Speaking: Bytes from the Big Apple Exhibits," American Libraries, August, 1996.
While most vendors downsized their booths for this very expensive venue, Microsoft's exhibit area covered 30 feet on both sides of the aisle—twice the size of its last ALA exhibit booth.

Dorman, David. "Observations on the North American Library Automation Marketplace," American Libraries, September, 1996.

Dreifus, Claudia. "The Cyber-Maxims of Esther Dyson," New York, N.Y.: New York Times Magazine, July 7, 1996.

Editors. "The Best Show on Broadway: ALA Conference is Full of Surprises." American Libraries. August, 1996.

Editors. "120th Anniversary of the American Library Association," Library Journal, July, 1996.

Editors. "New York Packs 'em In; Martinez Bows Out," Library Journal, August, 1996.

Elliott, Andrea and McKinley, Jesse. "A Day In The Life," New York Times, June 13, 2004.

Fiske, J. "The Work of a Librarian." Atlantic

Monthly. Vol. 38, _____, 18__: p. 480.

Gordon, Rachel Singer. "NEXTGEN: The Men Among Us." Library Journal, June 15, 2004, page 49. 82 percent of librarians are female, according to 2002 U.S. Statistical Abstract figures, and 21 percent of 2002 LIS grads were male, according to "Salaries Stalled, Jobs Tight" (LJ 10/15/03, p.28)

Greene, G. W. "The Public Library." North American Review, Vol. 45, page 116.

Haberman, Clyde. "NYC: At WNYC, Independence Has Its Price," New York Times, July ___, 1996

Harris, George T. "The Post-Capitalist Executive: An Interview with Peter F. Drucker." Harvard Business Review, May-June, 1993.

Howland, E. "The Public Library in the United States." Harper's, Vol. 54, page 722.

"Recent Improvements in Public Libraries." North American Review, Vol. 158, page 376.

"The Ideal Public Library." North American Review, Vol. 160: page 118.

James, Caryn. "Critic's Notebook: TV's Elvis Sightings," July 5, 1996. New York Times.

Jacques, Roy. Review of Post-Capitalist Society. The International Journal of Organizational Analysis, Vol. 1, No. 4 (October), pp. 427-439.

K.L. "Free Wiring Is One Thing, Expensive Hardware Is Another," American Libraries, November, 1996.

Kippen, David. "Confessions of a Copyright Warrior. The Bono Factor: Is a dead musician's legacy interfering with free speech?" San Francisco Chronicle, April 18, 2004.

Konrad, Rachel. "Trouble Ahead, Trouble Behind: Totalitarianism. Urban Pathology. The Death of creativity. These are the fears that keep John Perry Barlow awake at night." C/net News.Com, February 22, 2002.

Kuchment, Anna. "The More Social Sex: Why do women form more powerful relationships than men? It's all about survival." Newsweek, May 10, 2004.

Lee, Susan. "Peter Drucker's Fuzzy Future: The

big-thinking theorist's new book contains interesting nuggets. But as prophecy it's vague, grand, and ultimately unsatisfying." Fortune, May 17, 1993.

Livermore, G. "The Public Library." North American Review, Vol. 71, page 185.

Muschamp, Herbert. "A See-Through Library of Shifting Shapes and Colors: Enrique Norten's design for a Brooklyn Arts Center is a masterwork for New York." New York Times, January 19, 2003.

Newman, Andy. "Our Correspondent in Brooklyn: A Rare and Stirring Mixture," The Sophisticated Traveler, New York Times Magazine, New York Times, May 2, 2004.

Pareles, Jon. ""Blowing Off the Fetters of Styles as Boundaries," New York, N.Y.: New York Times, July 6, 1996.
CAPTION: George Clinton, left, performing with Bootsy Collins at Summerstage in Central Park on the Fourth of July.

America's founding fathers may not have envisioned the like of George Clinton and the P-Funk All-Stars, who played a sold-out Fourth of July benefit concert for Central Park Summerstage. But as a diverse, ambitious bunch of people cheerfully abetting the pursuit of happiness, P-Funk made a fine utopian model for America.

The rainbow-haired Mr. Clinton led a motley carnival of nearly two dozen musicians and singers, casually wandering the stage. Male musicians wore diapers, a burnoose, a nun's habit and a bridal gown. P-Funk looked disorderly and hedonistic, singing about "the funk," an amalgam of rhythm and sec, dancing and insubordination, knowledge and fun—about jettisoning the Puritan ethic...

Rawlinson, Nora. "1996 ALA Show in New York: Exceeding Expectations." Publisher's Weekly, July 15, 1996.

Reichel, Ruth. "Restaurants: Thai Food, a surprising carnival of hot and sweet spices, arrives raucously." New York, N.Y.: New York Times, July, 1996.

Rose, Frank. **Ghosts of 42nd Street?."** Fortune, June 24, 1996.

St. Lifer, Evan. "Born Again Brooklyn: Gates Wires the Library." Library Journal, November 1, 1996.

Sandomir, Richard. "Sports Business: O'Neal's Website is Underwhelming," New York Times, July 5, 1996.

Smith, Dinitia. "Librarians' Challenge: Offering Internet. The mission is still free information, but the means are new." New York, N.Y.: New York Times, July 6, 1996.
On the Fourth of July weekend, many Americans try to get away from it all. Not librarians. This weekend, 22,000 of them are attending the annual conference of the American Library Association in Manhattan. There are poetry readings, with exhibitions of a thousand new works. ("Not since the beats has there been such a revival of interest," reads the association's brocure.) There is a celebration of storytelling and a tour of "literary Greenwich Village."

But uppermost in the librarians' minds this weekend are not books but telecommunications. The business at hand, said Betty Turock, the departing president of the association, is "to retain the library as the central institution of a free society...

Solomon, Deborah. "Reanimated: For years, Walt Disney's nephew Roy was the passive heir, sitting on the sidelines of the company. But now he's leading a crusade to push out the chairman, Michael Eisner, and take back the kingdom." New York Times Magazine, February 22, 2004.

Teggert, F.J. "The First Advocate of Free Libraries." The Nation, Vol. 67, page 220.

Weber, Bruce. "In Times Square, Keepers of the Glitz: 3 Women Overseeing Block's Rebirth Promise to Return Its Splendor." New York Times, June 25, 1996.

Editors. "SIBL: NYPL's new Science, Industry, and Business Library," American Libraries, June/July, 1996.)

Editors. "Wired Libraries," New York Times, April 21, 2004.
In 1996, 28 percent of all libraries had PC's for public access to the Internet. Now, 95 percent of libraries offer Internet access. The Gates foundation accelerated the trend. There are now more than 120,000 Internet-connected PC's for public use in municipal libraries nationwide. Since 1998, the foundation has installed or paid for more than 47,000 PC's.

"Before we had the Internet and this building, the library was not considered a winner," said Mary Cosper LeBoeuf, the head librarian. "But now it is."

SPEED OF CARS AT CURVES: THE ALDERMEN WANT TO LESSEN THE DANGERS ON CABLE

ROADS. A Committee Directed to Prepare an Ordinance Regulating the Rate of Speed–The Old Reservoir to Give Way to the Public Library–Favorable Report on the Fulton Street Tunnel Project–The Fireworks Ordinance Suspended." New York Times, July 1, 1896.

...The County Affairs Committee reported favorably on the proposition to build the new public library in Bryant Park, and it was ordered that the old reservoir be removed after the new water mains have been laid in Fifth Avenue below Fortieth Street.

Alderman Brown introduced a resolution asking the County Affairs Committee to inquire of the Corporation Counsel as to the board's right to locate the library in Central Park.

The resolution created a laugh, but Alderman Brown pressed it, and it went through.

Film

Desk Set, 1957.
Efficiency expert Richard Sumner (Spencer Tracy) and his EMERAC computer are no match for quick-witted Broadcast network reference librarian Bunny Watson (Katherine Hepburn.)
Directed by Walter Lang
Produced by Henry Ephron
Screenplay by Phoebe Ephron, Henry Ephron
Based on Desk Set (play) by William Marchant
Starring Katharine Hepburn, Spencer Tracy
Distributed by   20th Century-Fox

Party Girl, 1995.
Aimless party girl Mary (Parker Posey) has to get a job working as a library page. Reluctantly mastering the Dewey Decimal System, she discovers an inner rage for order and applies it to organizing her wardrobe and putting on raves.
Directed by Daisy von Scherler Mayer
Written by Harry Birckmayer, Sheila Gaffney, Daisy von Scherler Mayer
Starring Parker Posey, Guillermo Díaz, Anthony DeSando, Liev Schreiber
Distributed by Sony Pictures
The Internet premiere happened on June 3, 1995, transmitted from Glenn Fleishman's Point of Presence Company (POPCO). Appearing live in the POPCO offices, Parker Posey welcomed Internet viewers and then introduced the film.

You're A Big Boy Now, 1966.
With parents played by Rip Torn and Geraldine Page, and a problematic girlfriend (Karen Black) young Bernard Chanticleer (Peter Castner) has a rough time coming-of-age while working as a roller-skating page at the New York Public Library. Filmed on location, Francis Ford Coppola's first feature film is a screwball comedy featuring a hit title song by The Lovin' Spoonful an an Academy-award nomination for Geraldine Page.
Directed by Francis Ford Coppola
Produced by Phil Feldman
Screenplay by Francis Ford Coppola
Based on You're a Big Boy Now by David Benedictus
Starring Elizabeth Hartman, Geraldine Page, Peter Kastner
Distributed by Warner Bros.-Seven Arts

Internet Links

Barlow, John Perry. "A Cyberspace Independence Declaration." Electronic Frontier Foundation, February 9, 1996.
https://projects.eff.org/~barlow/Declaration-Final.html

Goldberger, Paul. "The New Times Square: Magic That Surprised the Magicians." New York Times, Oct. 15, 1996.
http://www.nytimes.com/1996/10/15/arts/the-new-times-square-magic-that-surprised-the-magicians.html

Jacobs, Karrie. "Utopia Redux," WORD.com, April 18, 1996.
http://www.nettime.org/Lists-Archives/nettime-l-9604/msg00024.html

http://theshiftedlibrarian.com

www.lipsticklibrarian.com

www.new42.org
Welcome to the New 42nd Street. (includes chronology from early 1900s to 2000.)

Errata & Notes
Win Valuable Prizes!

Please note errors here and e-mail the author, Jeremiah D. Angelo, c/o
Federal Witness Security Program, Washington, D.C.

Whoever finds the most mistakes will reveive a
FREE
copy of
Return to Circa '96

Autographed by the author:
Jeremiah D. Angelo

Legal Mumbojumbo
We regret any lapses of decorum and mistakes in spelling. All natural fiber. Some settling of contents may
have occurred in transit. Product sold by weight, not volume. No animals were harmed during product testing. (See
SHOUTOUTS.) Author assumes no responsibility for harm or damage caused by the mis-use of this product. If
dissatisfied with product, return unused portion to the author for full refund.

000: Generalities

The *Hey Macarena!*
1996 Annotated Timeline

Dec. 7, 1995 – "The sleeping giant has awakened," said Bill Gates, announcing Microsoft's licensing of Java and the expansion of its Spyglass license to provide Internet Explorer for Windows 3.X, Macintosh, and UNIX.

January

Jan. 2 - AT&T announces elimination of 40,000 jobs, primarily through layoffs.

Jan. 5 - Congress approves legislation sending federal employees back to work after shutdown.

Jan. 8 - A massive blizzard hits the eastern half of the US. At least 50 deaths are blamed on the weather.

Jan. 15 - Russian troops attack Pervomayskaya, Russia, where Chechen rebels have been holding up to 100 hostages since Jan. 9.

Jan. 16 - Armed men in Trabzon, Turkey, hijack a Black Sea ferry, and demand that Russian troops stop fighting Chechen rebels.

Jan. 17 - Sheik Omar Abdel-Rahman and nine followers are handed long prison sentences for plotting to blow up New York-area landmarks.

Jan. 18 - Microsoft Corporation announced second-quarter revenues of $2.2 billion, a 48% increase over the same quarter a year ago.
- Lisa Marie Presley-Jackson files for divorce from Michael Jackson.

Jan. 21 - Yasser Arafat wins in a landslide election (88 percent of the vote) in first Palestinian election.

Jan. 23 - President Clinton delivers State of the Union address and urges Republicans to "finish the job" in achieving a balanced budget.

Jan. 29 - Navy F-14 fighter jet crashes in Nashville, Tenn., demolishing three houses and killing five people, including three on the ground.

Jan. 31 - The last Cubans held in refugee camps at Guantanamo Bay Naval Base board a plane for Florida.

001 Knowledge
002 The book
003 Systems
004 Data processing Computer science
005 Computer programming, programs, data
006 Special computer methods
007 Not assigned or no longer used
008 Not assigned or no longer used
009 Not assigned or no longer used
010 Bibliography
011 Bibliographies
012 Bibliographies of individuals
013 Bibliographies of works by specific classes of authors
014 Bibliographies of anonymous and pseudonymous
015 Bibliographies of works from specific places
016 Bibliographies of works from specific subjects
017 General subject catalogs
018 Catalogs arranged by author & date
019 Dictionary catalogs
020 Library & information sciences
021 Library relationships
022 Administration of the physical plant
023 Personnel administration
024 Not assigned or no longer used
025 Library operations
026 Libraries for specific subjects
027 General libraries
028 Reading, use of other information media
029 Not assigned or no longer used
030 General encyclopedic works
031 General encyclopedic works — American
032 General encyclopedic works in English
033 General encyclopedic works in other Germanic languages
034 General encyclopedic works in French, Provencal, Catalan
035 General encyclopedic works in Italian, Romanian
036 General encyclopedic works in Spanish & Portuguese
037 General encyclopedic works in Slavic languages
038 General encyclopedic works in Scandinavian languages
039 General encyclopedic works in other languages
040 Not assigned or no longer used
041 Not assigned or no longer used
042 Not assigned or no longer used
043 Not assigned or no longer used
044 Not assigned or no longer used
045 Not assigned or no longer used
046 Not assigned or no longer used
047 Not assigned or no longer used
048 Not assigned or no longer used
049 Not assigned or no longer used
050 General serials & their indexes
051 General serials & their indexes American
052 General serials & their indexes In English
053 General serials Germanic languages
054 General serials French, Provencal, Catalan
055 General serials & their indexes In Italian
056 General serials & their indexes In Spanish & Portuguese
057 General serials & their indexes In Slavic languages
058 General serials & their indexes In Scandinavian languages
059 General serials & their indexes In other languages
060 General organization & museology
061 General organization & museology In North America

Vocabulary Enhancement

apodictic, necessarily true: demonstrative without demonstration: beyond contradiction.

beghard, n. in Flanders or elsewhere from the 13th century, a man living a monastic life without vows and with power to return to the world.

beguine, beguine, n. a member of a sisterhood living as nuns but without vows, and with power to return to the world.

behaviorism, a psychological method which substitutes for the subjective element of consciousness, the objective one of observation of conduct of other beings under certain stimuli.

collieshangie, (Scot.) n. a noisy wrangling: an uproar: a disturbance.

colliquate, v.t. to melt: to fuse.

colliquesence, readiness to liquefy.

colloquial, pertaining to or used in common conversation.

colloquy, a speaking together: mutual discourse: conversation.

episode, a story introduced into a narrative or poem to give variety: an incident or period detachable from a novel, play, etc.: a part of a radio or television serial which is broadcast at one time.

062 General organization & museology In British Isles
063 General organization & museology In central Europe
064 General organization & museology In France
065 General organization & museology In Italy
066 General organization & museology In Iberian Peninsula
067 General organization & museology In eastern Europe
068 General organization & museology In other areas
069 Museology (Museum science)
070 News media, journalism, publishing
071 News media, journalism, publishing In North America
072 News media, journalism, publishing In British Isles
073 News media, journalism, publishing In central Europe
074 News media, journalism, publishing In France & Monaco
075 News media, journalism, publishing In Italy
076 News media, journalism, publishing In Iberian Peninsula
077 News media, journalism, publishing In eastern Europe
078 News media, journalism, publishing In Scandinavia
079 News media, journalism, publishing In other languages
080 General collections
081 General collections American
082 General collections In English
083 General collections In other Germanic languages
084 General collections In French, Provencal, Catalan
085 General collections In Italian, Romanian
086 General collections In Spanish & Portuguese
087 General collections In Slavic languages
088 General collections In Scandinavian languages
089 General collections In other languages
090 Manuscripts & rare books
091 Manuscripts
092 Block books
093 Incunabula
094 Printed books
095 Books notable for bindings
096 Books notable for illustrations
097 Books notable for ownership or origin
098 Prohibited works, forgeries, hoaxes
099 Books notable for format

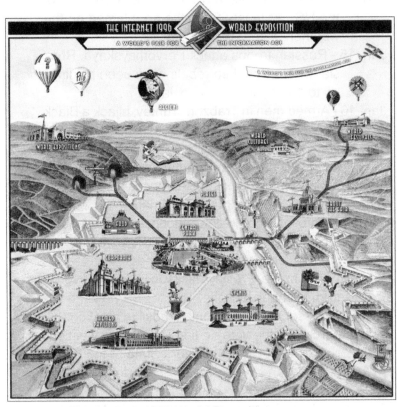

The Internet 1996 World Exposition
Throughout the year, a variety of events brought the fair into the real world. Japan decked Tokyo's Harajuku District with banners and parties, Taiwan opened public computers in 100 locations, and the Netherlands brought the fair to street festivals. At the end of the year, a closing ceremony was held in Tokyo, where the fair archives were archived to CD-ROM, blessed by a Shinto priest and put in a time capsule. http://park.org/About/Fair/index.text.html

100: Philosophy & Psychology

Rising Tide Lifts All Boats as FCC Levels Virtual Playing Field

Report on the Federal Communications Commission

Implementation of the Telecommunications Act of 1996
(In highly abridged monthly installments.)

- Public Notices requesting comments on applications to provide telecommunications services filed by two utility companies, CSW Communications, Inc. and Entergy Technology Comp. (OGC, released 2/13 and 2/23).
- Public Notice requesting nominations for Telecommunications Development Fund Board. (OGC and OCBO, released 2/13).
- Notice of Proposed Rulemaking to allow Bell Operating Companies (BOC) offering out-of-region interLATA service to be treated as nondominant under certain conditions. (CCB, released 2/14).
- Notice of Proposed Rulemaking proposing to eliminate 13 common carrier reporting requirements, and reduce the frequency of 6 other reports. (CCB, released 2/27).
-Order eliminating 30 day public notice requirement for private microwave license applications. (WTB, released 2/29)
- Establishment of Telecommunications Act home page at FCC web site (www.fcc.gov) to provide a central location for all public information regarding FCC actions to implement the new law. (OPA, 2/27). We have already had 68 hits on the home page and 1,849 hits on the Telecommunications Act implementation schedule that had previously been posted at the FCC's web site.

In Other News

- David Kaczynski, after reading the *Unabomber Manifesto* published in the New York Times and the Washington Post by the Unabomber and comparing it to letters written by his brother Ted, communicates his suspicions to the FBI that his brother is, indeed, the Unabomber.
- Microsoft announces that the installed base for Windows NT is over 4 million.

Feb. 1 - U.S. House of Representatives and U.S. Senate pass Telecommunication Bill of 1996.
Feb. 3 - Sgt. 1st Class Donald A. Dugan, 38, is killed in northern Bosnia after a piece of ammunition exploded in his hands, becoming the first U.S. soldier killed there while on duty.
Feb. 5 - Elizabeth Taylor files for divorce from Larry Fortensky, her seventh husband.

101 Theory of philosophy
102 Miscellany of philosophy
103 Dictionaries of philosophy
104 Not assigned or no longer used
105 Serial publications of philosophy
106 Organizations of philosophy
107 Education, research in philosophy
108 Kinds of persons in philosophy
109 Historical treatment of philosophy
110 Metaphysics
111 Ontology
112 Not assigned or no longer used
113 Cosmology (Philosophy of nature)
114 Space
115 Time
116 Change
117 Structure
118 Force & Energy
119 Number & quantity
120 Epistemology, causation, humankind
121 Epistemology (Theory of knowledge)
122 Causation
123 Determinism & indeterminism
124 Teleology
125 Not assigned or no longer used
126 The self
127 The unconscious & the subconscious
128 Humankind
129 Origin & destiny of individual souls
130 Paranormal phenomena
131 Occult methods for achieving well-being
132 Not assigned or no longer used
133 Parapsychology & occultism
134 Not assigned or no longer used
135 Dreams & mysteries
136 Not assigned or no longer used
137 Divinatory graphology
138 Physiognomy
139 Phrenology
140 Specific philosophical schools
141 Idealism & related systems
142 Critical philosophy
143 Intuitionism & Bergsonism
144 Humanism & related systems
145 Sensationalism
146 Naturalism & related systems
147 Pantheism & related systems
148 Liberalism, eclecticism
149 Other philosophical systems

150 Psychology
151 Not assigned or no longer used
152 Perception, movement, emotions, drives
153 Mental processes & intelligence
154 Subconscious & altered states
155 Differential & developmental psychology
156 Comparative psychology
157 Not assigned or no longer used
158 Applied psychology
159 Not assigned or no longer used
160 Logic
161 Induction
162 Deduction
163 Not assigned or no longer used
164 Not assigned or no longer used
165 Fallacies & sources of error
166 Syllogisms
167 Hypotheses
168 Argument & persuasion
169 Analogy
170 Ethics (Moral philosophy)
171 Systems & doctrines
172 Political ethics
173 Ethics of family relationships
174 Economic & professional ethics
175 Ethics of recreation & leisure
176 Ethics of sex & reproduction
177 Ethics of social relations
178 Ethics of consumption
179 Other ethical norms
180 Ancient, medieval, Oriental philosophy
181 Oriental philosophy
182 Pre-Socratic Greek philosophies
183 Sophistic & Socratic philosophies
184 Platonic philosophy
185 Aristotelian philosophy
186 Skeptic and Neoplatonic philosophies
187 Epicurean philosophy
188 Stoic philosophy
189 Medieval Western philosophy
190 Modern Western philosophy
191 Modern Western philosophy U.S.A.
192 Modern Western philosophy British Isles
193 Modern Western philosophy Germany
194 Modern Western philosophy France
195 Modern Western philosophy Italy
196 Modern Western philosophy Iberia
197 Modern Western philosophy U.S.S.R.
198 Modern Western philosophy Scandinavia
199 Modern Western philosophy
Other geographical areas

Feb. 8 - President Bill Clinton signs the Telecommunications Act of 1996.

Feb. 10 - "Deep Blue" supercomputer defeats Gary Kasporov in game of chess.

Feb. 12 - Bob Dole wins Iowa Republican caucuses.

Feb. 14 - Sen. Phil Gramm drops out of GOP presidential race.

Feb. 16 - U.S. District Judge Ronald L. Buckwalter bans government from enforcing the Communications Decency Act.

Feb. 17 - Gary Kasparov defeats "Deep Blue."

Feb. 20 - Bill Gates announces creation of the Internet Platform and Tools Division.

- Pat Buchanan wins New Hampshire primary by small margin over Dole.

- Gangsta-rapper Snoop Doggy Dogg and his former bodyguard are acquitted of murder in the shooting death of gang member.

Feb. 21 - Photographs from Hubble Space Telescope verify the existence of a black hole equal to the mass of 2 billion suns.

Feb. 24 - Steve Forbes wins the Delaware primary

Feb. 28 - Princess Diana agrees to divorce with Prince Charles.

Feb. 29 - Fire sweeps through a Peruvian commercial jet airliner sending it crashing into remote Andean mountain canyon killing all 123 passengers and crew.

February 8, 1996
First Netizens Tipper and Al Gore surf the 'net!

March FCC Report, abridged:
- Order eliminating the national broadcast radio ownership limits, and relaxing local radio ownership limits. (MMB, released 3/8, effective 3/15).
- Order eliminating numerical limits on national broadcast television ownership and raising national audience reach cap to 35 percent and changing the dual network rule. (MMB, released 3/8, effective 3/15).

200 Religion

- Order and Notice of Proposed Rulemaking regarding scrambling of sexually explicit adult video service programming, and Public Notice announcing that commission will not enforce or implement Section 505 of the 1996 Act (scrambling of sexually explicit programming) as a result of a court order. (CSB, released 3/8 and 3/13).
- Order repealing video dialtone rules, cross-ownership rules, and Section 214 requirements and Notice of Proposed Rulemaking regarding Open Video Systems (CSB, released 3/11).
- Order and Notice of Proposed Rulemaking regarding preemption of local zoning regulation of satellite earth stations. (IB, released 3/11).
- Order amending cable television ownership rules. (CSB, released 3/18).
- Notice of Proposed Rulemaking proposed that non-dominant long distance companies be relieved of tariff filing requirement as it begins review of regulatory regime for interstate interexchange telecommunications services. (CCB, released 3/25).
- Terminated inquiry into whether commercial mobile radio service providers should be required to afford equal access to long distance carriers for the provision of telephone toll services. (WTB, released 3/22).
- Notice of Proposed Rulemaking to allow broadcast stations to implement certain types of minor modification of their facilities and licenses without a construction permit. (MMB, released 3/22).
- On average, every day there have been 38,000 visits to out Internet site. There have been about 5,000 visits to our page of information on the Telecommunications Act of 1996, and more than 1,000 people have accessed our implementation schedule on line.

In Other News
- NetDay 96, a public-private partnership to connect schools to the Internet, organized thousands of volunteers to wire 3,000 California schools and their libraries. President Bill Clinton and Vice-president Al Gore volunteered, working to connect Ygnacio Valley High School in

201 Philosophy of Christianity
202 Miscellany of Christianity
203 Dictionaries of Christianity
204 Special topics
205 Serial publications of Christianity
206 Organizations of Christianity
207 Education, research in Christianity
208 Kinds of persons in Christianity
209 History & geography of Christianity
210 Natural theology
211 Concepts of God
212 Existence, attributes of God
213 Creation
214 Theodicy
215 Science & religion
216 Good & evil
217 Not assigned or no longer used
218 Humankind
219 Not assigned or no longer used
220 Bible
221 Old Testament
222 Historical books of Old Testament
223 Poetic books of Old Testament
224 Prophetic books of Old Testament
225 New Testament
226 Gospels & Acts
227 Epistles
228 Revelation (Apocalypse)
229 Apocrypha
230 Christian theology
231 God
232 Jesus Christ & his family
233 Humankind
234 Salvation
235 Spiritual beings
236 Eschatology
237 Not assigned or no longer used
238 Creeds & catechisms
239 Apologetics & polemics
240 Christian moral & devotional theology
241 Moral theology
242 Devotional literature
243 Evangelistic writings for individuals
244 Not assigned or no longer used
245 Texts of hymns
246 Use of art in Christianity
247 Church furnishings & articles
248 Christian experience, practice, life
249 Christian observances in family life
250 Christian orders & local church
251 Preaching
252 Texts of sermons
253 Pastoral office (Pastoral theology)

254 Parish government & administration
255 Religious congregations & orders
256 Not assigned or no longer used
257 Not assigned or no longer used
258 Not assigned or no longer used
259 Activities of the local church
260 Christian social theology
261 Social theology
262 Ecclesiology
263 Times, places of religious observance
264 Public worship
265 Sacraments, other rites & acts
266 Missions
267 Associations for religious work
268 Religious education
269 Spiritual renewal
270 Christian church history
271 Religious orders in church history
272 Persecutions in church history
273 Heresies in church history
274 Christian church in Europe
275 Christian church in Asia
276 Christian church in Africa
277 Christian church in North America
278 Christian church in South America
279 Christian church in other areas
280 Christian denominations & sects
281 Early church & Eastern churches
282 Roman Catholic Church
283 Anglican churches
284 Protestants of Continental origin
285 Presbyterian, Reformed, Congregational
286 Baptist, Disciples of Christ, Adventist
287 Methodist & related churches
288 Not assigned or no longer used
289 Other denominations & sects
290 Other & comparative religions
291 Comparative religion
292 Classical (Greek & Roman) religion
293 Germanic religion
294 Religions of Indic origin
295 Zoroastrianism (Mazdaism, Parseeism)
296 Judaism
297 Islam & religions originating in it
298 Not assigned or no longer used
299 Other religions

Concord, California. NetDay 96 continued throughout the year as a grass-roots effort to wire schools and libraries so that they could access the "on-line" world.

- Windows NT 4.0 Beta-2 released.

March 5 - Netscape holds DevCon, its developers conference, unveiling its strategy to make its browser and servers a platform capable of supplanting Windows on the internet.

- Dole sweeps "Junior Tuesday" primaries.

March 7 - Bob Dole wins New York Republican primary.

March 12 - Microsoft holds its Professional Developers Conference, announcing ActiveX as a counter to Java and a deal to put AOL in a folder on the Windows 95 desktop.

- Bob Dole sweeps "Super Tuesday" primaries.

Mar. 14 - President Bill Clinton commits $100 million to an anti-terrorism agreement with Israel intended to track down and root out terrorists.

- Steve Forbes drops his $30 million bid for Republican presidential nomination.

March 19 - Sen. Bob Dole clinches Republican presidential nomination with Midwest primary sweep.

March 22 – Astronaut Shannon Lucid blasts off on Space Shuttle Atlantis and successfully docks with MIR Space Station, beginning her record-setting 188-day mission.

March 25 - Beginning of an 81-day standoff between the FBI and antigovernment "Freemen" in Jordan, Montana.

- "Blood in the Browser War," an article in Newsweek by Steven Levy, puts new phrase into the Internet lexicon.

President Bill Clinton installing computer cables with Vice President Al Gore on NetDay at Ygnacio Valley High School in Concord, CA. March 9, 1996.
Public Papers of the Presidents of the United States: William J. Clinton (1996, Book I)

301 Sociology & anthropology
302 Social interaction
303 Social processes
304 Factors affecting social behavior
305 Social groups
306 Culture & institutions
307 Communities
308 Not assigned or no longer used
309 Not assigned or no longer used
310 General statistics
311 Not assigned or no longer used
312 Not assigned or no longer used
313 Not assigned or no longer used
314 General statistics Of Europe
315 General statistics Of Asia
316 General statistics Of Africa
317 General statistics Of North America
318 General statistics Of South America
319 General statistics Of other parts of the world
320 Political science
321 Systems of governments & states
322 Relation of state to organized groups
323 Civil & political rights
324 The political process
325 International migration & colonization
326 Slavery & emancipation
327 International relations
328 The legislative process
329 Not assigned or no longer used
330 Economics
331 Labor economics
332 Financial economics
333 Land economics
334 Cooperatives
335 Socialism & related systems
336 Public finance
337 International economics
338 Production
339 Macroeconomics & related topics
340 Law
341 International law
342 Constitutional & administrative law
343 Military, tax, trade, industrial law
344 Social, labor, welfare, & related law
345 Criminal law
346 Private law
347 Civil procedure & courts
348 Law (Statutes), regulations, cases
349 Law of specific jurisdictions & areas
350 Public administration
351 Of central governments
352 Of local governments
353 of U.S. federal & state governments

300 Sociology

A Chat With the Nerd-In-Chief
Chairman and CEO Bill Gates hosts an on-line chat on the Microsoft Network Wednesday, April 17, 1996, at the company's headquarters in Redmond, Wash., to celebrate the "cyberlaunch" of Libraries Online. Libraries Online is a partnership between Microsoft and the American Library Association to provide public access to the Internet.
Photo copyright Robert Sorbo/sorboimages.com

April FCC Report, abridged:
- Notice of Proposed Rulemaking on implementation of Section 207 of the Telecommunications Act, to prohibit state and local regulations that restrict a viewer's use of receiving devices for television broadcast signals and multi-channel multipoint distributions services. (CSB, released 4/4).
- Orders granting first three Telecommunications Act applications for utility companies to enter telecommunications. (CSW Communications, Inc., released 4/4; Entergy Technology Co., 4/12; and Entergy Technology Holding Co., 4/12 - all OGC).
- Order and Notice of Proposed Rulemaking implementing cable reform section of Telecommunications Act, including effective competition, subscriber notification and small cable system relief. (CSB, released 4/9).
- Order removing radiotelegraph requirement for global maritime distress and safety system equipped vessels. (WTB, released 4/12).
- Notice of Proposed Rulemaking to extend the license term of most television and radio [broadcast] stations to eight years. (MMB, released 4/12).
- Order implementing amended broadcast license renewal procedures under the Telecommunications Act and eliminating compar-

ative license renewal procedures and hearings. (MMB, released 4/12).

- Notice of Proposed Rulemaking proposing simple procedure for utility companies to enter telecommunications. (OGC, released 4/25).
- WTB held a consumer outreach forum (attended by about a dozen consumer groups) to discuss a variety of consumer concerns raised by the Telecommunications Act. (WTB, 4/23).
- The Commission placed on the Cable Services Bureau's Internet home page the initial comments received in the Open Video Systems proceeding which had voluntarily been filed on disk by commenters. Reply comments will be placed on the home page as well. (CSB, ongoing).
- In April, we averaged 39,000 visits per day to our Internet site. There have been more than 6,500 visits to our information page on the Telecommunications Act of 1996 and more than 1,554 people have accessed our implementation schedule on line. The Interconnection Notice of Proposed Rulemaking was posted on the afternoon of 4/19. Within 4 days, it already had received 800 visits. (OPA, ongoing).

In Other News

- Opening of $134 million San Francisco Public Library with 300 public access computer terminals.
- Ameritech Corporation of Chicago makes $2 million grant to the Library of Congress National Digital Library. The NDL plans to make 5 million documents available over the Internet by 2000. The funds will be used to digitize primary sources that document American history from libraries across the country.
- Apr. 3 - Near Lincoln, Montana, FBI agents arrest Theodore Kaczynski, prime suspect of the Unabomber bombings
     - Air Force jetliner carrying Commerce Secretary Ron Brown and American business executives crashes near Dubrovnik, Croatia, killing all 35 people aboard;
- April 4 - The Freemen in Montana meet with negotiators for the first time in standoff which began March 25 when agents arrested two Freemen leaders
- April 8 - SQL Server 6.5 released.
- April 11 - 7 year old pilot, Jessica Dubroff is killed while trying to be the youngest person to fly cross country.
- April 23 - A Bronx civil-court jury orders Bernhard Goetz to pay $43 million to paralyzed Darrell Cabey, one of four young men he shot on a subway car in 1984.
     - Three-night auction of Jacqueline Kennedy Onassis' possessions begins with a bidding frenzy.
- April 25 - Microsoft BackOffice Server 2.0 released.
- April 29 - Former CIA Director William Colby is missing after an apparent boating accident; his body was later recovered.

354 Of specific central governments
355 Military science
356 Foot forces & warfare
357 Mounted forces & warfare
358 Other specialized forces & services
359 Sea (Naval) forces & warfare
360 Social services; association
361 General social problems & services
362 Social welfare problems & services
363 Other social problems & services
364 Criminology
365 Penal & related institutions
366 Association
367 General clubs
368 Insurance
369 Miscellaneous kinds of associations
370 Education
371 School management; special education
372 Elementary education
373 Secondary education
374 Adult education
375 Curriculums
376 Education of women
377 Schools & religion
378 Higher education
379 Government regulation, control, support
380 Commerce, communications, transport
381 Internal commerce (Domestic trade)
382 International commerce (Foreign trade)
383 Postal communication
384 Communications & Telecommunication
385 Railroad transportation
386 Inland waterway & ferry transportation
387 Water, air, space transportation
388 Transportation Ground transportation
389 Metrology & standardization
390 Customs, etiquette, folklore
391 Costume & personal appearance
392 Customs of life cycle
393 Death customs
394 General customs
395 Etiquette (Manners)
396 Not assigned or no longer used
397 Not assigned or no longer used
398 Folklore
399 Customs of war & diplomacy

The Centennial -- wall paper printing press, Machinery Hall / photographed by the Centennial Photographic Company. Harper's weekly, 1876 Dec. 23. LC-USZ62-108122

400 Language

May FCC Report, abridged:

- Fifth Further Notice of Proposed Rulemaking in the matter of advanced television systems and their impact upon the existing television broadcast service. (MMB, released 5/20).
- Notice of Inquiry implementing mandate under Telecommunications Act to identify and eliminate market entry barriers for small businesses. (OGC, OCBO, released 5/21).
- Report and Order and Further Notice of Proposed Rulemaking in the matter of Definition of Markets for Purposes of the Cable Television Mandatory Television Broadcast Signal Carriage Rules - Implementation of Section 301(d) of the Act - Market Determinations. (CSB, released 5/24).
-Order granting Telecom Act application for utility company to enter telecommunications. (NU/Mode 1 Communications, Inc., released 5/30 - OGC).
- Conducted a round table discussion with representatives of local governments to facilitate their participation in proceedings under the Act. (OLIA, 5/16).
- Convened economics forum on interconnection with top economists and FCC's Chief Economist, 5/20.
- Public Notice asking for suggestions of forbearance. (CCB, released 5/20).
- OPA held a forum to educate the public on how to participate in FCC proceedings. (OPA, 5/31).

In Other News

May 11 - ValuJet Flight 592 reports smoke in the cockpit shortly

401 Philosophy & theory
402 Miscellany
403 Dictionaries & encyclopedias
404 Special topics
405 Serial publications
406 Organizations & management
407 Education, research, related topics
408 With respect to kinds of persons
409 Geographical & persons treatment
410 Linguistics
411 Writing systems
412 Etymology
413 Dictionaries
414 Phonology
415 Structural systems
416 Not assigned or no longer used
417 Dialectology & historical linguistics
418 Standard usage Applied linguistics
419 Verbal language not spoken or written
420 English & Old English
421 English writing system & phonology
422 English etymology
423 English dictionaries
424 Not assigned or no longer used
425 English grammar
426 Not assigned or no longer used
427 English language variations
428 Standard English usage
429 Old English (Anglo-Saxon)
430 Germanic languages German
431 German writing system & phonology
432 German etymology
433 German dictionaries
434 Not assigned or no longer used
435 German grammar
436 Not assigned or no longer used
437 German language variations
438 Standard German usage
439 Other Germanic languages
440 Romance languages French
441 French writing system & phonology
442 French etymology
443 French dictionaries
444 Not assigned or no longer used
445 French grammar
446 Not assigned or no longer used 447 French language variations
448 Standard French usage
449 Provencal & Catalan
450 Italian, Romanian, Rhaeto-Romantic
451 Italian writing system & phonology
452 Italian etymology
453 Italian dictionaries
454 Not assigned or no longer used
455 Italian grammar
456 Not assigned or no longer used
457 Italian language variations
458 Standard Italian usage
459 Romanian & Rhaeto-Romanic

after takeoff for Atlanta and attempts to turn around but crashes into the Florida Everglades, killing 104 passengers and five crew members.

May 13 - Canon PowerShot 600 digital camera introduced.

May 14 - Tornado kills more than 440 people and injures more than 33,000 while flattening 80 villages in northern Bangladesh.

May 21 - Some 500 passengers, many of them teen-agers, drown in Tanzania when a ferry hits a rock and capsizes in Lake Victoria.

May 23 - Ran Kropp reaches Mount Everest summit alone without oxygen after having bicycled there from Sweden.

May 29 - State appeals court overturns pandering conviction of "Hollywood Madam" Heidi Fleiss, ruling that jurors made trial a farce by engaging in vote-swapping misconduct to avoid deadlock.

May 30 - The former Sarah Ferguson and Prince Andrew are granted divorce.

460 Spanish & Portugese
461 Spanish writing system & phonology
462 Spanish etymology
463 Spanish dictionaries
464 Not assigned or no longer used
465 Spanish grammar
466 Not assigned or no longer used
467 Spanish language variations
468 Standard Spanish usage
469 Portugese
470 Italic Latin
471 Classical Latin writing & phonology
472 Classical Latin etymology & phonology
473 Classical Latin dictionaries
474 Not assigned or no longer used
475 Classical Latin grammar
476 Not assigned or no longer used
477 Old, Postclassical, Vulgar Latin
478 Classical Latin usage
479 Other Italic languages
480 Hellenic languages Classical Greek
481 Classical Greek writing & phonology
482 Classical Greek etymology
483 Classical Greek dictionaries
484 Not assigned or no longer used
485 Classical Greek grammar
486 Not assigned or no longer used
487 Preclassical & postclassical Greek
488 Classical Greek usage
489 Other Hellenic languages
490 Other languages
491 East Indo-European & Celtic languages
492 Afro-Asiatic languages Semitic
493 Non-Semitic Afro-Asiatic languages
494 Ural-Altaic, Paleosiberian, Dravidian
495 Languages of East & Southeast Asia
496 African languages
497 North American native languages
498 South American native languages

499 Miscellaneous languages

—So when did we get a paper shredder?

—It's a KeyCo thing. All departments must have paper shredders.

—How's it go?

—Put your paper in here and it comes out in strips into the wastebasket.

—Don't you have to turn it on?

—It's always on.

—Funny, libraries used to be about preserving information.

—Libraries are about preserving knowledge and wisdom. But you can't save everything.

—I think there's a difference between discarding…

—De-acquisitioning, you mean.

—Whatever—there's a difference between tossing out the trash and shredding it—know what I mean?

—We're not shredding everything—just financial records, annual reviews, By Statements, and updates. And patron records—for confidentiality.

—Dang! We're gonna need a bigger wastebasket!

Vocabulary Enhancement
deacquisition: de-, indicating a reversal of acquisition, the act of acquiring [L. acquirere, -quisitum-ad, to quaerere, to seek.]

June FCC Report, abridged:

- Order deleting Part 66 of the Commission's Rules, concerning consolidation, acquisition, or control of telephone companies. (CCB, released 6/4).
- Report and Order on Open Video Systems, providing a new opportunity for entry into the video programming distribution market. (CSB, released 6/3).
- Held the first meeting of the Telecommunications and Health Care Advisory Committee on June 12, 1996.
- Orders granting Telecom Act applications for utility companies to enter telecommunications. (Southern Information Holding Company, Inc., Southern Information 1, Inc., and Southern Information 2, Inc., released 6/14; Southern Telecom Holding Company, Inc., Southern Telecom 1, Inc., and Southern Telecom 2, Inc., released 6/14; and Allegheny Communications Connect, Inc., released 6/14 - all OGC).
- Conducted open forum on how to find FCC information on the Internet on June 24, 1996. (OPA, 6/13).

In Other News

June 2 - Rent, Bring in 'da Noise, Bring in 'da Funk' and The King and I dominate 1996 Tony Awards, each winning four.

June 3 - FBI turns off electricity at the Freemen ranch.

June 6 - Family of four become the first to leave the Freemen

500s Science

ranch since April.

June 13 - All 16 remaining members of the Freemen surrender to the FBI and leave ranch, ending the 81-day standoff.

June 16 - Russian voters go to the polls.

June 18 - ValuJet halts flight operations.

June 20 - Westinghouse Electric agrees to buy Infinity Broadcasting for $3.9 billion and combine the two biggest players in radio.

June 25 - U.S. Supreme Court orders Virginia Military Academy to admit women or forgo state support.

June 27 - Police officer charged with trying to hire hit man to kill football star Michael Irvin.

June 28 - Citadel votes to admit women.

501 Philosophy & theory
502 Miscellany
503 Dictionaries & encyclopedias
504 Not assigned or no longer used
505 Serial publications
506 Organizations & management
507 Education, research, related topics
508 Natural history
509 Historical, areas, persons treatment
510 Mathematics
511 General principles
512 Algebra & number theory
513 Arithmetic
514 Topology
515 Analysis
516 Geometry
517 Not assigned or no longer used
518 Numerical Analysis
519 Probabilities & applied mathematics
520 Astronomy & allied sciences
521 Celestial mechanics
522 Techniques, equipment, materials
523 Specific celestial bodies & phenomena
524 Not assigned or no longer used
525 Earth (Astronomical geography)
526 Mathematical geography
527 Celestial navigation
528 Ephemerides
529 Chronology
530 Physics
531 Classical mechanics Solid mechanics
532 Fluid mechanics Liquid mechanics
533 Gas mechanics
534 Sound & related vibrations
535 Light & paraphotic phenomena
536 Heat
537 Electricity & electronics
538 Magnetism
539 Modern physics
540 Chemistry & allied sciences
541 Physical & theoretical chemistry
542 Techniques, equipment, materials
543 Analytical chemistry
544 Qualitative analysis
545 Quantitative analysis
546 Inorganic chemistry
547 Organic chemistry
548 Crystallography
549 Mineralogy
550 Earth sciences
551 Geology, hydrology, meteorology
552 Petrology
553 Economic geology
554 Earth sciences of Europe
555 Earth sciences of Asia
556 Earth sciences of Africa
557 Earth sciences of North America
558 Earth sciences of South America
559 Earth sciences of other areas

Vocabulary Enhancement

episodal, episodial, episodic, episodical, pertaining to or contained in an episode: brought in as a digression: abounding in episodes. [Gr. *episodion–epi*, upon, *eisodos*, a coming in–*eis*, into, *hodos*, a way.]

hermetic, belonging in any way to the beliefs current in the Middle Ages under the name of Hermes, the Thrice Great: belonging to magic or alchemy, magical: perfectly close.

hermetically sealed, closed completely: made air-tight by melting the glass. [From *Hermes Trismegistos*, Hermes the thrice-greatest, the Greek name for the Egyptian Thoth, god of science, esp. alchemy.]

hob, a hub, a surface beside a fireplace, on which anything may be laid to keep hot.

hob, a rustic, a lout: a fairy or brownie (as Robin Goodfellow): a clownish fellow: a male ferret: mischief.

hobgoblin, a mischevious fairy, a frightful apparition.

play hob, raise hob, to make confusion.

hobbledehoy, an awkward youth.

hobnob, at a venture: hit-or-miss: with alternate or mutual drinking of healths.

–v.i. to associate or drink together familiarly: to talk informally (with)

hysteria, a psychoneurosis in which repressed complexes become split off or disassociated from the personality, forming independent units, partially or completely unrecognized, giving rise to hypnoidal states and manifested by various physical symptoms, such as tics, paralysis, blindness, deafness, etc., general features being an extreme degree of emotional instability and intense craving for affection.

hysteric
hysterical
hystericky
hysterics, popularly, alternate paroxysms of laughing and crying.
hysteroid

560 Paleontology Paleozoology
561 Paleobotany
562 Fossil invertebrates
563 Fossil primitive phyla
564 Fossil Mollusca & Molluscoidea
565 Other fossil invertebrates
566 Fossil Vertebrata (Fossil Craniata)
567 Fossil cold-blooded vertebrates
568 Fossil Aves (Fossil birds)
569 Fossil Mammalia
570 Life sciences
571 Physiology
572 Human races
573 Physical anthropology
574 Biology
575 Evolution & genetics
576 Genetics & evolution
577 General nature of life
578 Microscopy in biology
579 Collection and preservation
580 Botanical sciences
581 Botany
582 Spermatophyta (Seed-bearing plants)
583 Dicotyledones
584 Monocotyledones
585 Gymnospermae (Pinophyta)
586 Cryptogamia (Seedless plants)
587 Pteridophyta (Vascular cryptograms)
588 Bryophyta
589 Thallobionta & Prokaryotae
590 Zoological sciences
591 Zoology
592 Invertebrates
593 Protozoa, Echinodermata, related phyla
594 Mollusca & Molluscoidea
595 Other invertebrates

596 Vertebrata (Craniata, Vertebrates)
597 Cold-blooded vertebrates Fishes
598 Aves (Birds)
599 Mammalia

The grand display of fireworks and illuminations: at the opening of the great suspension bridge between New York and Brooklyn on the evening of May 24th, 1883, Currier & Ives. LC-DIG-pga-04849

July FCC Report, abridged:

- Order and Notice of Proposed Rulemaking adopting measures to protect consumers from deceptive toll-free call practices and proposing additional minor modifications to maximize consumers' protection from confusing or deceptive practices relating to the provision of interstate information services. (CCB, released 7/11).
- Conducted public forum on July 23, 1996, on Antitrust and Economics Issues involved in BOC InterLATA Entry.

In Other News

July 2 - Lyle and Erik Menendez are sentenced to life in prison without parole for shotgun deaths of their parents.
- Power outage hits customers from Canada to the Southwest.

July 3 - Blaze destroys fireworks store in Scottown, Ohio, full of Fourth of July shoppers, killing eight and injuring 12.

July 4 - Russian President Boris Yeltsin sweeps to victory.

July 5 - Dolly the sheep, the first mammal to be successfully cloned from an adult cell, is born. Dolly the Sheep was named after Dolly Parton, the country/western singer, because the cell used to clone Dolly was a mammary cell.

July 6 - A jet engine of Delta Flight 1288 blows apart and rips into cabin, killing mother and son and forcing pilot to abort takeoff from Pensacola, Fla.

July 9 - Ross Perot announces candidacy for Reform Party's presidential nomination.

July 11 - Air Force jet trying to make an emergency landing

600s Technology

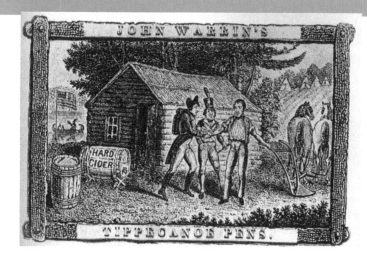

601 Philosophy & theory
602 Miscellany
603 Dictionaries & encyclopedias
604 Special topics
605 Serial publications
606 Organizations
607 Education, research, related topics
608 Invention & patents
609 Historical, areas, persons treatment
610 Medical sciences Medicine
611 Human anatomy, cytology, histology
612 Human physiology
613 Promotion of health
614 Incidence & prevention of disease
615 Pharmacology & theraputics
616 Diseases
617 Surgery & related medical specialities
618 Gynecology
619 Experimental medicine
620 Engineering & allied operations
621 Applied physics
622 Mining & related operations
623 Nautical engineering
624 Civil engineering
625 Engineering of railroads, roads
626 Not assigned or no longer used
627 Hydraulic engineering
628 Sanitary & municipal engineering
629 Other branches of engineering
630 Agriculture
631 Techniques, equipment, materials
632 Plant injuries, diseases, pests
633 Field & plantation crops
634 Orchards, fruits, forestry
635 Garden crops (Horticulture)
636 Animal husbandry
637 Processing dairy & related products
638 Insect culture
639 Hunting, fishing, conservation
640 Home economics & family living
641 Food & drink
642 Meals & table service
643 Housing & household equipment
644 Household utilities
645 Household furnishings
646 Sewing, clothing, personal living
647 Management of public households
648 Housekeeping
649 Child rearing
650 Management & auxiliary services
651 Office services
652 Processes of written communication
653 Shorthand

slams into a house in Pensacola, Fla., setting home on fire, killing a 4-year-old boy and badly burning his mother.

July 17 - TWA Flight 800 explodes over Long Island, NY, killing 230 passengers.

July 18 - Shaquille O'Neal abandons the Orlando Magic to sign seven-year, $120 million deal with the Los Angeles Lakers.

July 27 - A pipe bomb explodes at the Olympics in Atlanta, killing one person and injuring 111.

July 29 - Windows NT 4.0 released to marketing.
   - Child Protection portion of the Communications Decency Act is struck down as too broad by a U.S. federal court.

July 31 - After Clinton announcement that he would sign it, 98 Democrats join House's Republican majority to pass historic welfare overhaul bill.

The Wide Awake Parade was formed in 1860 by Republicans in the Northern states to help nominate Abraham Lincoln as the President of the United States. http://en.wikipedia.org/wiki/Wide_Awake_Parade

Vocabulary Enhancement

hysteroidal

hysteromania, hysterical mania, often marked by erotic delusions and an excessive desire to attract attention.

hysterical pregnancy, (see **pseudocyesis**)

[Greek *hystera*, the womb, with which hysteria was formerly thought to be associated.]

Jenny, a generic name for a country lass (Scot.): a womanish man (Scot.)

jeremiad, a lamentation: a tale of grief: a doleful story. [From Jeremiah, reputed author of the Book of Lamentations.]

neurosis, originally, nervous activity, distinguished from or associated with mental: functional derangement through disordered nervous system: mental disturbance characterized by a state of unconscious conflict, usually accompanied by anxiety and obsessional fears (also called psychoneurosis): loosely, an obsession

654 Not assigned or no longer used
655 Not assigned or no longer used
656 Not assigned or no longer used
657 Accounting
658 General management
659 Advertising & public relations
660 Chemical engineering
661 Industrial chemicals technology
662 Explosives, fuels technology
663 Beverage technology
664 Food technology
665 Industrial oils, fats, waxes, gases
666 Ceramic & allied technologies
667 Cleaning, color, related technologies
668 Technology of other organic products
669 Metallurgy
670 Manufacturing
671 Metalworking & metal products
672 Iron, steel, other iron alloys
673 Nonferrous metals
674 Lumber processing, wood products, cork
675 Leather & fur processing
676 Pulp & paper technology
677 Textiles
678 Elastomers & elastomer products
679 Other products of specific materials
680 Manufacture for specific uses
681 Precision instruments & other devices
682 Small forge work (Blacksmithing)
683 Hardware & household appliances
684 Furnishings & home workshops
685 Leather, fur, related products
686 Printing & related activities
687 Clothing
688 Other final products & packaging
689 Not assigned or no longer used
690 Buildings
691 Building materials
692 Auxiliary construction practices
693 Specific materials & purposes
694 Wood construction Carpentry
695 Roof covering
696 Utilities
697 Heating, ventilating, air-conditioning
698 Detail finishing
699 Not assigned or no longer used

August FCC Report, abridged:

- Order implementing Section 207 of the Telecommunications Act, to prohibit state and local regulations that restrict a viewer's use of receiving devices for television broadcast signals and multichannel multipoint distributions services, and preemption of local zoning regulation of satellite earth stations. (CSB, released 8/6).
- Order implementing several self-effectuating additions and revisions to FCC's rules relating to pole attachments. (CSB, released 8/6).
- Order implementing the provision of the Telecommunications Act that governs the use of data regarding alarm monitoring service provides. (CCB, released 8/7).
- Adopted a Second Report and Order and Memorandum Opinion and Order to implement the dialing parity, nondiscriminatory access, network disclosure and numbering administration requirements of the Telecommunications Act. (CCB, released 8/8).
- Further Notice of Proposed Rulemaking released regarding the implementation of digital television (DTV). (MMB, released 8/14).

In Other News

- Windows NT 4.0 released. Final code count: 16 million lines.
- Aug. 4 - State drug enforcement agents in San Francisco raid club that openly sold marijuana to AIDS and cancer patients.
- Aug. 5 - Olympus D-300L and Olympus D-200L digital cameras introduced.
- Aug. 10 - Bob Dole completes Republican ticket by announcing former HUD secretary Jack F. Kemp as his running mate.

700s The Arts

Aug. 11 – *Hey, Macarena* (Bayside Boys Mix) hits #1 on Billboard Weekly Chart of Best-Selling Albums.

Aug. 12 - Microsoft releases Internet Explorer 3.0.

Aug. 19 - Netscape releases Navigator 3.0.

Aug. 14 - Republican National Convention nominates Jack Kemp for vice president and Bob Dole for president.
- Festival-goers pack a bridge in Arequipa, Peru, for riv-

701 Philosophy & theory
702 Miscellany
703 Dictionaries & encyclopedias
704 Special topics
705 Serial publications
706 Organizations & management
707 Education, research, related topics
708 Galleries, museums, private collections
709 Historical, areas, persons treatment
710 Civic & landscape art
711 Area planning (Civic art)
712 Landscape architecture
713 Landscape architecture of trafficways
714 Water features
715 Woody plants
716 Herbaceous plants
717 Structures
718 Landscape design of cemeteries
719 Natural landscapes
720 Architecture
721 Architectural structure
722 Architecture to ca. 300
723 Architecture from ca. 300 to 1399
724 Architecture from 1400
725 Public structures
726 Buildings for religious purposes
727 Buildings for education & research
728 Residential & related buildings
729 Design & decoration
730 Plastic arts Sculpture
731 Processes, forms, subjects of sculpture
732 Sculpture to ca. 500
733 Greek, Etruscan, Roman sculpture
734 Sculpture from ca. 500 to 1399
735 Sculpture from 1400
736 Carving & carvings
737 Numismatics & sigillography
738 Ceramic arts
739 Art metalwork
740 Drawing & decorative arts
741 Drawing & drawings
742 Perspective
743 Drawing & drawings by subject
744 Not assigned or no longer used
745 Decorative arts
746 Textile arts
747 Interior decoration
748 Glass
749 Furniture & accessories
750 Painting & paintings
751 Techniques, equipment, forms
752 Color
753 Symbolism, allegory, mythology, legend
754 Genre paintings
755 Religion & religious symbolism
756 Not assigned or no longer used
757 Human figures
758 Other subjects
759 Historical, areas, persons treatment

erside fireworks show as stray rocket sends high-tension line crashing into the crowd, unleashing 10,000 volts that electrocute 35 people and causing many of their bodies to burst into flames.

Aug. 17 - Military cargo plane carrying gear for President Clinton crashes and explodes in flames shortly after taking off from Jackson Hole Airport in Wyoming. Eight crew members and Secret Service employee are killed.

Aug. 19 - Ralph Nader is nominated as Green Party's first presidential candidate.

Aug. 28 - Democrats nominate President Bill Clinton and Vice President Al Gore for second term.
- 15-year marriage of the Prince Charles and Princess Diana ends in divorce.

760 Graphic arts Printmaking & prints
761 Relief processes (Block printing)
762 Not assigned or no longer used
763 Lithographic processes
764 Chromolithography & serigraphy
765 Metal engraving
766 Mezzotinting & related processes
767 Etching & drypoint
768 Not assigned or no longer used
769 Prints
770 Photography & photographs
771 Techniques, equipment, materials
772 Metallic salt processes
773 Pigment processes of printing
774 Holography
775 Digital Photography
776 Not assigned or no longer used
777 Not assigned or no longer used
778 Fields & kinds of photography
779 Photographs
780 Music
781 General principles & musical forms
782 Vocal music
783 Music for single voices The voice
784 Instruments & Instrumental ensembles
785 Chamber music
786 Keyboard & other instruments
787 Stringed instruments (Chordophones)
788 Wind instruments (Aerophones)
789 Not assigned or no longer used
790 Recreational & performing arts
791 Public performances
792 Stage presentations
793 Indoor games & amusements
794 Indoor games of skill
795 Games of chance
796 Athletic & outdoor sports & games
797 Aquatic & air sports
798 Equestrian sports & animal racing
799 Fishing, hunting, shooting

Vocabulary Enhancement

neurotic, of the nature of, characterized by, or affected by neurosis: loosely, obsessive: hypersensitive: a person with neurosis

newell (Spenser) a new thing. [A combination of novel and new.]

—Use *newell* in a short dialogue sequence.

—I don't get where this book fits in the Dewey Decimal system. It's partly fact and partly fiction.

—Call it friction. Or fraction. A fraction of the truth.

—Call it a *newell* and Edmund Spenser would know just what you mean.

Library Journal, Nomber 1, 1996.

September FCC Report, abridged:

- Adopted a Report and Order streamlining procedures for utility companies to enter in the telecommunications industry (OGC, released 9/12).
- Order and Notice of Proposed Rulemaking released reducing accounting reporting requirements for common carriers. (CCB, released 9/12).
- Notice of Inquiry adopted regarding access to telecommunications service, telecommunications equipment, and customer premises equipment by persons with disabilities. (WTB, released 9/19).
- Common Carrier Bureau held a public form on September 12, 1996,

800: Literature

to discuss access charge reform and universal service issues raised by the Telecom Act of 1996.
- Common Carrier Bureau and Office of General Counsel held a public forum on September 17, 1996, to discuss enforcement issues raised by the Telecom Act of 1996.
- Office of General Counsel and Office of Communications Business Opportunities held a public forum on September 24, 1996, on market entry barriers for small businesses.

800 Literature & Rhetoric
801 Philosophy & theory
802 Miscellany
803 Dictionaries & encyclopedias
804 Not assigned or no longer used
805 Serial publications
806 Organizations
807 Education, research, related topics
808 Rhetoric & collections of literature
809 Literary history & criticism
810 American literature in English
811 Poetry
812 Drama
813 Fiction
814 Essays
815 Speeches
816 Letters
817 Satire & humor
818 Miscellaneous writings
819 Not assigned or no longer used
820 English & Old English literatures
821 English poetry
822 English drama
823 English fiction
824 English essays
825 English speeches
826 English letters
827 English satire & humor
828 English miscellaneous writings
829 Old English (Anglo-Saxon)
830 Literatures of Germanic languages
831 German poetry
832 German drama
833 German fiction
834 German essays
835 German speeches
836 German letters
837 German satire & humor
838 German miscellaneous writings
839 Other Germanic literatures
840 Literatures of Romance languages
841 French poetry
842 French drama
843 French fiction
844 French essays
845 French speeches
846 French letters
847 French satire & humor
848 French miscellaneous writings
849 Provencal & Catalan
850 Italian, Romanian, Rhaeto-Romanic
851 Italian poetry
852 Italian drama
853 Italian fiction
854 Italian essays
855 Italian speeches
856 Italian letters
857 Italian satire & humor
858 Italian miscellaneous writings

In Other News

- Windows 95 OSR2 released.
- Monica Lewinsky meets Linda Tripp after being transferred to the Pentagon.

Sept. 3 - The United States launches 27 cruise missiles at "selected air defense targets" in Iraq as punishment for Iraqi invasion of Kurdish safe havens.

Sept. 4 - Anti-aircraft fire lights the skies of Baghdad, hours after the United States fires a new round of cruise missiles into southern Iraq and destroys an Iraqi radar site.

Sept. 5 - Russian President Boris Yeltsin acknowledges he needs heart surgery.
-Hurricane Fran slams the Carolinas.

Sept. 7 - Rapper Tupac Shakur and Death Row Records Chairman Marion "Suge" Knight are shot in car cruising in Las Vegas. Shakur died the next day.

Sept. 10 - Ross Perot picks economist Pat Choate to share Reform Party presidential ticket.

Sept. 13 - Launch of Disinformation® website, a search service for information on current affairs, politics, new science and "hidden information." Funded by Telecommunications, Inc. (TCI, now part of AT&T), who paid for placement on Netscape's then ubiquitous search page. Some three weeks after launch, John Malone, CEO of TCI, learned of Disinformation and immediately ordered it closed down.

Sept. 14 - Bosnians go to polls.

Sept. 17 - O.J. Simpson's civil trial begins.

Sept. 18 - Food and Drug Administration declares French abortion pill RU-486 safe and effective.

Sept. 21 - John F. Kennedy Jr. marries Carolyn Bessette in secret ceremony in Cumberland Island, Ga.
- Clinton signs Defense of Marriage Act.

Sept. 22 - Virginia Military Institute's Board of Visitors votes 9-8 to end its 157-year-old male-only admission policy.

Sept. 26 - Astronaut Shannon Lucid returns to Earth in Space Shuttle Atlantis after six months of weightlessness.

Sept. 27 - Taliban capture capital city, Kabul, Afghanistan.

859 Romanian & Rhaeto-Romanic
860 Spanish & Portuguese literatures
861 Spanish poetry
862 Spanish drama
863 Spanish fiction
864 Spanish essays
865 Spanish speeches
866 Spanish letters
867 Spanish satire & humor
868 Spanish miscellaneous writings
869 Portuguese
870 Italic literatures Latin
871 Latin poetry
872 Latin dramatic poetry & drama
873 Latin epic poetry & fiction
874 Latin lyric poetry
875 Latin speeches
876 Latin letters
877 Latin satire & humor
878 Latin miscellaneous writings
879 Literatures of other Italic languages
880 Hellenic literatures Classical Greek
881 Classical Greek poetry
882 Classical Greek drama
883 Classical Greek epic poetry & fiction
884 Classical Greek lyric poetry
885 Classical Greek speeches
886 Classical Greek letters
887 Classical Greek satire & humor
888 Classical Greek miscellaneous writings
889 Modern Greek
890 Literatures of other languages
891 East Indo-European & Celtic
892 Afro-Asiatic literatures Semitic
893 Non-Semitic Afro-Asiatic literatures
894 Ural-Altaic, Paleosiberian, Dravidian
895 Literatures of East & Southeast Asia
896 African literatures
897 North American native literatures
898 South American native literatures
899 Other literatures

9/11/1996

An FBI investigation into two relatives of bin Laden, begun in February 1996, is closed. Four of the 9/11 hijackers lived at 5913 Leesburg Pike at the same time the two bin Laden brothers were there. Abdul bin Laden was the U.S. director of the World Assembly of Muslim Youth. A high-placed intelligence official told a London paper, "There were always constraints on investigating the Saudis. There were particular investigations that were effectively killed." An unnamed US source tells the BBC, "There is a hidden agenda at the very highest levels of our government." The Bosnian government later says a charity with Abdullah bin Laden on its board had channeled money to Chechen guerrillas with the tacit approval of the CIA. The investigation into WAMY is restarted two days after 9/11/2001, after the bin Laden family has left the U.S.A. (CCR, Project Censored, Greg Palast)

October FCC Report, abridged:

-Public Notice announcing appointment of private sector board members to the Telecommunications Development Fund. (OGC, OCBO released 10/1).

- Adopted an Order amending the FCC rules to remove restrictions against corporate licensees having alien officers or directors. (OGC, released 10/9).

- The Federal-State Joint Board on Universal Service held an open meeting on October 17, 1996 to address universal service associated with implementation of Section 254 of the Telecommunications Act of 1996.

- Adopted an Order approving the open video system certification of Bell Atlantic-New Jersey, Inc. (CSB, released 10/17).

- Adopted a Report and Order ruling that non-dominant interexchange cariers will no longer file tariffs for the interstate domestic long distance services. (CCB, released 10/31).

- Office of General Counsel held a public forum on October 2, 1996 to discuss key issues stemming from implementation of Section 103 (added a new Section 34 to the Public Utility Holding Company Act of 1935) of the Telecom. Act.

In Other News

- Al-Jazeera, Arabic television news channel based in Qatar, starts broadcasts.
Oct. 1 - Federal grand jury indicts Unabomber suspect Theodore Kaczynski in 1994 mail bomb slaying of ad executive.
Oct. 2 - The Electronic Freedom of Information Act Amendments are signed by President Bill Clinton.
- Peruvian plane slams into Pacific, and all 70 passengers and crew are believed killed.
Oct. 6 - President Bill Clinton and Senator Bob Dole meet in Hartford, Conn., for first presidential debate.
Oct. 7 - Fox News first newscast goes out to 17 million cable subscribers. Fox News is a division of News Corporation, whose major shareholder and director of operations is Australian billionaire Rupert Murdoch.
Oct. 14 - Dow Jones industrial average closes above the 6,000 mark for the first time, less than a year after it cleared the 5,000 barrier.
- In the Oct. 14 issue of The New Yorker, novelist Nicholson Baker accuses San Francisco Public Library of dumping thousands of books in its move to the new high-tech building.
Oct. 16 - Bob Dole challenges President Clinton's ethics and honesty in final debate

900 Geography & History

901 Philosophy & theory
902 Miscellany
903 Dictionaries & encyclopedias
904 Collected accounts of events
905 Serial publications
906 Organizations & management
907 Education, research, related topics
908 With respect to kinds of persons
909 World history
910 Geography & travel
911 Historical geography
912 Graphic representations of earth
913 Ancient world
914 Europe
915 Asia
916 Africa
917 North America
918 South America
919 Other areas
920 Biography, genealogy, insignia
921 Not assigned or no longer used
922 Not assigned or no longer used
923 Not assigned or no longer used
924 Not assigned or no longer used
925 Not assigned or no longer used
926 Not assigned or no longer used
927 Not assigned or no longer used
928 Not assigned or no longer used
929 Genealogy, names, insignia
930 History of ancient world
931 History of ancient world China
932 History of ancient world Egypt
933 History of ancient world Palestine
934 History of ancient world India
935 History of ancient world Mesopotamia & Iranian Plateau
936 History of ancient world Europe north & west of Italy
937 History of ancient world Italy & adjacent territories
938 History of ancient world Greece
939 History of ancient world Other parts of ancient world
940 General history of Europe
941 General history of Europe British Isles
942 General history of Europe England & Wales
943 General history of Europe Central Europe Germany
944 General history of Europe France & Monaco
945 General history of Europe Italian Peninsula & adjacent islands
946 General history of Europe Iberian Peninsula & adjacent islands
947 General history of Europe Eastern Europe Soviet Union
948 General history of Europe Northern Europe Scandinavia
949 General history of Europe Other parts of Europe
950 General history of Asia Far East

Oct. 17 - Boris Yeltsin fires security chief Alexander Lebed, one day after former general was accused by rival of building his own rogue army.

October 20 - Casio QV-300 digital camera released.

Oct. 22 - 30 people are killed and 80 injured when flaming Boeing 707 jet slices through dozens of homes minutes after taking off from Ecuador's Manta airport.

Oct. 23 - Bob Dole unsuccessfully urges Ross Perot to quit the Presidential race and endorse GOP ticket.

Oct. 26 - Prosecutors clear guard Richard Jewell in Olympic bombing case.

Oct. 31 - Brazilian jetliner Flight 402 crashes into a residential neighborhood in Sao Paulo shortly after takeoff, igniting a fire that engulfs apartments, homes and cars and killing all 95 people on board.

951 General history of Asia China & adjacent areas
952 General history of Asia Japan
953 General history of Asia Arabian Peninsula & adjacent areas
954 General history of Asia South Asia India
955 General history of Asia Iran
956 General history of Asia Middle East (Near East)
957 General history of Asia Siberia (Asiatic Russia)
958 General history of Asia Central Asia
959 General history of Asia Southeast Asia
960 General history of Africa
961 General history of Africa Tunisia & Libya
962 General history of Africa Egypt & Sudan
963 General history of Africa Ethiopia
964 General history of Africa Morocco & Canary Islands
965 General history of Africa Algeria
966 General history of Africa West Africa & offshore islands
967 General history of Africa Central Africa & offshore islands
968 General history of Africa Southern Africa
969 General history of Africa South Indian Ocean islands
970 General history of North America
971 General history of North America Canada
972 General history of North America Middle America Mexico
973 General history of North America United States
974 General history of North America Northeastern United States
975 General history of North America Southeastern United States
976 General history of North America South central United States
977 General history of North America North central United States
978 General history of North America Western United States
979 General history of North America Great Basin & Pacific Slope
980 General history of South America
981 General history of South America Brazil
982 General history of South America Argentina
983 General history of South America Chile
984 General history of South America Bolivia
985 General history of South America Peru
986 General history of South America Colombia & Ecuador
987 General history of South America Venezuela
988 General history of South America Guiana
989 General history of South America Paraguay & Uruguay
990 General history of other areas
991 Not assigned or no longer used
992 Not assigned or no longer used
993 General history of other areas New Zealand
994 General history of other areas Australia
995 General history of other areas Melanesia New Guinea
996 General history of other areas Other parts of Pacific Polynesia
997 General history of other areas Atlantic Ocean islands
998 General history of other areas Arctic islands & Antarctica
999 Extraterrestrial worlds

Vocabulary Enhancement

pseudocyesis, a psychosomatic illness marked by many of the symptoms of pregnancy

pseudopod, a psychic projection: a pseudopodium

pseudopodium, a temporary process sent out by the protoplasm of a unicellular organism or phagocyte, for locomotion or feeding

psychoneurosis, a functional disorder of the mind in one who is legally sane and shows insight into his condition.

Macdonald, A.M. OBE BA(Oxon).
Chambers Twentieth Century Dictionary.
Littlefield, Adams & Co. Totowa, New Jersey. 1901-74.

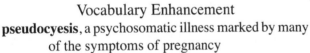

—Use *pseudopod* in a sentence.

—The characters and events in most works of fiction are *pseudopods* of the author's psychoneurosis.

December FCC Report, Abridged:

- Second Further Notice of Proposed Rulemaking seeking comment of possible changes to the local television ownership rule, radio-television cross-ownership rule, and the grandfathering of television local market agreements. (MMB, released 11/7).
- The Federal-State Joint Board adopted universal service recommendations. (CCB, released 11/8).
- Adopted a Notice of Proposed Rulemaking to implement the infrastructure sharing provisions of the Telecom Act. (CCB, 11/22).
- Mass Media Bureau and the Office of Engineering and Technology convened a public forum on the economics of mandated standards for digital television on November 1, 1996.

In Other News

Nov. 8 - Bill Clinton defeats Bob Dole to be re-elected as President—first 2 term Democrat President since Franklin Delano Roosevelt.

Nov. 9 - Evander Holyfield upsets Mike Tyson to win heavyweight boxing title.
    - Returning to the White House the day after his re-election, Bill Clinton greets 21-year old intern Monica Lewinsky.

Nov. 15 - Michael Jackson marries the woman carrying his baby—his plastic surgeon's nurse, Debbie Rowe, in an Australian wedding ceremony.

Nov. 17 - A Russian space probe fired toward Mars hurtles back to Earth.

Nov. 19 - A commuter plane landing at Baldwin Municipal Airport in Quincy, Ill., collides at runway intersection with a small private plane approaching take off, igniting a fireball that kills all 14 people aboard both aircraft.

Nov. 23 - An Ethiopian Airlines Boeing 767 cartwheels into the waves off Comoros Islands, killing 123, after hijackers struggle for controls even as one engine and then the other run dry and stop.

Nov. 30 - 150,000 people fill the streets of Belgrade to

Vocabulary Enhancement

psilanthropism, the doctrine that Christ was a mere man
psilanthropic
psilanthropist
psilanthropy
[Greek: *psilos*, bare, *anthropos*, man]
Phillipic, one of the three orations of Demosthenes against Philip of Macedon: any discurse full of **invective**, (See **Jeremiad**.)
rebellow, (Spenser) to bellow in return: to echo back a loud noise.
riverrain, of a river or its neighborhood.–n. riverside dweller.–adj.
rivery, of or like a river.
river-god, the tutelary deity of a river. (e.g. Mark Twain and the Mississippi River.)

92s Biography

—Use psilanthropic in a sentence.
—He was a psilanthropic philanthropic kinda guy.

protest Serbian President Slobodan Milosevic.

FCC December Report, Abridged:

- The Board of Directors convened the first meeting of the Telecom-munications Development Fund (TDF) on December 3, 1996. (As of October 29, 1996, TDF has $6.6 million from the up-front payments businesses submit to participate in the FCC spectrum auctions.)
- Adopted a Notice of Proposed Rulemaking to determine policies for Bell company manufacturing of telecommunications and customer premises equipment. (CCB, release 12/10).
- Adopted a Second Order on Reconsideration concerning imple-mentation of the local competition provisions in the Telecom Act, specifically the obligation of incumbent local exchange carriers to provide access to their operational support systems functions. (CCB, released 12/13/96).
- Adopted an Order implementing a standard for the transmission of digital television. (MMB, released 12/27/96).
- Public forum on issues concerning the use and management of pub-lic rights-of-ways conducted by the Cable Services Bureau, Common Carrier Bureau, Wireless Bureau and the Office of General Counsel on December 16, 1996.

In Other News

- Microsoft announces that 732,000 copies of NT Server 4.0 sold in 1996.
- Tickle Me Elmo becomes the hottest selling toy for Christmas, some stores charging up to $30 for the prized gift.

Dec. 14 - Freighter rams into shopping mall on Mississippi River, injuring scores.

seriality

series, n. a set of things in line or i succession, or so thought of: a set of things having something in common, esp. of books in similar form issued by the same house: a set of things differing progressively.

–adj. **serial**, forming a series: in series: in a row: in install-ments: of publication in installments.

–n. a publication, especially a story, in installments.

–v.t. **serialize**, to arrange in series: to publish serially.

–ns. **serialization**, publication in installments.

serialist, a writer of serials.

seriality.

–adv. **serially**.

–adj. **seriate**.

–advs. **serially; seriatim**, one after another.

[L. *series–serere, sertum*, to join.]

Tug boats hold the ship steady against the Mississippi River wharf in New Orleans Dec. 14, 1996, after the Bright Field struck the Hilton Hotel river walk, causing a portion of the building to collapse. (Photo by Eliot Kamenitz, NOLA.com / The Times-Picayune archive) TIMES-PICAYUNE /LANDOV

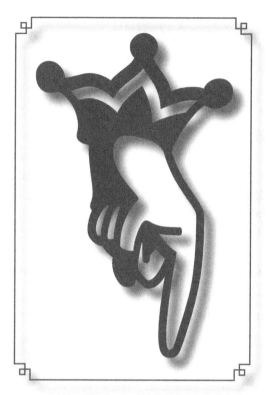

R B
P L

Your attention, please.

Don't forget to Vote!

November 8, 1996

Non-profit organization
U.S. Postage Paid
Permit #123

Friends of
River Bend Public Library
1010 Meredith Willson Blvd.
River Bend, Iowa 51234

Mr. & Mrs. John Q. Public
1776 Live Free or Die Ave.
River Bend, Iowa
54321

A few words about
Intiative #1:
"Shall River Bend bond for $20 million
dollars to build a

21st Century Library?"

(See other side.)

If You Love River Bend

Vote Yes! For the children. Yes! For the Future.
Yes! For the 21st Century Library.
Vote Yes. Vote Early. Vote Often.

November 8, 1996

Intiative #1

Intiative #1: Shall River Bend bond for $20 million dollars to build a 21st Century Library?

YES! If not for yourself then Yes! for the kids. Can you even remember what it was like when you were a child? Hanging out in the library basement killing time till the Saturday afternoon matinee. It was the middle of July, hot as blazes, and you could be catching crawdads up a creek, riding a bike to the Natatorium, or playing 500-Up with whoever showed up at the park that day; but failing these and national holidays, you always knew in the back of your mind that somewhere the Library waited patiently.

The library is the place where, when there's no place else to go, they have to take you in. Didn't Robert Frost say something like that once? Hey—You could go to the library and look it up. Maybe learn something new. You just never know.

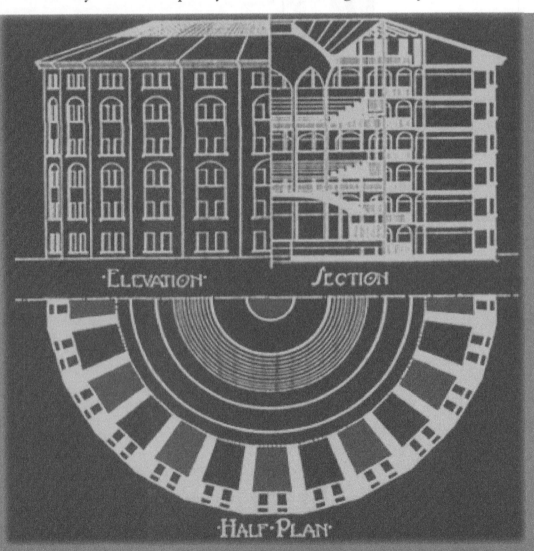

·ELEVATION·   SECTION

·HALF·PLAN·

Raise the Magnolia!

Raise the Magnolia!
c/o Derrick the Dude
Pier 31, River Bend,
Iowa 51234

Non-profit Organization
U.S. Postage Paid
River Bend, Iowa
Permit #1234

Mr. & Mrs. John Q. Resident

123 Piccolo Row, River Bend, Iowa 51234

Bring back the good old days.

This was the sort of moment captured by George Caleb Bingham in *Raftsmen Playing Cards* (1847): a pastoral haze envelops a static tableau of cardplayers, stout fellows, hardworking men at rest, leaning on their elbows, legs splayed at random. Adrift in mist, they seem exempt from ordinary time—much as Huck and Jim do in *Huckleberry Finn* (1884), Mark Twain's refiguration of his boyhood of the 1840s, when it seemed always to be Saturday or summer.

The river as a realm of male camaraderie, an escape from the schedules and norms of bourgeois civilization (schoolmasters, bosses, mothers, wives)—these themes all link Bingham's painting with Mark Twain's novel. But there is another thematic connection as well; it may suggest one reason riverboat gambling has preserved an almost mythic stature as an American ritual. That is the tendency, common to Bingham, Mark Twain, and other artists, to imagine the river as a timeless, parallel universe of play.

Lears, Jackson. *Something for Nothing: Luck in America.* New York: Viking Penguin, 2003.
Dewey Decimal: 363.42 L4386s

Initiative # 2
Shall River Bend bond for $20 million dollars to raise and restore the *Magnolia*, a historic riverboat gambling casino?

If you love Liberty

Vote YES!

Initiative #2 will provide funds to restore the *Magnolia*, a riverboat queen present at the 1886 Dedication Ceremony of the Statue of Liberty. Outfitted for a new life as a 21st Century floating casino, the *Magnolia* will create jobs and return tax on investment for a new generation of freedom-loving Americans.

Vote YES!
Raise the Magnolia!

Invisible Prisons

Giovanni Battista Piranesi (1720-1778) trained as an architect, moved from his home town of Venice to Rome: the center of the Enlightenment.

Piranesi not only found beauty in the obvious monuments, he saw it in "the sewers, the walls, the aqueducts, the paved roads" of the city as well. But it is the *Carceri*, (Invisible Prisons) for which he has become best known. These engravings of Piranesi's imagined prison interiors are stark views into the artist's own tormented inner world.

These hellish views, sold as souvenirs to tourists, became touchstones for a later generation of surrealist artists known as the Dadaists, such as this fellow in the window, believed to be May Ray. Or maybe Chagall....

Non-profit Organization
U.S. Postage Paid
River Bend, Iowa
Permit #1235

Magna Dolorum

Concerned Citizens
for Public Safety
& Initiative #3

1234 Security Lane
River Bend, Iowa 54321

·ELEVATION·   SECTION

You Can Never Be Too Safe!
Vote for Initiative #3

Mr. & Mrs. John Q. Public
1234 Fiddler's Dell
River Bend, Iowa
54321

Initiative #3

Shall River City bond for $20 million dollars to build the Panopticon?

River Bend Panopticon

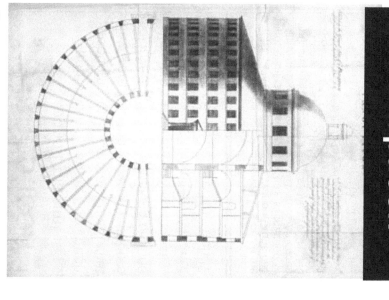

River Bend's Panopticon will be modeled on this historic design by Jeremy Bentham, with an educational Visitor Center and Gift Shop.

Hence the major effect of the Panopticon: to induce in the inmate a state of conscious and permanent visibility that assures the automatic functioning of power. So to arrange things that the surveillance is permanent in its effects, even if it is discontinuous in its action; that the perfection of power should tend to render its actual exercise unnecessary; that this architectural apparatus should be a machine for creating and maintaining a power relation independent of the person who exercises it; in short, that the inmates should be caught up in a power situation of which they are themselves the bearers.

–Michel Foucault, *Discipline & Punish: The Birth of the Prison*

11-Year Growth Projection
Shows Bright Future for Prison Industry!

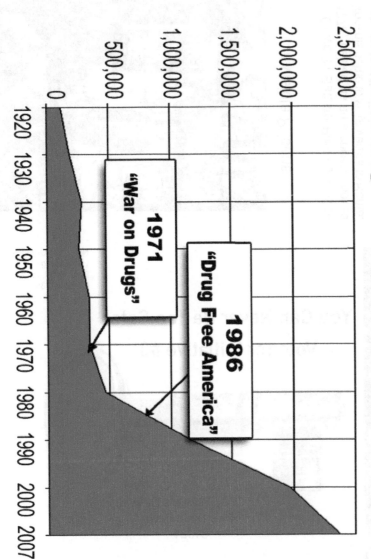

River Bend
Panopticon

Magna Dolorum!

People can't handle too much freedom. You know that. That's what laws are for. And growing numbers of law-breakers are making prisons America's fastest growing industry. The potential is unlimited. Why not help River Bend get in on this trend?

Out of the get-tough on crime era arose the nation's War on Drugs. The War on Drugs has not eliminated crime, but has succeeded in filling up the nation's prisons. By 1982 American prisons held 412,000 inmates, a leap of 91,000 in only 2 years. By mid-1992 that figure had grown to 855,958. At this rate, half of America will be behind bars in the year 2050.

Prisons by Lois Warburton, Lucent Books, Inc. 1993

The United States now incarcerates between 1.8 and 2 million of its citizens in its prisons and jails on any given day, an over 5 million people are currently under the supervision of America's criminal justice system. That's more prisoners than in any other country in the world....Todays' 2 million prisoners represent a prison and jail system ten times larger than that which existed a mere twnty-nine years ago.

The Perpetual Prison Machine: How America Profits from Crime by Joel Dyer, Perseus Books Group, 2000.

Permissions, Licenses, Coyright Notices, & Photo Credits

Title page:
U.S. Marshalls Service

Contents Page:
Melvil Dewey. New York Public Library [1] Print Collection portrait. Stephen A. Schwarzman Building / Print Collection, Miriam and Ira D. Wallach Division of Art, Prints and Photographs file. This image is available from the New York Public Library's Digital Library under the strucID 568918

Summer *riverrun*:
page 2: AP photograph 96100901682 - Microsoft CEO Bill Gates announces the launching of "Libraries Online," a 10.5 million philanthropic initiative to help library systems in economically disadvantaged communities nation-wide provide public access to the internet and multimedia personal computers, in New York Wednesday, Oct. 9, 1996. At right is New York Mayor Ryudolph Giyliani. (AP Photo/Adam Nadel)
page 3: Book cover from POST-CAPITALIST SOCIETY by PETER F. DRUCKER. Copyright © 1993 by Peter F. Drucker. Reprinted by permission of HarperCollins Publishers.

With regard to the cover from MANAGING IN A TIME OF GREAT CHANGE by Peter F. Drucker (Dutton 1995), we were unable to locate contractual information to help us determine who controls rights to the cover/jacket. Therefore, while we would have no objection to the use of this material as described in your request, we are unable to grant a license for its use.
page 5: Smolan, Rick. 24 Hours in Cyberspace: Painting on the Walls of the Digital Cave, 1996. (With CD-ROM). Digital Wall in Singapore, photo credit: R. Ian Lloyd. http://www.againstallodds.com/cyber24.htm
page 8: Dick & Jane copyright and trademark Pearson Education, Inc. Used by permission of Pearson Education, Inc. All rights reserved.
page 10-11 Goteborg Bookfair, Germany, Copyright 2014 by Jacub Opas. All rights reserved.
page 110: Gorsline. *What People Wore: A Visual History of Dress from Ancient Times to 20ᵗʰ Century America.* New York, N.Y.: Viking Press, 1952. Dewey Decimal: 391 G6745w

Fall *riverrun:*
cover photo: Tug boats hold the ship steady against the Mississippi River wharf in New Orleans Dec.

14, 1996, after the Bright Field struck the Hilton Hotel river walk, causing a portion of the building to collapse. (Photo by Eliot Kamenitz, NOLA.com / The Times-Picayune archive) TIMES-PICAYUNE /LANDOV
page 8. Gorsline, Douglas. *ibid.*
page 12: Gorsline, Douglas. *ibid.*
page 14-15: Gorsline, Douglas. *ibid.*
page 15: The "Charles P. Chouteau"—a sternwheeler of the seventies carrying a record cargo of cotton. (Stanton's "American Steam Vessels")
Quick, Herbert, Quick, Edward. *Mississippi Steamboatin': A History of Steamboating on the Mississippi and Its Tributaries.* New York. Henry Holt and Co., 1926. Dewey Decimal: 387 Qu
page 10: Still life
Date Created/Published: c1887.
Medium: 1 print : lithograph, color.
Summary: Tobacco label showing lock in shape of a heart hanging from a door, with a key hanging on a nail by the lock.
Reproduction Number: LC-USZC4-5657 (color film copy transparency)

Vote for the 21st Century Library
Jeremy Bentham's Panopticon penitentiary, drawn by Willey Reveley, 1791

Raise the Magnolia!
Raftsmen Playing Cards by George Caleb Bingham, St. Louis Art Museum.
Excerpt used as illustration for Raise the Magnolia! brochure from SOMETHING FOR NOTHING: LUCK IN AMERICA by Jackson Lears, copyright © 2003 by Jackson Lears. Used by permission of Viking Penguin, a division of Penguin Group (USA) LLC.

Build the Panopticon
Chart from U.S. Bureau of Justice Statistics BulletinNCJ 219416 - Prisoners in 2006

Dayplanner:
page 152 Gorsline. *ibid.*
page 156 *Hey Macareena* website:
Los Del Rio: *Macareena*
https://www.youtube.com/watch?v=XiBYM6g8Tck
page 162 Gorsline. *ibid.*
page 163 Gorsline. *ibid.*
page 164 Gorsline. *ibid.*
page 165 Gorsline. *ibid.*

Shout Outs

**Utah Division of Arts & Museums
Original Writing Competition**
Established in 1958, the competition identifies and awards Utah writers for works of fiction, nonfiction, and poetry in the form of short stories, essays, poems, and full-length manuscripts for readers of all ages. There is no entry fee for the competition, and it is open to all Utah residents.

**Vinnie Kinsella &
the Manuscript Editing Class of 2006 at
Ooligan Press, Portland State University**
Thanks to their close reading and personal feedback, the original version of this book was substantially reconsidered, re-written, re-jiggered, cut, trimmed, shaved, showered, and shampooed. Unnecessary characters were deleted. Important characters were brought into sharper focus, and a back-story invented for the narrator. The professional evaluation and practical suggestions I received improved the manuscript in every way.
Emily Bowles
Karen Brattain
Elizabeth Buelow
Karli Clift
Allison Collins
Audrey Coulthurst
Ryan Hume
Susan Landis-Steward
Cameron Marschall
Cassie Richoux
Joanna Schmidt
Rachel Tobie
Jamie Webster
Erin Woodcock

Public libraries, librarians, and support staff—you know who you are, even if nobody else appreciates you—who maintain traditions of literacy and democracy. Let Freedom reign.

This space available
at
Reasonable Rates.

Inquire: Jeremiah D. Angelo,
Prop.

Great Works of Innovative Fiction Published by JEF Books

✦

Collected Stort Shories by Erik Belgum

Oppression for the Heaven of It by Moore Bowen [2013 Patchen Award!]

Don't Sing Aloha When I Go by Robert Casella

How to Break Article Noun by Carolyn Chun [2012 Patchen Award!]

What Is Art? by Norman Conquest

Elder Physics by James R. Hugunin

Something Is Crook in Middlebrook by James R. Hugunin [2012 *Zoom Street* Experimental Fiction Book of the Year!]

Tar Spackled Banner by James R. Hugunin

OD: Docufictions by Harold Jaffe

Othello Blues by Harold Jaffe

Paris 60 by Harold Jaffe

Apostrophe/Parenthesis by Frederick Mark Kramer

Ambiguity by Frederick Mark Kramer

Meanwhile by Frederick Mark Kramer

Minnows by Jønathan Lyons

You Are Make Very Important Bathtime by David Moscovich

Xanthous Mermaid Mechanics by Brion Poloncic

Return to Circa '96 by Bob Sawatzki [2014 Patchen Award!]

Short Tails by Yuriy Tarnawsky

The Placebo Effect Trilogy by Yuriy Tarnawsky

Prism and Graded Monotony by Dominic Ward

For a complete listing of all our titles
please visit us at experimentalfiction.com

CPSIA information can be obtained at www.ICGtesting.com
Printed in the USA
BVOW11s1652080215

386776BV00002B/2/P

9 781884 097065